THE BROKEN PLACES

BLAINE DAIGLE

WICKED HOUSE PUBLISHING

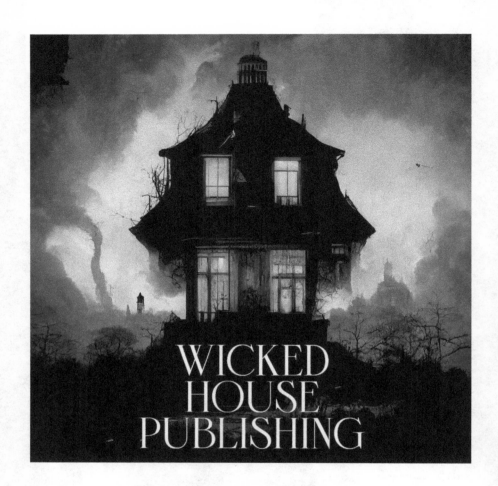

WICKED
HOUSE
PUBLISHING

The Broken Places
By Blaine Daigle

Wicked House Publishing

Cover design by Christian Bentulan
Interior Formatting by Joshua Marsella

Contents

For Tate, Benton, and Talia

DECEMBER 1999-YUKON

ONE
A NATURAL PART OF THESE WOODS

Deep within the dark, ancient heart of the Yukon, a storm raged. Snow, harsh and wild, clawed at the small cabin tucked within a dark cove of trees. This cabin had stood deep in the frigid grip of the taiga for well over a century. Even through the annual winter storms that seemed tethered to the solstice, when the freezing winds battered and rammed its structure with merciless intent, the cabin never wavered in its structural integrity. Its wood never cracked. Its chimney never buckled. Everything looked exactly as it did on the cold day in 1857 when William Burdette built the place atop the frozen ground.

A vast blanket of icy wind and thick snow howled beyond the wooden walls. The blinding snow fused with the empty, black night and became an opaque sheet draped over the natural world as the wind chill dropped to twenty degrees below zero. But inside the dwelling there lived a lofty warmth. A fire burned through the thick logs inside the stone fireplace, bellowing smoke out the top of the chimney where it was caught, cooled, and whisked away in the white. The fire held the misery from the outside winds at bay; as the cold, dead fingers of winter felt for a crack in the armor. A way in.

Warm and comfortable, eight-year-old Ryne Burdette slept nestled away in the upstairs loft. A quiet peace simmered within the cabin while the hearse of the Yukon winter shrilled and screamed outside its doors.

* * *

Ryne's eyes opened to the creaking of a door downstairs. The faint reach of the fireplace threw a soft, orange glow against the window next to him, through which the forest loomed across a cold, unlit land. The place called to him, so far away from the noise of home. Far away from the chaotic school hallways and clamor of everyday life. A serenity lived in its quietness. On most nights, the sky above the Yukon taiga glistened with stars, or the occasional echoes of the northern lights. But tonight, the stars had vanished, and no light graced the sky.

The fire crackled and danced inside the stone.

"Dad?" Ryne called out as he wiped the sleepiness from his eyes. No answer. Stretching his arms far behind him, he called out again.

He listened for the familiar voice, deep and articulate with a softness normally reserved for mothers. The voice of the man who'd hugged him goodnight hours earlier. Nothing came.

Sliding out of bed, his feet, warm inside thick socks, met the wooden floor. He walked over to the banister and glanced below to the living area. His father slept on the couch. He was wrapped in a thin sherpa, his head sunk deep into the pillow. He didn't like the cabins' beds and preferred to sleep on the couch next to the fire when they visited. And there he was, fast asleep.

His mouth dry, Ryne descended the steps downstairs, still fighting the deep sleep from which he had awoken. In his groggy state, the quietness surprised him. The storm had arrived just hours earlier with a fury Ryne had never witnessed, at least not in person. He'd seen hurricanes on TV hitting the Gulf Coast. Tornadoes ripping through the Midwest. Blizzards smothering small northern towns. But this storm was different. The sturdiest of trees became rag dolls; tossed and shredded in the vortex of ice. *Angry*, Ryne thought. It felt *angry*. The world outside the cabin had sounded like a train thundering by, but silence filled the warm air inside, save for the crackling of the fire.

Reaching the floor below, he shuffled to the kitchen and opened the refrigerator, poured a glass of milk, and took a long gulp. The thick liquid filled his belly, and sleepiness returned to him. Eyes heavy and lips wet, he turned back to the stairs where the orange flicker from the fireplace adorned the walls with a dancing glow. Ryne stopped in front of the bedroom tucked beneath the loft.

The door was open. The bed was empty.

"Uncle Rod?" he said into the darkness, but the heavy silence and dancing flames were the only replies.

He turned away from the bedroom and looked across the living space of the cabin. On two sides, double-pane windows stretched from the floor to the ceiling. Most of the cabin had an open layout. The living area, the kitchen, the stairs to the loft, and the loft itself shared no hard boundaries. The only closed-off rooms were the empty bedroom beneath the loft and the bathroom.

As he moved toward the bathroom, Ryne rubbed his eyes to push away the sleepiness. The light inside the bathroom was off. He knocked at the door.

"Uncle Rod?"

He scanned the cabin again. A worried trickle crept down the nape of his neck and pulled him away from his drowsy haze. His eyes settled on the front door. After the night had fallen, his father locked the deadbolt. Ryne had watched him do it.

Now, the door was unlocked.

A lump formed in his throat and choked his breath as his heart shifted gears in his chest. He walked over to the couch and tried to shake his father awake. His eyes stayed locked on the door.

"Dad," he said. "Dad. Uncle Rod went outside. Dad?"

The sleeping man stirred and rolled but didn't wake. The entire day spent tracking deer through the woods held the man asleep. It had been Ryne's first hunt, and as he looked down the barrel of the rifle at deer after deer, his father's voice had been soft in his ear. "No, not that one." They'd frozen through hours of that before the buck had emerged into view, and his father had nodded. "That one." The squeeze of the trigger. The explosion of the round. The shock against his shoulder. The animal falling into the snow. Clean. His father had dragged the deer all the way back to the cabin and cleaned the carcass himself, showing Ryne how to slide the knife beneath the hide just right. How to keep the hair off the meat. But it had taken its toll. Exhaustion had defeated him.

Ryne gave up trying to rouse his father and moved towards the door. *Why would he go outside?* The thought lived alone within his sleepy mind as the icy chill slowly dug its way into his spine and methodically descended each vertebra, digging its nails into the bone.

He turned the handle and pushed the door open.

The cold air hit him like a brick and shocked him alert. No wind blew across his face, and the air was clear aside from the immense fog of his breath. A slight buzz of light emanated from the cabin's windows. Outside the reach of light was a still, quiet cold more frigid than the deepest freezes the Earth could offer. The world blacked out into nothing.

Nothing but a figure at the tree line. A scene unfolded on the brink of the light's reach, just within the grasp of his vision.

Squinting, the details emerged. A slow, dark procession. The thick yellow jacket, the black arctic pants, and the black balaclava his father got Rod as a birthday gift last year. All of these lay discarded in the snow next to the naked man. It was his Uncle Rod, down on his knees facing the surrounding forest. Speaking into the dark trees. His voice soft in the dead night. The words unfamiliar. To Ryne's ears, they sounded like a chant.

Like a prayer.

Something else formed in the night. A dark shadow, moving just beyond the praying man, vaguely visible in the dark. Jagged shapes reached into the air above the shadow. Like a vast set of antlers.

"Uncle Rod?" Ryne's voice cracked and broke apart the cold.

Rod's head whipped around; his eyes wide in the fading glow of the cabin's light. The shadow rose high into the air, and the night erupted with the sound of splintering wood. Its form shrouded by the shadows of the trees. Not a deer, but something else. Something so dark it made the night's blackness seem almost angelic.

Frost bit deep into the boy's skin. He could not move. His eyes were unable to leave the empty holes in the night air. The cabin door exploded open behind him, his father screaming out.

"Ryne! Get inside!"

His father's voice was a distant echo as new forms emerged within the tree line. He felt the gazes of things unknown as the forest became a canvas of shadow.

Rod was still on his knees. The dark figure stared straight at Ryne, and the sea of shadow focused its gaze intently on him, as he heard a whispering echo through the trees. He felt arms wrap around him and yank him up and around, back inside.

The door closed, and the warmth returned. A wave of sleepiness overtook him as his father shook him awake.

"Ryne, wake up!"

"Dad? What's going on?"

The door behind his father opened, and Rod stepped back inside, closed the door behind him, and locked the deadbolt. He was fully dressed, the yellow jacket and black pants dotted with snow.

"What *was* that?" Ryne asked.

"What was *what*?"

"The animal. Outside, with the antlers."

The men looked at each other. The ferocity of his father's face was a piercing siren.

"It was a deer, Ryne," Rod said. "Got caught in one of the snares I laid out earlier. I was letting it go."

"A deer?"

"Yeah, kid. Just a reindeer."

"Why didn't you have clothes on?"

"What?"

"You weren't wearing any clothes."

"Were you sleepwalking?" asked his father. "You walked right out the front door."

"No, I was awake. I was looking for Uncle Rod," Ryne said.

"Never go outside at night in these woods. Never. You could've wandered into the trees and gotten lost and froze to death or been attacked by a wolf. Never go outside at night. Do you understand me!"

"I'm sorry, Dad. I thought he was in trouble."

"I'm fine, kid."

"I don't care if either of us is in trouble. You *do not go outside!* Is that clear?"

"Yes, sir."

5

His father held him tight for a few seconds, but the boy sensed his father's anger. Not at him, though. The man's fury was directed elsewhere. He grabbed the unfinished glass of milk from the counter.

"Here, finish this off and go back to bed."

He gulped down the milk and made his way back towards the loft. Before going up, he turned and faced his uncle.

"Just a deer?" he asked.

Rod smiled. "Just a natural part of these woods, Ryne. Nothing to worry about."

"OK," said the boy. He went back up the stairs. He tucked himself in beneath the thick blanket as warmth returned to his fingers, toes, and face. The bedroom door downstairs closed, and the sounds of arguing from inside the bedroom filtered out.

"What the hell were you thinking?"

"I had to. I couldn't wait any longer."

"I gave you every chance when we went to town earlier."

"I'm sorry."

The storm returned. Its wrath reclaimed whatever calm had come, and, through his window, he saw the outside world fade back into the white.

A sudden, severe sleepiness arose within Ryne. Had he been dreaming? The boy pulled the blanket to his chin and tucked his knees into his chest. He thought of the hunt, the feeling of the trigger against his finger. The smile on his father's face. Rod was right. A deer caught in a trap. Nothing more. Nothing less. Anything else he had seen had been a trick of his exhausted mind.

Outside the window, the branches of trees whipped and cracked. As his eyelids grew heavy, an owl sat perched in the nearest tree. Tucked safely inside a hole in the bark as the world screamed, it gazed through the window at him.

"Rory, you don't have much longer. He needs to..."

"No."

"Well, you don't have...."

"I said no. He is my son. That is not your call to make."

"Not yours either, to be frank. Ryne has a part to play, whether you want to admit that or not. He is part of this family. It's not in your hands or mine.

It never was, and it never will be. You can fight all you want, but one day, you will have to make your peace. Best to accept it now."

In the warm bed of the upstairs loft, eight-year-old Ryne Burdette's eyes grew heavy and closed. Outside, the storm resumed its rage upon the wild, and Ryne fell back asleep under the gaze of the empty, black eyes of the owl.

THE FIRST NIGHT

TWO

WOLF'S BONE

December 2019-Yukon Territory

The old red truck moved with a hiss across the icy asphalt while the cold wind whispered through the spruce and out into the thin December air of the Yukon sky. The road was raised upon the soft accents of the taiga's hills, and on either side stood skyward trees oppressed with snow of days gone. No shoulder extended beyond the edge of the road, and the spruce trees rose high and vast, suffocating the road into one never-ending path. The forest stretched outward into the horizon, glazed in a hanging fog frozen upon the wind by the slightest grip onto the fragile limbs of old and weary trees, while the dull sun slumped from unseen gallows in the winter sky. It wouldn't be there much longer before it sank back into the abyss and gave way to the encroaching darkness.

Ryne Burdette felt the crunch of the truck's tires as they dug through the ice. The heater on full blast, the red relic subjected its three occupants to every bump and crack in the old roads, plowing its way toward nowhere. He took a sip of coffee from his thermos. He'd been driving for nearly eight hours now and was fighting sleep as the fading light outside held a weight on his eyelids. Shawn Ackerman sat in the passenger seat, awake, and playing a game on his phone, shivering under a thick, white jacket. Shawn had offered to drive many times during Ryne's shift, but he had no real idea where they were going, and Ryne didn't trust himself to stay awake long enough to guide him. Behind them, Noah Stratton slept stretched across the entire back row, his jacket zipped up tight over his beard. Noah had driven before Ryne's leg, putting forth a valiant ten-hour shift up to Beaver Creek. He'd earned the rest. Occasionally, Shawn would look up from his phone and stare into the endless sea of ice and spruce.

"I didn't think it was *this* far out here."

But it was, and Ryne knew all too well. They were getting close. He just needed one last push of caffeine, and they would arrive safe and sound.

"Another hour. Tops."

The music playlists had long since grown stale over the three-day slog, and the radio held on to weaker and weaker signals as they pushed further and further north. The current station was originally a fairly clear classic rock station, but, as they entered the heart of the Canadian North, static had become the primary soundtrack of the trip. From time to time, the static would break open, and, for brief moments, a weather forecast would announce itself.

The signal was broken and choppy, but momentary clarity provided the pieces necessary to complete the puzzle—a system that was barely moving, with strong winds and heavy snowfall. After a while, Ryne grew tired of the static and turned the radio off, continuing the drive in silence. He understood that some things never changed. These storms always came with the solstice. Just the way things were in this part of the world.

Off in the distance, a storm was brewing. Moving slowly. Crawling malevolently toward the town of Wolf's Bone, preparing in earnest to meet the men in the red truck.

* * *

"How bad do you think it's going to get?"

Tucked inside his jacket, Shawn's gloved hands wrung and massaged each other. The weather report had been full of static and hard to decipher, but he realized something formidable loomed somewhere in their path. The man on the radio had sounded so damn cheery. Like he'd waited his entire life to broadcast a warning for a storm of this magnitude. A powerful storm was bad enough; but coupled with the weather outside the car made this a precarious situation.

But the concern didn't seem to extend to Ryne. "It'll probably get a little rough, but it won't be too bad. It's the solstice; I don't know why, but there's always a storm that hits this time of year."

"Are you sure the cabin is going to be okay?"

"It's been fine every other time these things hit."

Shawn let it go. If anyone knew the weather patterns of Wolf's Bone, it was Ryne. But he had a pit in his stomach. It had formed the second the weatherman's voice came through with any clarity. As he thought about the possibility of being stuck inside a remote cabin in the middle of a serious winter storm, the pit grew deeper.

"I promise," said Ryne. "We'll stock up on firewood and starter logs. The fireplace in the cabin is great. You can wear a T-shirt and shorts inside and be fine."

"If you say so." He shifted in his seat, and a stinging grip locked up his knee. His face tightened with pain as he attempted to stretch his leg as much as possible, but there wasn't enough room without reclining the seat.

Shawn turned around and saw Noah sleeping across the back row. Under a heavy blanket, his breath escaped in wisps through his high zipped jacket.

"Hey, Noah. Heads up, I need to lean the seat back."

"Screw you, I'm sleeping," came the groggy response.

Shawn rolled his eyes and reached down between the door and the seat to the release catch.

"Geronimo," he said, pulling the lever up and releasing the catch. The seat dropped onto the sleeping Noah, planting his face in the cold leather seat.

"I hate you," said Noah. He pushed his way out from beneath the seat and sat up. His beanie came off his head and his dark hair was in shambles.

"Good lord, man, you look like a crackhead," said Shawn.

"I'm going to shoot you. Sometime during the next few days, I'm going to see a deer, take aim, and then...whoops, Shawn's down."

"You won't kill me. You're not a good enough shot."

"I know. But it'll hurt like a bitch."

Ryne smiled, and the pit in Shawn's stomach quelled for a moment. How many months had passed now since he'd seen any sort of happiness grace his friend's face? The days all seemed to blend and blur with their collective misery. The sorry sights they were.

"Seriously, though. I need to stretch my leg out."

A loud pop sounded as Shawn extended his leg, the surgical patchwork of his knee shifting beneath his skin. He grimaced with pain. The joint hurt bad enough during the warmer months of the year, but the pain was almost unbearable in the cold.

"That sounds bad," said Noah.

"It feels bad, too."

"Are you ever going to get that thing fixed?" asked Ryne. "Like, actually fixed?"

"I have another small procedure in January. Supposed to clear out some fluids that are still causing issues. Hopefully, it'll work, and I'll be back on my feet in a few weeks."

"Or— just hear me out," said Noah as he changed his position to lie behind Ryne's seat, "whenever I shoot you; I'll just aim for your leg. Then, if I miss; I'll probably kill you. If I hit; I'll blow your leg off. It won't hurt anymore, and you can get a peg leg. It'll be great. I don't think the Pirates need a center fielder, but they could definitely use a mascot. It's a win-win for everyone involved."

The three of them together again, laughing and joking as they'd done before the last year had stripped them of that joy, felt right. Normal. Like the scars, at long last, might be healing, scabbing over with the bonds of life-time brotherhood.

But a dark cloud hung over the trip, one that had persisted for almost a year. Shawn hoped with everything in him that the three of them could take this weekend and finally evaporate that cloud, or, at the very least, let it rain itself dry.

* * *

Ryne mentally prepared himself for the long, sweeping curve in the road, the last before their destination would appear on the white horizon. He steadied his hands and made the turn across the slick asphalt, his eyes intently focused on the curve in front of him as his hands studied the wheel for slippage. But the tires held, and the red truck glided safely along the black ice and into the final opening of the trees.

Shawn reached into the backseat and shook Noah. "Hey, wake up."

Noah stirred out of his sleep.

"My turn again?" he asked.

"No, we're here," said Ryne as the truck pulled out of the long curve in the road, breaking free of the tunnel of trees as it moved into the town of Wolf's Bone.

The town rose from the taiga as a forgotten relic, clustered within a small, cleared valley between ageless forests and ancient hills. Three roads snaked their way between snow-covered buildings, which had not changed at all since the very first day Ryne's feet had fallen upon the vast land. As they approached the split separating the main street from the first set of housing, a strange conflict formed within him. The first set of buildings, with their brick faces and flat roofs above large set-in windows, reminded him very much of times in which his family had still been intact; before internal strife rotted its foundation beyond repair. These buildings had withstood the decay of time with startling success, and a feeling in his gut ignited a small spark of appreciation. A feeling that was strange for a place from which most of his positive memories had evaporated long ago.

The buildings on the ridges above reminded him of the other side of his memory and flooded the burning nostalgia. Residential homes remained frozen in the same spots as they had always been, existing as slightly more dignified shanties with their walls of worn-out wood discolored by the ice seeped deep into the grains, and low metal roofs. There was little space between the huts, and it was hard to imagine that civilized people called those places homes. These dwellings were spread all along the edges of Wolf's Bone, stretching to its furthest borders where civilization met wilderness. As a child, Ryne had asked his father how many people lived in the town. Two hundred and fifty had been the answer, give or take a few. Had his father been alive to hear the question now, he wasn't sure the answer would have been any different. Ten years had passed since he'd set foot in this place, but nobody had bothered to remind Wolf's Bone.

They continued down the right fork, which was straighter and quicker, although both ended up in the same place. Ryne looked to his left to see Conway's Deli, one of the first establishments a visitor passing through the town would see. A building made of timber and red brick that was seemingly untouched by time, it was a small restaurant that served hunted game from the vast forests surrounding the small town. But Wolf's Bone did not see many visitors. People moved about the streets, heavily clothed against the vicious winter. They moved slowly, deliberately, and with little purpose outside of the next step in their path. Few people bothered to engage in conversation with each other, let alone even look up from their feet. Watching them shamble through the cold, he remembered the reverence in his uncle's voice when he would speak of the town's inhabitants in stark contrast to the vitriol his father used to spew on the same subject.

As the red truck continued down the street, their dispositions changed. They stopped moving and glanced upwards, staring at the vehicle as though it was either the first time they had seen it, or the first time they had seen it in quite a while. A peculiar behavior from the peculiar inhabitants of this peculiar place, and it made a part of his skin crawl into itself.

Shawn must have noticed it as well. His sharp jaw was tight, and there was a movement under the scruff he called a beard—he ground his teeth, an old habit of nervousness. His blue eyes darted left-to-right in quick succession—a wary animal lost in tall grass.

The truck continued through the town and approached its zenith. A church, by far the town's largest building, loomed at the reunion of the two roads. Only a few cars occupied its parking lot, but through the windows a light filled the space where many shadows moved within.

It was a place of great contention in Ryne's family. Raised Catholic since birth, Ryne had never seen the inside of the place. Rory took the faith very seriously and had Ryne's entire life, a practice Ryne continued up until the past year. His father had always forbidden him from attending during the annual trips to Wolf's Bone. Rod, however, was a constant visitor. The mass, if one were to call it a mass, was held every morning, and Rod would get up during the earliest sign of sunlight and make the drive back into town to attend. On one occasion, Rod tried to coerce Ryne into going with him. Upon his father's realization, the trip ended immediately. He'd asked his father many times what was so wrong with the church, never receiving anything resembling an actual answer.

Now, ten years since his last visit to Wolf's Bone, the church stood as the paragon of old buildings staying new in a town forgotten by time.

"That's a big ass church," said Shawn.

"Didn't think the people this far north were particularly into Jesus," said Noah.

"It's not a Christian church," said Ryne.

Shawn blinked. "It sure as hell looks like one."

"It's not."

"What do they worship?" asked Noah.

"Don't know. Dad never told me."

To the right of the church was a grocery store. An inconspicuous building of old, treated wood that stood in line with everything else. Ryne pulled the truck into the parking lot and the three of them got out. The air was a wet, biting cold upon their faces. A special type of cold. The kind that ignored the modern clothing technology had designed to make war with the wind. The kind that cuts its way into the skin like a razor, taking its time as it slices and splits its way to the bone. The kind of cold Ryne only ever experienced in the core of the Yukon, in this town so far from the rest of the world.

They hurried through the frozen parking lot and into the warm embrace of the grocery store.

THREE

FAMILY SYSTEMS

I t started with his mother.

Even before everything else, it had started with her. He remembered the day eight years before, like a scar newly fleshed over. The smell of the hospital and wishing that he would never have to endure that smell ever again. Seeing her in the bed, fragile as glass, the hair gone from her, lost in the echoes of useless fights. The vitality stripped from her face. How she smiled weakly through the pain, knowing that her end was near. How she had shared one last meal with her son and husband before drifting off into somewhere unknown and unreachable. The emptiness started that day.

He remembered that it hadn't broken him, not completely, but it had provided the first crack.

The first time he'd been to this sleepy town in the Yukon wild, Ryne had been eight years old. Rory and Rod had agreed he was old enough to go on his first hunt and packed up everything for a week-long trip to Rod's cabin, located a few miles into the wild surrounding Wolf's Bone.

They drove the same truck Ryne himself now drove two decades and hundreds of thousands of miles later. Miles from the memory of arriving in the town for the first time and, hungry, asking to stop and eat at Conway's Deli, only to have his father tell him they never ate there. They would buy all their food from the grocery store. The same grocery store in which he stood motionless in thought before the frozen foods section.

No longer a hungry eight-year-old child, Ryne had grown into a tall and imposing figure. His dark hair wrapped and curled around the tips of his ears, and he was a week overdue for a shave. It had been this way for a while now. Over the past year, these small moments of everyday care had taken a backseat to malaise and melancholy. His broad shoulders now slumped formlessly into his jacket, his eyes a dull blue against his darker features, hiding a once furious intensity that had long since faded into weary apathy.

The last few trips to the cabin had been the worst as the strife between Rod and Rory had grown stronger. Yet, they still made the annual trip. Until ten years ago when they finally stopped. Until the venom turned too toxic. Ryne was never quite sure exactly what had come between them so intensely—Rory would never say—but the aftermath had left the remnants of the Burdette family in shambles. After that, everything else had fallen apart like so many dominoes, and a decade of angry absence fell by the wayside. Six months ago, they'd reconciled for one more trip to Wolf's Bone.

It was only after the remains from a fiery car wreck a few miles out of town had been identified, that Ryne was informed he was now the last remaining member of the Burdette family. A fact that relieved one part of his soul, while butchering the other.

Breaking out of his trance, he opened the freezer door and grabbed a pizza. There were cuts of venison to his left, laid out and packaged, looking delicious. But old habits died hard, and he heard his father's voice in his head, quelling the water salivating in his mouth. Ryne had never consumed a single bite of meat in Wolf's Bone, at least none from the town itself. That had been Rory's thing, drilled into Ryne's psyche. He'd always said that the hunters in the area still used bullets lined with lead, rendering the meat unclean. It was only on the rare occasion when Rory would actually shoot a deer instead of letting it pass by that Ryne had eaten from the land. The guilt swelled within him as he stared at the chops of meat, and the memory of just how much his father had cared, and how distant Ryne had become after his mother's death, became moving pictures in his mind. A film he couldn't rewind.

He closed his eyes and turned away from the deli, tossing the frozen pizza into the basket. It wouldn't make a difference anyway. He'd feel wrong eating it. This place may have been home to family members he never knew, but he was an outsider. As loud as his father's voice was, his uncle's was there too. Darker. Deeper.

The meat is for locals.

The family left Wolf's Bone permanently two years before Ryne was born and emigrated south of the border to Pullman, Washington. From what he understood and remembered, this had presented a significant conflict between his father and uncle. Rory wanted to leave while Rod insisted the family stay where they belonged. However, Rod eventually relented and left the town alongside his brother, settling a few miles down the road in Moscow, Idaho. Ryne always wondered why Rod couldn't have just stayed behind in Wolf's Bone. Rod's answer was simple—the family stayed together, no matter what.

But now there was no more family. The years had passed, the funerals came and went, and now the only thing left of the Burdette lineage was a tall, dark-haired, once-proud, now defeated shell, thinking to himself in a freezer window.

* * *

Noah bobbed his head to a song in his mind, while Shawn looked through piles of starter logs looking for the best of the bunch. It wasn't an absent-minded task. They'd both made this trip before. Not to Wolf's Bone, but the hunting trips shared between the three of them dated back a couple of decades now, and there were procedures that needed taking care of.

Friends since kindergarten, they'd bonded over a mutual love for baseball and the outdoors. For Shawn, Ryne had always been a constant North Star of normalcy. Shawn's own family was in tatters. He hadn't seen his father since his seventh birthday, which was fine by him, as he had no use for the mean-drinking piece of shit. His mother was still so scarred from their relationship, that most of the time she may as well have been somewhere else entirely; even as they'd sat on the same couch.

Ryne's house was different. His parents seemed, strangely enough, to like each other. He'd spent so many nights at their home that he kept clothes there. It became a home in which he felt safe, as every child should.

That remained the case as long as Ryne's Uncle Rod wasn't around. Even through youthful eyes, Shawn could tell that the relationship between the brothers was rotting, and the sense of normalcy in the home would dissipate whenever Rod would stop by for a visit.

Noah spoke from behind him, breaking Shawn out of the trance. "It's just three nights. Do you think we need this many?"

"Ryne said we did."

"But do we really?"

Shawn loaded the handpicked stack of starter logs into the buggy. "You don't remember Kalispell?"

"Honestly? Not really." His face twisted as he searched for the memory. A futile effort. Noah's memory was terrible before his accident; but had gotten worse since. "I remember it was cold."

"It was a little more than cold."

"I'm just saying we could be spending money on better things right now than something we are literally going to be surrounded by."

"You really don't remember. We tried that last time. The fire wouldn't catch cause of all the snow. Damn near froze to death."

Shawn turned, and a sharp pain shot through his knee. A familiar pain, one embedded so deep within it may as well have been a part of him, but familiarity didn't make it any less excruciating. His knee buckled, and Noah's hands grabbed his shoulders, halting his fall.

"I'm fine," said Shawn, the words spat through clenched teeth.

"Did you bring your brace?"

"I hate wearing that thing."

"Did you bring it?"

"No, mom."

The pain coursing through Shawn's knee was more than a physical blemish. It was a constant reminder of the life he'd worked for, bled for— the life taken from him by the cruelty of circumstance. He had two passions in life: baseball and hunting. He'd played ball since he was old enough to swing a bat and felt love at the first grip of his fingers around the padded handle. The game spoke to him in a way nothing else could. The sound of a ball smacking perfectly into the glove's pocket gave him the best kind of goosebumps. It represented a way out of the hell he went home to every day and a pathway to the ultimate dream—to make money doing something you love. And he did love it. A special freedom lived between those lines. A freedom that cut the ties to everything he wanted gone and removed the mad puppeteer guiding his miserable world. A place where he could be the person that he always felt he truly was. No longer a wounded, scared animal in his own home. On the field, he was an apex predator. That was his territory. And he defended it well.

As the years went by, Shawn's potential became apparent. Throughout high school, he either tied or broke every school record in the books. By the time his senior year came around, pitchers no longer pitched to him. He signed to travel west to Seattle and play for the University of Washington, but a phone call from the Pittsburgh Pirates in the third round of the Major League draft made that a moot point. There had been a signing party hosted by the Burdette's. There was cake, ice cream, and a contract signed by a young man with a smile as wide as the Puget Sound.

He still looked the part. Almost as tall as Ryne; his frame remained slender and muscular, held in shape through years of hopeful workouts and physical therapies. But while his arms were still strong, his money had been his legs. And that check voided on a warm summer night with a sickening pop.

He'd always believed at twenty-eight he would be standing in centerfield at Wrigley Field or Fenway. Instead, he stood in a grocery store in the middle of the Yukon while his childhood friend kept this once elite athlete from buckling under his own weight.

"You need to wear the damn brace," said Noah.

"I said I'm fine," said Shawn as he regained his form and stood up, immediately regretting his tone. He knew Noah was trying to help. Just Noah being Noah. But he'd never needed help before, and it made him intensely uncomfortable to need it now.

The two men began making their way back to the rendezvous point with Ryne.

"I slept for a good while," said Noah. "How was he?"

"Hardly said a word. Ever since we left, he's barely talked. Did he say anything when the two of you were awake?"

Noah shook his head. "You sure this isn't a mistake? Bringing him back here?"

"He needs a break from everything. It's not ideal, but it's better than him just sitting alone in Pullman."

"Yeah, I get that. But what happens in three days? What happens when we go back, and he's back in the same place he was in before? I mean, this is like using a band-aid when you need stitches."

Ryne came into view, and Noah stopped talking.

"You guys got what you need?" asked Ryne.

"Yeah," said Shawn. "Should be enough for the next few nights."

They moved down the aisle towards the front of the store. The eyes of folks bundled up in heavy garb found their forms and followed them along their way. Eyes hidden by heavy hoods over dark faces charred the air between them, burning a hole into him as he moved through their space. They were outsiders, and outsiders were always scrutinized, and never trusted. Ryne's uncle had always been that way. Shawn balled his hands into fists beneath the heavy sleeve of his jacket.

As if Ryne heard his thoughts, he spoke low and steady, "Just get everything in the cart, and we'll get the hell out of here."

But Shawn was beyond that. He refused to stand there and let himself be studied and watched. He understood the natural inclination to look at something or someone new, but this was ridiculous. Every eye in the store rested upon them now with intense glares. As if they were some priceless pieces of art hung in a museum.

"Can we help you?" he called to the wandering eyes.

All eye contact broke away, and the people dispersed throughout the store.

"Really? Anything at all?"

"Shut the hell up, Shawn," Ryne snapped beneath his breath.

Shawn stopped talking but did not drop his guard. He was on edge. This place may have been home to Ryne's family, but he and Noah had never been here before, and he didn't know any of these people. They were hours away from any outside contact should something happen, which made him extremely uneasy. The others should understand. After all, if anybody understood how everything can go to complete shit in a matter of moments, it was the three of them.

Ryne finished paying, and they hurried out the front door, leaving behind the unsteady eyes. Reaching the truck, they loaded everything into the bed beneath the tarp cover, with the drinks going in a cooler which, ironically, would keep them from freezing and bursting open on the fifteen-mile drive into the woods.

The cold calm of the world was then broken apart by the striking of a bell. A church bell. One cleanly struck knell resounded through the thin, snowy air and out into the trees. The sound died away and was then joined by another knell, deep and heavy. A shrill wave that stretched on forever. The doors to the church opened, and people began leaving the old building. Orderly, practiced. The steps of people who made this walk daily. Religiously. As they poured from the building, Shawn couldn't help but notice the stark contrast between the people in the church and the people in the grocery store. These people did not share the ragged, decrepit appearance. They looked like the kinds of people you wouldn't find in a place like this, dressed nicely with heavy overcoats shrouding ties and dress shirts.

Shawn noticed something else as the congregation spilled out that he neglected to realize before. Every soul he'd seen in Wolf's Bone, from the moment they arrived at the grocery store, wore the dark complexion of Indigenous peoples—natives still living in a land their ancestors had lived on and died for. The faces leaving the old doors of the church were white. It was only in the newly stark contrast that he'd even noticed.

As the men prepared to load themselves into the cabin of the truck, a voice from behind them called out.

"Ryne Burdette?"

Shawn turned to see a man in a police uniform moving towards him. The man's head reached well above even his, a thick gut poking above the belt. Ryne looked puzzled before a spark of recognition flickered in his expression as he put the familiar pieces together.

"Constable Whitting."

The man in the uniform made his way to the truck, wearing a big grin under a thick beard, greyed at the tips. In a few long and heavy strides, he reached them and stuck out his hand to shake Ryne's. Ryne obliged.

"It's been a while, eh," Whiting said. "You have certainly grown a bit since the last time I saw you. How long has it been since you've been here?"

"Ten years," Ryne said. "But I didn't see you last time. Probably closer to fifteen."

"Fifteen years, wow. Boy, you sure shot up, eh?"

Shawn stood with one foot in the truck and one on the icy asphalt of the parking lot. He was ready to go, but it was somewhat calming to see someone with a friendly disposition after what happened in the grocery store.

Behind him, however, Noah was not nearly as comfortable. Shawn saw his hand squeeze the door handle. His grip tightened enough that the exposed skin between his gloved hands and the end of his jacket sleeve blanched bone white. Shawn reached out and pressed on his shoulder, which lessened his grip and seemed to calm him. Shawn understood. The last time Noah had been this close to a man in a uniform, he was dead.

"And who have you got with you?" the constable asked Ryne.

"This is Shawn, and this is Noah. Friends from back home."

Shawn and Noah provided courtesy nods in the constable's direction.

"You guys headed to the cabin?"

"Yeah," said Ryne. "For a few nights."

"Good, good. Listen, I wanted to say the whole town was sorry to hear of your uncle's passing. He was a special man. Not many people leave this place and still get held in good graces, but Rod was one of those."

"I appreciate that, and I'm sure he would too."

"And also, we heard about what happened with, you know, the baby."

Shawn's ears perked, and he saw Ryne lose his breath, struggling for a few seconds before finding it again.

"Thank you," said Ryne, his voice quiet, suffocated. "I appreciate that."

A canned response, one Ryne had taught himself to repeat on demand. Shawn knew it didn't mean a damn thing, and it shouldn't, but there was a genuine surprise held within the practiced tone, as if there was information known that shouldn't have been.

"Well," said the constable. "You guys be safe. If you need anything, just radio in, and I'll be right out." He pulled out a piece of paper and wrote a radio frequency. "The old tower still works. Lost power for a while, but we got it back not too long ago. Here, I'll write down the frequency you need to use."

"Thank you."

"It's good to have you back, son." Whiting patted Ryne on the shoulder and made his way back towards his truck. "Watch out for the wolves, eh," he called as he wedged his body into the cabin.

Ryne turned away, shaking.

Shawn spoke up. "Hey man, you o..."

Ryne cut him off, slamming the door.

"Let's get the fuck out of here."

The truck kicked back to life and pulled back onto the main road. The road led right and would eventually take them out of Wolf's Bone altogether and further east, but as they cleared the last building, Ryne turned left into a small opening in the trees and powered through the fresh snow on the path to the cabin in silence.

FOUR
THE DEER

R yne stared directly ahead as the truck pushed its way through the snow-covered trail, his eyes furious and his jaw tight. Whitting had no right to bring up the baby. Absolutely no right. His blood boiled beneath his skin, and, despite the fierce cold outside the window, he ran hot with anger.

"Ryne," Shawn's voice. "Ryne, slow down."

Red. That's all he saw—a consuming, fiery red. The purifying flame of unbridled fury simmering within his temples. It burned the at backs of his eyes as he gripped the steering wheel so tightly his fingers hurt.

"Ryne?"

He remembered the last time this much anger pulsed through his veins. He had been in a hospital room—*that* hospital room.

"Ryne!"

"Fuck!" Ryne slammed the brakes and punched the steering wheel as hard as his strength would allow. Over and over. Nobody in the truck stopped him. A small bit of anger subsided into darkness as he wailed on the wheel, before he finally stopped and slumped forward in a panting heap.

"Ryne," Noah said from the back. "You okay, man?"

"Let him come back," said Shawn. "Few seconds."

Ryne leaned his head back. Cold sweat dripped down his face, and his jaw relaxed.

"I'm good."

The truck sat motionless in the path. They'd been driving for about four miles into the trail, and Wolf's Bone rested well beyond their rearview. Now, the only plane of existence was a world of snow and spruce.

Noah let out a deep sigh from the backseat.

"You beat the absolute *shit* out of that steering wheel, dude."

Against his own mind, the corner of Ryne's mouth curled into a smile, and a quiet laugh escaped his pursed lips. Shawn couldn't help but join in.

"Seriously, how bad do your hands hurt?" Noah asked.

"Pretty fucking bad," Ryne laughed.

"Can we get going, Ali?" Shawn asked. "I'm cold."

"I'm not cold."

"Well, you just went ten rounds with General Motors," said Noah. "Can we go?"

Ryne put the truck back into gear and continued down the path.

He felt stupid having lost his cool, but he'd been festering for a while. A year spent holding everything in as much as possible, trying to create a brave face for everyone who still cared. The effort consumed him, and the parts of him that hadn't yet been devoured by the abyss were sometimes unrecognizable. Some nights he would watch himself from inside his own mind and wonder just who the hell he was even looking at. Like a prisoner within himself, horrible thoughts were born from his cell, and he had spent the past year watching helplessly as those horrible things escaped and shaped this new man out of putrid clay. He put on his old face and pretended everything was fine. Played the role of the recovering griever. Put on a show to fool anyone who cared enough to look.

But now the prison cell was gone, changed into a wall of trees and snow; and there were few people left to fool. And those who remained were sitting in the truck with him, and no mask would fool them. Through the years, the friendship between them had held tight despite distance and occupation. The sense of dissolution and breaking had never occurred to him. When Shawn's baseball dream died, Ryne and Noah were on the first plane to Pittsburgh. When Noah had his accident, the others were at the hospital that afternoon. After the miscarriage, Shawn and

Noah stopped their lives on the spot and returned to offer a shoulder once again.

It was this deep affinity they shared which made this weekend all the more needed—and all the more difficult.

Six months had passed since the accident took his father and uncle. Along with the normal inheritances left by Rory, he'd also received a surprise from Rod. Despite the relationship between the two of them dissipating into little more than a faint vapor, Rod had gifted all of his worldly possessions to Ryne. Rod didn't have much, but he still had the cabin. Now it was Ryne's.

He shouldn't have wanted anything to do with the place. There were still memories held in Wolf's Bone that he would have happily forgotten, times in which the shiny veneer of his family life would show its deep fissures. And besides, he had built an entire life for himself. Had the accident happened a few months prior, he would have sold the cabin the second it became his.

But that was before. The wheels of loss had already been set in motion early in the dark hours of one December morning. Maxie didn't leave until four months later, but those seeds were firmly planted into strong soil that morning. He didn't blame her, and the part of himself that he still recognized hoped she didn't blame him, but he couldn't fault her if she did. He saw himself in the mirror every day and understood that what looked back at him; truthfully what remained, was nothing more than an empty, cracked jar of who he used to be. The drive he once possessed for his job as a teacher and coach had vanished. He no longer got joy out of seeing young minds grow and expand under his tutelage. When his performance at work flatlined, the school didn't offer him a new contract. No reaction. He barely even remembered the conversation. All he recalled was nodding his head and walking, ending the meeting before they finished telling him how concerned they were about him.

The last time he had made this drive, a different man sat behind the wheel. That was ten years ago. Now, he returned a broken one.

He didn't like this empty jar and wanted nothing more than to mend the cracks, refill its contents, and return to some semblance of who he used to be. But there were too many broken pieces, spread too far across the emptiness. Repair wasn't an option, but perhaps restarting was. That was why he'd decided to make this trip, why he wanted the last people in the world he had left to be here—to say goodbye.

* * *

It was dark now. The road through the forest was narrow and shrouded by dark figures of old trees stretching up above the path, a bright moon casting their shadows across it. A light snow misted on the wind, but the night was crisp and clear.

In the backseat, Noah stared out of the side window as the snow-tipped spruce passed by. His breath caught every time Ryne hit a slick spot on the iced path. That was his life now—anxiety for the sake of anxiety. The worst part was that the feeling taking over his body every time he sensed his life teetering at the end of his own sanity was a feeling he couldn't joke away.

As he looked outside at the deep layers of snow sitting atop the frozen ground, he thought about a story he read a long time ago about a man who described his experience of being caught in an avalanche. He remembered the vivid depiction concerning how *fast* ice moved. The story framed the moving cold as the devil himself, incomprehensibly fast and unrelentingly violent. But Noah knew better. Yes, ice was fast. But ice had to get going, build up momentum, and reach top speed before that beast emerged to take you.

Grain, on the other hand, moved in the blink of an eye.

Noah knew all too well how fast everything could change—the speed at which someone's entire world could be uprooted and obliterated in a matter of seconds, with no warning other than the crunch of the grain crust as a foot breaks through.

Four years had passed since he'd died, but he still struggled to shake the anxiety that took him over following the ordeal. The panic birthed from the bottom of the silo had grown and now ate at him from the inside. He'd always tried to be as optimistic of a person as humanly possible. It was easy for him to do. Everyone has their gifts. He wasn't the athlete, nor was he the brains of any group, but perspective came easily to him. He understood how to take a hopeless situation and make something positive come from it. Not an enormous gift, but it played a monumental role in building Noah Stratton's reputation as one of the hardest workers anybody would ever claim to know. It wasn't strength, and it wasn't intelligence—it was grit. Pure willpower. A trait he once possessed in spades.

Spending two hours suffocating to death in the bottom of a grain silo can dissolve the grit of many, and he was no exception. None of them were. The shadow was different for each of them, a different tragedy, but the truth was that neither of them were the same people that had spent two weeks hunting in Kalispell as a senior trip ten years ago. Hell, it seemed so long ago that Noah could barely remember it. Maybe it was brain damage from the accident, or maybe they had drifted so far away from the people they were then that the memory had become a mirage. For that reason, Noah was unsure what they hoped to accomplish here.

It was Ryne, the most recent victim of this metamorphosis, who came up with the idea. Get out of Washington and spend a few days away from the world. Shawn had supported the idea, but Noah wasn't convinced. Ryne didn't even like Wolf's Bone. He also knew that Ryne's family history was much darker than he let on. Shawn only had his own broken home to compare it to, and Noah understood that perspective, but he'd been around as well and had always known something wasn't quite right with the Burdette family. It was as though the lifeblood of the home was colored with secrets. The foundation molded from half-truths and withheld information. It was the two brothers, mostly. Even when they were being cordial to each other, there was a toxin in their voices. Restrained, but there, nonetheless. Inaudible to anyone who didn't know what normal sounded like.

The death of Rory and Rod should have been the end of it all. God, he hated thinking that way, but he couldn't deny the truth. The final anchor had fallen away, and Ryne should have been able to float off into a better life. But it wasn't that simple, and their deaths weren't the reason they were here now. It was *a* reason, but not *the* reason. *The* reason was the entire picture framing each of their lives over the years. For Noah, it began with the grain. For Ryne, it had started long before that. Only festering and coming to a head over the past year. Shawn couldn't see. His home was so shattered that he couldn't see the cracks in the Burdette family facade. Noah could.

The passing view of trees suddenly slowed and came to an abrupt stop as Ryne hit the brakes. The seat belt locked against Noah's chest and his head snapped forward, hitting the back of the passenger headrest.

"Ryne, what the..." His gaze found its way beyond the windshield, his voice drifting off into soundlessness at the sight in front of them.

In the middle of the narrow road stood a reindeer. It faced the truck head-on and stared through the glass. An old buck, massive against the white backdrop, antlers raised high into the air, curving outward and then inward at the top. Long tufts of hair hung beneath its neck as the snow stuck to the tips of the brown-grey mane. A set of black, penetrating eyes upon its face.

"Is it gonna move?" asked Shawn.

"Flash your lights," said Noah.

Ryne flashed the lights on and off, both high and low beams, but the deer didn't move. Not a single inch. It just stood in the snow, filling the space between the darkness and the glow of the headlights. Its black eyes gazing upon them.

Ryne hit the gas and revved the engine. There was no reaction from the animal blocking the way.

"Move, dumbass," said Ryne.

He put the truck into gear and lurched forward, slamming the brakes again before it could hit the deer. Still, the animal did not move.

"Is he in a trance or something?" asked Shawn.

Noah stared at the stolid animal, and a trickle of ice crept through his bones. The hairs on his arms stood beneath his jacket. He'd heard the claim all his life—wild animals were unpredictable. In his experience, however, wild animals were very predictable if you watched and observed them enough, with some extraordinary exceptions. When an animal broke away from the tried-and-true methods and actions of its nature, there was always a specific reason. This was either the single bravest deer evolution could craft, or something was very wrong with it.

* * *

Looking at the deer, Shawn felt the same uneasiness he'd felt in the grocery store. Everything about the animal fit well within the dark cabinets of the unnatural. To see a deer frozen in headlights was one thing; but for it to not react to the flashing lights? For it not to move when the truck had lurched forward?

Whatever the reason, he was growing quite tired of those black eyes looking at him. There was something so intensely off about them. They didn't reflect the headlights and disappeared into the night when Ryne turned the lights off. They were *nothing*. Vacant of any sort of liveliness in an otherwise living thing.

Ryne turned off the headlights again and blared the horn, but the animal did not blink or recoil at the sudden explosion of sound. It didn't even seem to recognize the sound being made, as though it was somewhere else entirely. Just looking at them.

"Fuck this," Shawn said. He opened the door into the snowy dark.

"What the hell are you doing?" asked Ryne.

"Getting it to move."

His heart beat fast and hard against his breastplate as he left the warm truck and emerged into the frozen world outside. Blood pumped through his veins like a generator, keeping a warmth that fought the bite of the soft, freezing wind.

Through the clear, cold night, the animal's gaze shifted to Shawn.

It wasn't in a trance. It wasn't an animal caught in the headlights. The beast was purposely holding its ground. Its black eyes lacerated the crisp night as small flurries of snow danced in the blackness of the frozen breeze.

His heart continued to race, faster now as the eyes of the deer followed him while he moved to the back of the truck. The air in front of him became a cloudy haze with every breath, but the darkness of the animal's eyes could not be shrouded. Step by careful step, Shawn made his way along the side of the truck to the back corner. He fumbled with the tarp while his eyes never left the animal.

It didn't follow him. Still standing in front of the vehicle, it only looked his direction. But that was enough. Cougars, bears, wolves, he had shared the forest with all sorts of predatory beasts, but he'd never felt more unnerved than he did now under the watchful gaze of this deer.

He blindly felt for his target. The animal watched him. His hand ran across the hard roughness of the plastic case. He unlocked the latches, opened the case, and pulled out the rifle inside. He carefully lifted the weapon out of the bed of the truck. Raising it to eye level, he pulled the bolt back and heard the round settle into place.

"Oh, come on," said Ryne from the cab.

"Don't be stupid," said Noah.

"Relax, I'm not going to kill it. Just scare it."

He retraced his steps back to the front of the truck at a cautious pace and moved around the open passenger door as Ryne and Noah looked on.

Even holding the weapon, his nerves tightened and stung as he stepped in front of the grill and into the headlights. The animal stood its ground, and its eyes met his. He had never seen anything so black.

A deep darkness fell from the trees above him, cloaking the path in the black and white of night and snow. He would need to be careful. Raising the gun to his shoulder, he removed the safety and aimed slightly to the right of the animal's head. He planted his feet and prepared for one of two possibilities: either the animal would be so spooked or shaken from the rifle's blast that it would run off, or it would attack. Any normal deer would take option one.

But this was a different beast, and doubt ran through his head. Something was *wrong* with this animal. He needed to be able to move quickly to defend himself and get back into the truck.

He readied his aim. The deer looked at him, and there was something in the blackness of its eyes. Something almost familiar. Something unnerving.

He squeezed the trigger.

A crack blasted through the trees. Violent reverberations filled the air and hung there briefly before fading away. As the soundlessness of the forest returned, he stared in awe at what was in front of him. The deer had not run, nor had it attacked.

It simply stood there. It hadn't moved a single inch.

This was wrong. This was wrong in so many ways. A tightness formed within his chest as the animal's eyes leered into his own.

Something snapped inside him. A long-held moral standing now unraveled from his very being. He raised the gun again, despite everything in his core telling him to put it down. He aimed, this time at the animal's face. Right at those black eyes.

This isn't right, he told himself. *Don't do this. You know better.*

But he could not look at those eyes anymore.

He squeezed the trigger, and another blast erupted through the night air. The bullet found its mark; and the space between man and beast filled with gore and bone. The animal fell in a heap in the snow, and the snow turned red.

Behind him, he heard the door to the truck open.

"Shawn, what the hell!" said Ryne.

"I couldn't look at that thing any longer," he said. "Let's load it up."

"Come on, man," said Noah. "You can't be serious."

"We shot it. That means we use it. You know that."

"I didn't shoot shit."

The deer took their combined strength to move. With effort, they dragged it to the back and placed it on the tailgate before tying it down with straps.

Ryne looked at Shawn in disgust, and Shawn didn't blame him. He had crossed a line. But he could not stand that animal's gaze any longer. And besides, they would use the deer like they were supposed to, so his karma would remain intact.

As he got back into the truck, he glanced at the darkness of the trees enclosing the path. For a moment, he thought he saw something in the black. A set of antlers. And then, as quickly as it had appeared, it vanished back into the black of night.

FIVE

THE CABIN

Nobody said a word for the rest of the drive. The snow covering the path was thick, and Ryne would occasionally have to hammer the accelerator and shift aggressively to push the vehicle through. Darkness swallowed the scenery outside the backseat window as Noah ruminated on the depths of their isolation. The wilderness stretched around them, suffocating the land to the farthest extremes of vision, devouring all exits but the one narrow path. Their phones would be useless once they got to the cabin. Hell, they'd already been useless an hour before they'd arrived in Wolf's Bone. The only way to contact someone would be by radio.

All this made Noah nervous by itself, but the bulk of his anxiety resided within what had not yet arrived. The radio signal had been choppy on the drive into Wolf's Bone. Ryne had downplayed its severity, but brief moments of clarity simmered at the top of Noah's mind. A storm was moving in. A strong one. A variable he hadn't prepared himself for, and this lack of preparation placed him on a very thin edge.

What would happen if the shit hit the fan? If the storm got bad enough that even the radio was useless? If nobody could get to them? Ryne seemed to trust the cabin's structure, but not many structures held Noah's faith. Not anymore.

His thoughts boiled in the boundless cauldron of the land. They were only about two hundred miles south of the Arctic Circle, and the vastness of the forest surrounding them compelled a distinct and terrifying feeling of smallness. They were useless specks against an ancient landscape that tolerated man's existence but did not respect it. Fewer people lived here than in any other province in Canada. The space between them and anything resembling the civilized world, save for the shanty village of Wolf's Bone, was unfathomable. The blood in his veins cooled at the thoughts. He felt like an interloper in a place man was never meant to go.

"We're here," said Ryne.

The cabin formed into shape out of the trees. Squatting in the snow, two stories with a long, steep wood-shingled roof that stretched up and over the frame like a tent. A porch wrapped around the cabin's entirety, and windows reached upwards on both side walls. According to Ryne, the cabin was built in 1856 and had never been added to, only updated; and it showed. The walls were aged, dark brown logs held by craftsmanship and a thick black adhesive almost invisible in the darkness. The windows had obviously been changed to a tempered, more insulated glass. But the frames around the windows were old, bent and contorted at the edges, pressed to their limit to fit the new glass. A small shed sat to the right with an old wooden door that looked like it belonged to one of the shanty homes back in town.

Ryne pulled the truck up to the cabin, placed it in park, and applied the parking brake for good measure.

The snow beneath Noah's feet crunched as he stepped out of the truck and onto the frozen ground. Panic spread with a sudden quickness through his nerves as the sound of the grain crust breaking beneath his weight was summoned from the darkness of his memory and became a siren in his head. All sounds were instantly drowned out and replaced by the single crunch that preceded the sudden burial years earlier. An intense restlessness overtook his muscles, his lungs constricted by some outside force pressing in on his chest.

He gripped the lining of the truck bed and breathed slow and deep. The panic came quickly, but it wouldn't last long. He just had to remember that there was solid ground beneath his feet, however many breaths it took. He gathered himself and mentally recited lines from a poem he had always liked.

The woods are lovely, dark, and deep. But I have promises to keep, and miles to go before I sleep.

Another deep breath, slow exhale, and repetition of the mantra. The panic filtered out of him, slinking back into its dark place with the promise that it would return upon the next inevitable trigger.

Shawn looked at him with concern in his eyes but, with a dismissive wave of his hand, Noah assured him he could handle it on his own. He'd been at war with the panic for two years now and had developed his own system for dealing with it. Breathing and repeating the poetic line in his head helped calm him during the first few attacks after the accident, but the panic was getting more devious, more intrusive with time. The attacks never lasted long, but their severity increased and required deeper breaths, longer exhalations, and more repetitions. He shuddered to think about how much longer he would be able to keep it at bay.

Ryne pulled the tarp off the bed of the truck, and they grabbed their bags, moving cautiously, avoiding the faceless carcass tied to the tailgate.

They made their way to the porch. Noah looked around the back and saw where both sides of the wraparound met in the back before continuing on a long wooden walkway that carried off into the trees.

"Where does that go?" he asked.

"Leads down to the lake," said Ryne.

Noah's eyes locked on the dark path. A sliver of panic, lingering like a stubborn mist, still crawled around the corners of his mind. Maybe a walk and some fresh air would help.

"Mind if I throw my stuff down inside and go see it?"

"Knock yourself out."

"Where's the flashlight?"

'What's wrong, scared of the dark?" asked Shawn.

"Yes. Very much so, thank you."

"In my bag," said Ryne.

"I'll get started on the deer," said Shawn.

* * *

Standing on the cabin's open floor, a familiar wave rushed through Ryne, and he couldn't help but feel connected by even the most fragile of heartstrings.

Shawn had rightly decided it was his duty to clean the deer and stood outside making the preparations to do so. Noah wanted to walk to the lake. But there was nowhere for Ryne to go, no task to perform, no sight to see.

He stood silently next to the couch, love seat, and recliner that had stayed in the same area for his entire life. Change wasn't a popular concept in Wolf's Bone, and the cabin was no exception. The cloth covering the furniture was the old horrific shades of yellow and blue popular in the 1960s, and the Formica counters and handmade wooden cabinets of the kitchen formed a garish contrast with the dark, treated log walls holding back the outside wild.

He took a deep breath and let it go; the air drifted from his lungs. So many memories. Not all good, but he was running out of space for the bad ones. His family had always been torn into two halves, and each of those halves held a distinct name. Rory and Rod. It was in this cabin that those two worlds collided more than anywhere else. And within those collisions came the best and the worst of what the Burdette family offered.

As a young boy, the trips to the cabin were the highlights of his winter, if not the entire year. The only child from either branch of his grandfather's lineage, he remembered having a special kinship with both his father and uncle when they were still tethered to the natural world. Days were spent stalking through thick snowfall looking for game, and nights spent sleeping beside a campfire listening to the two brothers recount stories from their childhoods, making for a warm and comfortable blanket from the cold of the rest of the world.

But a strangeness always permeated the air around his family. The two men were far from loving brothers in their everyday lives. Meetings back home would often end in sharp words or blunt fists. Heavy tension thickened the air during family Thanksgiving dinners, and Rod would often procure the wrath of Ryne's mother for skipping Christmas and telling Ryne that his family shouldn't be celebrating *that* day.

In Wolf's Bone, however, all appeared forgiven. The brothers put aside their differences and seemed to enjoy each other's company, with Ryne along for the ride. But as time went on, his childhood slipped into the abyss of the past, and the warm blanket became frozen with tension and contempt. The more venomous the brother's relationship became, the more the cabin itself seemed poisoned by their anger.

He looked up at the upstairs loft. The only room was on the cabin's second floor. Directly above the one bedroom, open to everything. He remembered being up there, holding a pillow over his ears as the old sanctuary below became a debate floor without rules. Just wishing it would stop. Wishing it could go back to how it used to be. How it was supposed to be.

At twenty years old, he'd sat in the hospital with his father as his mother withered away into the darkness of cancer. Rod never showed up. No call, no text, no late-night visit of apology. Nothing but silent indifference. Rory never asked where his brother might be at the lowest moment of his life, and Ryne figured that was the final fracture in their brotherhood.

But family is a strange thing. Like a snake caught in a trap. There is always that need, that compulsion to reach out and offer a hand of assistance, while your better sense screams that you're inviting a bite. Because despite best efforts, some things—like Wolf's Bone and the cabin— never change. Even after everything, Ryne had come back.

He wouldn't sleep in the loft anymore. It made him uneasy sleeping next to that tall window. Like the forest was looking in on him. Tree branches stretched towards the window like hands reaching.

It was stupid. Childish. Immature and unbecoming. But it was there, nonetheless.

He walked into the room below the loft against the back wall. The bed took up all but four feet on three sides of the room. A single lantern sat on a small nightstand. Four bedposts rose upwards from each corner, hand-crafted out of the same dark wood as the walls. Ryne wondered how old this bed was and how long it had rested the long-gone members of his family.

He set his bag on the ground, unzipped the small compartment on the side, and pulled out a brown box. Flat and wide, his father's hands had crafted it years ago. Inside was a small, but poignant, little artifact. A dream-catcher. Light and delicate to the touch, the rings made of the molded bones of an owl, bent and preserved with tender care. Small tufts of fur from the many animals found within the Yukon taiga wrapped tightly within small, white feathers. Strips of velvet from deer antlers, processed into a thin twine and stretched across the frame into an intricate pattern that resembled some strange sigil.

He hung the dreamcatcher upon the bedpost closest to where he would sleep. At the base of the string, it moved stiff and soft and fragile.

Along with the cabin, he inherited his childhood home in Pullman and his uncle's trailer in Moscow. Both homes were sold now, and all material items auctioned away. He'd rid himself of everything as quickly as he could. All that remained for him in memory of his family's legacy was the cabin and the dreamcatcher.

* * *

The moon had risen completely above the tree line, the last vestiges of daylight smothered above the smooth ice of the frozen lake. Noah sat at the end of the long dock. The frigid night blew a sharp wind over the ice that slapped him in the face. But he smiled. The cold caught in his beard, and a tingling sensation raced through the veins of his face. A lightness in his chest. The panic leaving his body.

For him, the cold was a welcome home. Every summer, he worked under the warm sun and longed for the return of the crisp taste of oncoming winter that never arrived fast enough. Here? In this place? Perpetual winter. He had no idea what the Yukon summers were like, but he liked to think that the cold was always here. Like a friend who didn't want to leave. He imagined that even the summers had a certain bite to it, a promissory note that the cold would soon arrive again. It was a simple affection, really. He remembered back home the beauty of the grass as the seasons changed. The grass would die, as all things did, and turn a hard amber. The reeds, hanging onto the last gasp of summer's spent warmth, would stretch up above the grass and blow in the winter wind that raked its way across the Palouse.

While it was an enjoyable hobby, Noah was never an avid hunter. That was Shawn and Ryne's thing. Noah preferred the outdoors because he appreciated the simple beauty of a land created by happenstance. The combination of so many random events unfolding to create a type of art touched a spot in his soul that many things proved unable to reach.

Most of all, he enjoyed the outdoors because they were open. Even in the darkness, he could see the vast expanse of the beautiful Yukon taiga, illuminated by a moonlit sky filling with deep stars. The hills of spruce rising from the pristine ice, thickening into a forest; that was the only thing in existence until the horizon line where the world fell off into an uncertain place. And the air was clean. All those years working, building houses, and pushing items in factories. His lungs always heavy with the presence of something unwelcome. Sawdust, soot, that thick grime that saturated every single shop he'd ever stepped foot in. The suffocating oil inside the grain silos.

No, this was him. This was the air he wanted. Brisk and clean, untouched by man's greasy hands, pure as the driven snow that covered this exquisite landscape. The beauty of the creation almost drowned the isolated feeling he'd felt earlier. He wished he could stay in the wilderness. After his accident, he found himself wishing that more and more often. The epiphany he experienced while choking to death in grain oil had forced him to reconsider everything he'd ever known, thought, or felt. He now knew what happened when the lights went out, and all that did was draw him closer to the wild.

But despite the landscape stretching out before him and all the beauty within it, Noah sensed a presence of something that did not belong. There was an extra snap to the cold, different from anything else he'd ever experienced. The ice appeared so unsettlingly thin; he could swear he saw ripples of water as something moved beneath the frozen veneer. His smile abandoned him, and he shivered as the tips of his frozen fingers burned beneath ineffective gloves. The image of the deer in the road was stapled in his mind, and the eeriness of it all played a constant tone within his freezing core.

A random, frightening thought intruded into the inner sanctum of his mind. A sudden urge to step out onto the ice. Just to see if it would hold. He shook the thought away from his consciousness and rose to his feet, his joints cracking with the effort. He gave one last long look at the lake and surrounding landscape, wondering if the unwelcome presence was him.

* * *

The knife slid into the leg of the deer hanging from the large tree that held its roots at the base of the surrounding tree line. Shawn dragged the knife upwards towards the elbow of the animal. Cleaning and quartering a deer had never been an issue for him. He'd always possessed a particular talent for the act. With the right knife in his hands, his wrists, strengthened and emboldened from years swinging a bat, would provide the support necessary to complete the gruesome process quickly. He had already moved past the part of the process that made every girl he'd ever dated squirm—the dressing. The entrails of the deer had been buried beneath a thick patch of snow just beyond the edge of the trees. Now came the act of cleaning the animal.

But, as Shawn ran his blade up the sides of the animal towards the fastened back legs, his hands shook with nervousness. He hadn't wanted to shoot the deer. There was no sport in it, no honor in it. Like those assholes back home who paid hundreds of dollars to hunt on fenced land where they chased and cornered the terrified animal and fired away before spending more money to have someone clean the poor thing. These people would drive home so satisfied with themselves for a cheated kill.

That was how Shawn felt now. Like he was cleaning an animal he had no right to clean. This wasn't a fair hunt. No, this was a last resort. Still, he'd pulled the trigger, so the responsibility fell on him. That was the quintessential difference between him and those other people. They would've left the animal dead in the snow, rotting away in the cold. He couldn't think of a more insulting action.

His knife reached the top of the back leg near the fastener. He cut around the leg to the bone and pulled the hide from the meat. He planted his feet and pushed hard against the ground to steady himself as he pulled. His knee throbbed, but the cursed joint held firm enough for him to remove the hide. Inside the deer, the meat shined in the darkness.

That meat had long been the lifeblood of his family. Through the eyes of a child, he'd watched his father drink his way through job after job as the food in the refrigerator became replaced with cases of beer. His mother had no say on the subject. It didn't matter that she wanted to feed her kids. He would never let her spend any of *his* money. That money was reserved for the poison of men not meant for families. His mother wilted away, as did his sisters. They looked like ghosts. Lived like them, too.

Hunting very well may have saved his life. His trips into the woods with Ryne and Rory Burdette usually resulted in something coming home. It

41

was there he learned the particular skill required to retrieve clean, hairless meat from a hunted animal. Where he learned the most important thing about this lifestyle. What you kill, you eat. No exceptions. To waste meat was spitting in nature's face for a precious gift. It was a duty, a responsibility he had taken seriously from those early moments of life. Through these lessons, a bond formed between the neglected boy and his surrogate family. Shawn always felt like a burden in his own home, but Rory never looked at him that way. He entrenched these lessons into Shawn just as he had to his own son.

He would hunt as many weekends as possible. Then, when his father would drink himself into a coma and pass out on the couch, he would grab the venison hidden in the back freezer. He would cook the meat, just enough for himself, his mother, and his sister. Not his father. That bastard deserved nothing. The day he had finally left; Shawn cooked a gourmet meal for his family. He thanked the forest for everything it gave him and held a profound respect for it. If he were to ever have children, he would teach them that respect. He would instill those values in them.

But he couldn't deny that something felt very different here. The whole situation was wrong. He shot and killed an animal, but it hadn't behaved like an animal. No, this deer had behaved like a stubborn child; unwilling to move until Shawn moved for it. As he looked at the meat glistening in the deepening Yukon night, a darkness filled his mind. He didn't want to eat this meat. A violation of everything he built his life around, but he couldn't help it. He stood for a long while in front of the hanging deer trying to reconcile his thoughts.

The most unsettling thing Shawn had ever experienced on a hunt was the first time he heard a cougar screaming. Bone-chilling. As though there was some poor woman out in the wild being held in place and torn open. He'd been engulfed in fear and, thinking he had just witnessed the sounds of a murder, ran as fast as he could back to Ryne and Rory. Rory laughed and explained what he had heard.

From then on, it wasn't scary. Shawn understood the sound as a natural part of the forest. He'd heard the scream many times following that day, but it no longer held any effect on him. An animal, nothing more. A reason to be cautious, sure. But not scared.

But this was different. This was the antithesis of natural. There was nothing rational, nothing sensible, nothing usual or explainable about the deer. It had been so unnatural that it almost seemed human. Like something somebody would do to prove they weren't scared. Playing chicken. Taunting.

A shudder went through him every time he looked at the carcass. He would clean it, but he didn't know if he could eat it. These thoughts festered within his mind as he slid the knife into the backstrap next to the spinal column and began to cut.

SIX

WHISPERS

As the night continued its forward march, Ryne stood next to the burning campfire a few yards off the porch of the cabin. He grilled the meat of the deer on a grill tray laid over the open flame as light flurries of snow fell around him like thin curtains in the dark. Inside, the atmosphere had been pleasant, with Noah and Shawn sitting at the living area table playing a card game, throwing insults back and forth in-between catching up with new stories about the lives they'd led between tragic reunions. Their camaraderie eased Ryne and seemed to bring the others some comfort as well. The specter of the deer was gone for now, out of sight and out of mind. He could have stayed inside, but the impending conversation weighed upon him. The campfire provided clear air and a crisp resolve.

Venison sat on the grill for Noah and himself, while Shawn only wanted a salad. He'd acted strange about eating the deer, but Ryne hadn't pressed him. In fairness, even Ryne contemplated making something else for himself. As stupid as he found Rory and Rod's rule about eating the meat here, it didn't change the fact that the custom was seared deep into his being, and he would be lying if he said he didn't feel wrong going against the wishes of his father.

Beyond the flames was the grip of night. The clouds had rolled in and covered the moon, birthing an impenetrable darkness broken only by the dim glow stretching from the high windows of the cabin. As the meat crackled and spat in the pan, Ryne checked his surroundings. The aroma of the searing meat would carry on the wind, and this deep into winter, there were plenty of hungry mouths in these woods.

But, for now, the night was silent. Empty. A place of quiet reflection. The feeling of inevitability laid claim to his thoughts. There was a hard conversation on the near horizon, and he had no idea how it would be received. Maybe they'd understand. Get it. Respect his decision and realize his logic. He hoped with everything he had that they would. He needed them to.

The silence was broken as a crack echoed softly in the night—a limb, snapped by something out in the trees. Ryne's entire body went rigid, his eyes wide and alert. He scanned the tree line, which stood shrouded in black. Nothing moved but the soft flurries dancing upon the faint breeze. The woods were quiet again, but a tension, tight and compressed, twisted around his nerves. A sense that he was not alone by the campfire. That something stalked its way carefully and quietly between the trees, wrapped in night and watching.

Slowly, he backed up onto the porch, every step a careful measure, never taking his eyes off the dark trees. He reached back and knocked on the door behind him. The door opened, and Shawn stuck his head out.

"What's up?"

"Get the rifle."

"Why?"

"Just get the goddamn gun," Ryne hissed. "There's something out here."

Shawn hurried back into the cabin and returned a few seconds later with the gun. Ryne felt blindly for a grip on the weapon. Neither of them dared take their eyes off the dark. His hand finally found its hold and took the gun. He raised the stock to his shoulder and took aim.

Another crack. Light footsteps breaking through the frozen snow layer. Soft and careful; but booming in the quiet of the night. Ryne followed these steps, not with his eyes, but with his ears. The woods taught him long ago that he couldn't trust his eyes. Not at night. They would see shadows that weren't there. But his ears wouldn't. Sound was sound and couldn't be manipulated by darkness; only amplified. His blood cold, he listened for the track.

If it was a wolf, then he had to be careful not to hone-in entirely on one sound. Wolves rarely traveled alone. Even if this was a party away from the main pack, there would be more than one for sure.

The sound moved across the tree line towards the spot where Shawn had buried the deer's entrails in the snow. A noise like digging, quick and frantic. But he couldn't see anything. Then the sound stopped.

He should hear low panting or growling now—especially if they had found the discarded guts. But he heard nothing. Nothing but silence and the soft footsteps on the crusty snow.

He felt a new coldness within him. Deep in his marrow. Something seemed off here. Wrong. His eyes focused hard, and then widened as he noticed something else. The trees had stopped moving. There had been a gentle sway against the cold wind before. But now they stood motionless. Like statues standing guard.

It was as if they were watching him as well.

The footsteps changed direction. Ryne listened, the stock of the rifle firm against his shoulder and his eyes tracing down the barrel to the sight. Whatever was in the trees was making its way towards the cabin. Then Ryne heard what he didn't want to hear. The footsteps broke their rhythm.

Another set of steps coming from the left.

"There's more from this way," whispered Shawn behind him, his head turned to the right.

All sides now converged on the cabin.

"If there's anybody out there, say something now," Ryne said. But they were fifteen miles into the wild. Whatever was closing in on the cabin was no man. Couldn't be.

Ryne squeezed the trigger and fired off a blind shot into the trees.

He heard the splintering crack as the bullet hit some distant bark. As the echo from the shot and the strike died away, the ringing in his ears slowly subsided. The silence of the woods returned, and the trees resumed their quiet sway.

"Are they gone?" Shawn asked.

"I think so," said Ryne.

"Wolves?"

"Yeah," he said, finally lowering the weapon. "Yeah, had to be. Probably hungry."

"Let's go inside. I think the food is done," said Shawn as smoke bellowed from the campfire. Ryne quickly placed the venison on a metal tray and smothered the campfire. He looked back at the trees continuing in their soft dance with the wind. He looked for any lingering shadow, listened for any remaining footstep. But it was just the night. Just the cold. Just the trees.

* * *

Shawn ate his salad as Noah sat on the couch and ripped into the grilled backstrap. After ten hours of nothing but snacks and jerky, everyone was starving. In the recliner across from them, Ryne stared down at the backstrap on his plate. He looked lost, as though he'd been unable to shake the encounter's grasp.

Shawn couldn't figure out why. A hungry pack moving in on a camp wasn't uncommon, especially during the winter. But Ryne's reaction suggested something different, something not of the usual experiences. He seemed unnerved.

Shawn supposed that maybe the animals had gotten closer than he'd realized. Neither he nor Ryne actually saw the wolves. But the night was devouring and, with only the small campfire to light the land, they could have missed something close to them—especially something with gray fur against the snow. Still, he wasn't worried. While his anxiety had been out of control in recent hours, he didn't fret about the possibility of wolves. Wolves were natural parts of the land. He could easily explain and analyze natural predator behavior. It made sense in every way the deer had not. This familiarity bred a warm comfort in him.

Ryne picked around his food. His fork clattering against the ceramic plate, pushing around the backstrap. His eyes turned up, and he put the fork and plate down on the table.

"Hey, guys?" he said. "Thank you for coming up here. I know you have lives, and this was kind of a last-minute thing, but I want to let you know how much I appreciate it."

Both Shawn and Noah stopped eating. "No problem, man," said Noah. "Whatever you need, you know we've got you."

"I know," said Ryne. "Which is why I wanted to tell you guys how much I appreciate everything before I tell you the reason we're here."

Shawn and Noah gave each other a look. A nonverbal conversation. *The reason we're here? What was he talking about?*

"The past year has been tough. Really tough. The baby, my job, my dad, the divorce. I don't have much left, and I know part of that blame is on me, most of it, actually. I should have handled things better. Should have been a better husband, better worker, better friend. I'm not the same person I was before. It's taken me a while to admit this, but this past year broke me."

Shawn didn't like where this was going. Without a doubt, Ryne had lived a rough year, but he survived it. Now, his words seemed poisoned. Defeated. Like someone who's lost a fight before the first punch.

"So, I figure the best thing to do is to tear it down and build it back from scratch. That's why I wanted us all to come up here. I wanted to spend one last weekend with you guys. Because I'm not going home with you."

"What?"

"Care to explain that one a little further?"

"I'm staying here," said Ryne. "In the cabin. It's mine, it's paid off, there's no rent. My uncle left me everything. There's nothing back in Washington for me."

"The hell do you mean there's nothing back in Washington?" said Shawn. "You've got a life back—"

"I sold the houses. I paid off the apartment lease. Everything else I gave to Maxie in the divorce. I have nothing left there."

Anger pulsed within his veins.

"And what do you have here, huh? You think you're Grizzly Adams or something? There is nothing here! Just a bunch of empty space to mope around in. At least back home you've got people who care about you."

"Ryne," said Noah. "Look, man, I get that it's been a rough year, but this is not the way. You're trying to make yourself numb and you're never going to get there."

"It's not about feeling numb..."

"No, it's about you giving up," said Shawn.

"Shawn, calm down," said Noah.

"No, this is insane. He's acting like he's the only one of us that lost something."

"What you lost and what I lost are two very different things," said Ryne.

"Don't talk down to me. This isn't some fucking competition. This is you feeling sorry for yourself and straight giving up. You don't think I've suffered, fine. Then you've got a short memory. But Noah was dead. And he didn't quit. It's still in his head. Or don't you see that? You see the way he shakes? He didn't quit. Not like you're talking about."

"I didn't want this..."

"I don't care what you wanted. I'm not about to sit and watch you give up on yourself."

"I'm not giving up," Ryne said. "That's not what this is."

"Yes, it is," said Noah, his voice soft and distant. "You can dress it however you want, but we all know where this is headed."

"Besides," added Shawn. "Why would you stay here, anyway? You don't even like it here."

Ryne sat down soundlessly, his eyes to the floor.

"I don't like it anywhere, Shawn. At least here I can be alone."

"And you think this is a good thing?"

"No," said Ryne. "But I think there are worse things. I'm trying to figure out how to best handle all this."

"And quitting on everything? That's your plan?"

"No, rebuilding my life is my plan. This might not be permanent, but I don't know when I'll be coming back. I need to fix myself first before I fix anything else."

A fury burned behind Shawn's eyes. His breathing was heavier now, and a migraine drilled through the base of his skull. This road had a clear destination, and he wasn't about to let Ryne drive down it.

"This is bullshit," he said. "I can't talk to you like this. You sound just like you did..."

The words broke away even as they formed in his throat. Noah looked at him, his eyes wide with dreadful anticipation. Shawn could read those eyes like a book. *Don't say it*, they said. *I know you want to, but don't.*

"I sound just like what?" asked Ryne, his voice hard. Solid.

"Nothing," said Shawn.

"No, you have something to say. Say it."

"Ryne--"

"Be a man, and fucking say it."

Shawn looked at his friend. His brother, for all intents and purposes. Looked through him to his center. Noah shook his head, but Shawn didn't care. He was over it. Beyond it. The only thing left to say was a hard truth.

"You sound just like you did when Maxie left."

Ryne's face boiled with hatred for the words that dared leave his mouth, but Shawn wasn't done.

"This crap has got to stop. You don't think clearly when you get in these moods. You say shit you don't mean, and you fuck up good things--"

Ryne threw the glass plate across the room where it crashed against the wooden wall, breaking apart into dozens of jagged ceramic teeth falling to the floor.

Shawn didn't budge.

"And you do stupid shit like that," he said.

Moments passed without a word. For most of those moments, Shawn thought Ryne would start swinging. Their friendship never went that far, but Shawn had never crossed a line the way he just did, and he knew it. But it needed to be done. If this is what it took to save his friend's life, then he would wear it. He might have to. Shawn could see the stress on Ryne's face, the tremble in his shoulders. The space between them was heavy.

The quiet passed, and he saw Ryne's shoulders relax.

"I'm sorry," he said. "But that's what I'm doing."

"At least sleep on it," said Noah.

"I will, but I'm not promising anything." He started walking towards the bedroom but stopped at the door.

"Shawn," he said, his voice dark, restrained. "I get what you're saying. I really do. But I don't think you get what I'm saying. I'll sleep on this, but you sleep on what I've said tonight, too. And one more thing. Do not ever speak to me about that again."

Shawn said nothing. Ryne went into his room and closed the door, ending the conversation for good.

"Did you have to go there?" asked Noah.

"Yes," said Shawn. "He's going to kill himself out here. Not directly, and not quickly, but this plan will kill him. We have to talk him out of this."

"What if we can't?"

"I'm not leaving until we do."

He made his bed on the couch. Noah said something incomprehensible to himself and climbed the stairs to the loft. The lights of the cabin dimmed away. Became a fog of embers in the fireplace. Shawn gazed at these embers, burning and dying within each other as all things do. He hoped he wouldn't dream. That he would close his eyes and be instantly transported to a morning where logic and sense ruled again. Instead, he lay helpless on an old couch while his best friend drifted violently away. It took a while, but his eyelids grew heavy as the last of the embers died, and he fell asleep to the image of the deer in his mind. Its black eyes cutting through him as midnight closed in.

* * *

It was a few minutes past one in the morning when Ryne stirred, awoken by the sound of a soft voice floating through the cabin. He sat up and rubbed his eyes, surely hearing some remnant of a dream. He just needed a moment to recuperate himself.

But the voice didn't stop. It drifted along the cold air of the room, seeping through the gentle space. He got out of bed, his feet freezing against the cabin floor even inside his socks. He wrapped himself in the bed comforter, pulled it tight around his body, and opened the bedroom door.

Shawn was already awake, his breath smoke in the dark air. The moon, full and bright, shined down through the loft window above. Noah made his way down the stairs, shivering.

"What is going on?" he asked.

"Shh!" said Shawn. "Listen."

The voice sang along. A hum, quiet and eerie, ethereal in its lightness, coming from all directions simultaneously, like it was floating in the cabin air on moving particles. Ryne's ears focused as the sound materialized into a familiar realm, and his heart galloped against his breastbone.

It sounded like a child singing.

"I'm not the only one hearing this, right?" asked Shawn.

"No," said Ryne.

"Am I crazy," said Noah. "Or does that sound like a kid?"

Ryne looked around but couldn't pinpoint the direction the sound was coming from. It was barely audible, but it was there—bleeding through the walls.

Shawn stood; his eyes locked on the far window. Ryne followed his gaze out of the glass into the moonlit night, and his breath caught somewhere in his chest.

Within this newly lit forest was the most bizarre sight he had ever seen.

Surrounding the cabin were dozens of animals. Reindeer, wolves, beavers, muskrats, foxes, wolverines, mountain goats, and bears—all standing outside the cabin, looking in.

Shawn whispered something, but his voice was choked and inaudible. Like the air had been vacuumed from his lungs.

The sound continued moving softly throughout the cabin. A faint echo off distant trees.

Ryne stood frozen. In his periphery, he saw Shawn, entranced by the uncanny sight, and Noah, standing further back, his face tight and his eyes unblinking. His belly rose and fell with heavy breaths.

"The woods are lovely, dark, and deep. But I have promises to keep, and miles to go before I sleep," Noah said, his voice choppy and soft.

The animals stared into the cabin, unmoving. Noah continued his breathless chant.

In the strangeness, a realization crept into Ryne's mind. Listening carefully, he could swear that the sound was coming from outside.

From the animals.

That was crazy. That was the kind of thing insane people talk about when receiving their pills in the asylum. No reason, no path existed that would invite the possibility. The sound could not be coming from the forms outside.

And yet, he couldn't escape the blackened thought that they were.

Then, a dark cloud moved in front of the moon and consumed everything in shadow. The animals' figures were briefly outlined in the blackness and then faded into the night. The sound stopped, and the cabin was quiet again.

"Can we please light a fire?" asked Noah. "Please?"

Ryne tossed a new starter log into the fireplace and, with a trembling hand, struck a match and tossed the flame in. The log caught quickly, and warmth and light imbued the cabin.

"What in God's name was that?" asked Shawn.

"I don't know," said Ryne.

"There were bears," said Noah. His unblinking gaze hadn't left the window.

"Bears?" asked Shawn.

"They shouldn't have been there," said Noah. "It's below zero outside in the dead of winter. The bears should be hibernating. Why were there bears?"

The fire grew and cracked in the quiet cabin. The voice was gone, the animals vanished, and all that remained of the encounter was a thick blanket of unnerving disquiet that slowly molded itself around them all. Ryne could almost feel it tightening, constricting him.

"We should try to get some sleep."

* * *

Upstairs in the loft, Noah tossed and turned in his sleep. Hours had passed since the strange encounter, and they were all emotionally exhausted. They agreed to discuss the matter of Ryne staying in the cabin more over the next two nights. Shawn was still upset, but an unspoken understanding lingered. Nobody was in any kind of position to think clearly. Not after the deer. Not after the animals.

Everything about the day had been strange. From the wintry welcome of Wolf's Bone to the deer in the road. Now, the sight that had manifested outside the cabin. The chill in his bones hadn't subsided, and his teeth hurt from clenching and grinding so much. He searched for a reason. A purpose. He convinced himself of some rational explanation for the strange behavior, and the more he thought about it, the more he could mold it into a relatable shape in his mind. These were true wild animals. Human interaction was something alien to many of them. The Yukon was sparsely populated, so many of the animals had most likely never even seen a human before. That could be the cause of the strange behavior.

It had to be.

Noah didn't like Ryne's decision either, but he couldn't say he agreed with Shawn's methods. But that was Shawn. You always knew where you stood with him. Noah understood the stakes. Ryne was lost and broken, but Noah had disagreed with the trip in the first place, and now he was justified in his concern. Letting Ryne stay behind was the equivalent of rolling a boulder down a hill. Once it got started, there was nowhere else to go.

They had two more nights. Two nights to bring Ryne out of that shadow.

They needed to put everything into perspective. There was a logical explanation for what was going on and wasting time trying to find it wasn't helping anyone. They had to come to grips with that and move on to the important problem. Noah tossed again, his belly full and satisfied with the backstrap and his head fuzzy with sleepiness.

Somewhere off in the distance, a deep rumbling of thunder rolled across the land as he drifted off to sleep under the black winter sky.

SEVEN

PHANTOMS

R yne woke from a dreamless night to the sizzling sound and fatty aroma of bacon frying in a hot pan. The ice outside the window had created a frozen glaze over the glass, impenetrable by the human eye. But the room was warm, and he had sweat through his thermal pajamas. He had always been fascinated by how much one little fireplace could turn the cabin into a sauna.

The thought of the previous night cooled his sweating body. He had fought sleep while wrestling with the facts of what he'd seen, what he'd heard, until, eventually, he had exhausted all options and fell asleep with more questions than answers.

The heavy specter of the conversation preceding the strangeness of the night still loomed thick as well. His friends were upset, especially Shawn, but he meant what he'd said. Nothing waited for him back in Pullman. Those dark and empty rooms of his old home were now filled with the lives of someone else. And while he could not have been more appreciative of the friendship he shared with Shawn and Noah; they were both small lights in a life of agonizing darkness. A life he wanted nothing more to do with. Yes, Wolf's Bone had soured in his mind over the years, but the cabin provided him a chance to pretend the place didn't exist. Sure, he would need to make routine trips into the town for necessities, but he would be alone. That was all he wanted.

His eyes struggled to adjust to the absent light in the room, but he made out a dim glow beyond the frosted window. He checked his watch. Noon. The sun had risen an hour ago. He got up and changed into shorts and a short-sleeved shirt before walking into the living area.

Sunlight poured through the windows, illuminating the interior of the cabin with a bright glow. Shawn stood by the fireplace watching the bacon sizzle atop the grill tray. Noah sat on the couch and ate away at a thick strip of meat. It must have been more backstrap from the deer.

"We bought bacon?"

"No," said Shawn. "I packed some before we left and kept it at the bottom of the ice chest."

"Sweet," he said as he sat on the sofa next to Noah.

"That deer may have been one of the weirdest things I've ever seen," said Noah. "But it is delicious."

"Glad you like it," said Shawn, placing strips of bacon on a plate and handing it to Ryne. "Because it is all yours. I'm not touching that thing."

"Your loss." Noah ripped away another thick piece. "My gain."

Ryne worried about Noah. He didn't handle difficulty the same way he used to. He'd always been so resilient, even as a kid. Tough, in a way the others weren't. The three of them all had different reactions when things would go to shit. Ryne would usually recoil into silence, wrapping every thought into an emotional ball and burying it deep inside before an inevitable private explosion. Shawn, the fireball, would get angry and loud, even combative. Noah had always been the balance. Placed perfectly between them. His presence kept the group in check more times than not.

At least, that was the Noah he remembered.

But that person was long gone. When Ryne's phone rang following the accident, he was told his friend was dead, pronounced on the scene by the first responders. And then, a miracle out of thin air, he was alive. Just like that. It defied explanation, but it had happened, nonetheless. He'd stepped across the veil and then returned. But there was always this feeling, even an understanding— that Noah hadn't come back, not fully. The spunky, head-strong, go-getter had perished under a sea of grain. What lived now was a phantom of his friend. A ghost holding up imaginary and impossible weight.

But despite all the weight upon his shoulders, Noah seemed to be holding it well for the time being. Relaxed and unfazed, he ate tenaciously, with an appetite Ryne hadn't witnessed in years. It felt good to see him this way. It had been far too long.

They finished their food in relative silence aside from the crackling fire and the smacking sounds of their eating. There was a coldness against Ryne's neck as he felt Shawn's gaze. He wasn't interested in the discussion behind those eyes and had no desire to revisit or reassess last night's argument. Shawn would never understand. He talked a big game about not giving up, but his existence painted a perfect counterpoint. Three years. It had been three years since Shawn blew his knee out. Ryne had seen him endure multiple rounds of intense physical therapy and attend tryout after tryout, all to no avail. Time and time again, scouts tried to tell him the truth, as unfortunate as it was. His career was done. The injury had stolen his greatest skill set. His uniqueness had vanished; and he'd become no different a player than any other minor leaguer.

And yet, he refused to leave this constant, miserable struggle to reclaim what he no longer possessed. Just as Noah and Ryne lost parts of themselves, so had Shawn. And he reeked of desperation. He had put all his eggs in an incredibly fragile basket. Circumstance had obliterated that basket, and he must have realized he wasn't really qualified to do anything else. And through all the boisterous talk, he wore his fear all over his face. The very thought of the uncertain future terrified him. Shawn could throw as many stones as he wanted, but first he'd need to shatter his own glass walls. But he would never do it. He was cursed to haunt the space inside those walls. Cursed to forever look at the reflection of what might have been. Another phantom.

When Ryne looked at the three of them, that's what he saw. Phantoms.

He glanced towards the window. Off in the distance, a large charcoal gray cloud, opaque and goading, loomed across the horizon.

"The storm is getting close."

Noah looked up from his meal and out the window, and Shawn's accusatory glance broke away and refocused on the coming storm.

"It's been sitting out there since yesterday," said Noah. "Why is it moving so slow?"

"Is it usually like this?" asked Shawn.

The doors of memories opened within Ryne's head as he searched for anything comparable to what blackened the distant sky; but he found no memory, no file on record to explain the visual beyond the trees. "No," he said. "The storms could get rough, but that thing is barely moving. It's just building up. I've never seen one stalled like that."

"I hate to bring this up," said Shawn. "But maybe we should get out of Dodge."

Ryne turned, looking Shawn in the eye for the first time all morning. "We talked about this."

"We might *need* to leave."

"I told you—I'm not leaving."

"Oh, for God's sake. Do you not see what I see?"

"It's a storm, Shawn. What about going hunting? The only hunting we've done is you blowing some deer's face off."

"Look man, I want to go hunting too, but I'm not blind enough to not see those clouds coming in."

"It's a storm," Ryne repeated. "I've been through plenty like that up here. Hunted through them, too."

"You *just* said that you don't remember one moving like this."

"I don't, but it's been years."

"I feel like you'd remember something like that."

Ryne stopped talking. The conversation wasn't going anywhere, but neither was he.

"Jesus, we can rent a room at the inn in town if you want to stay in this godforsaken place so much. All I'm saying is we shouldn't try to ride out the damn apocalypse in a hundred-year-old cabin!"

"Ryne, come on," said Noah. "Just listen for a second."

"I'm not leaving," said Ryne quietly, raising his eyes again to meet Shawn's. "If you want to go, then you can go, but I've already told you where I stand. Don't ask me again."

The two of them glared at each other. This didn't need to happen. This last weekend with the boys didn't need to be like this. But he'd messed up. He never should have said a word. He should have enjoyed these few days before driving down to the airport in Whitehorse and giving them the plane tickets that he'd purchased weeks ago. Let them be mad. Let them be upset. And then let them go. Like ripping off a band-aid.

That's what he should have done.

"Fine," said Shawn, his teeth tight, his voice a furious whisper. "You want to stay here? We'll stay here. But we need to prepare. We need more firewood and food."

"I thought you guys got enough yesterday?"

"I mean, we got what we thought we needed. But we weren't counting on that," said Shawn, pointing in the direction of the dark clouds. "Who knows how long we'll be stuck here."

"He's right," said Noah. "I know your family had some weird thing about not buying meat from town, but I don't think we have a choice. If we get snowed in..."

"What about the hunt?" said Ryne. "We only have a few days."

"Dude, we may be stuck here for more than a few days," said Noah. "We'll have time to hunt, but we need to make sure we're at least ready for that thing."

"Why don't you and Noah go into town and get as much stuff as you can," said Shawn. "I'll stay here and try to get as much dry firewood as I can find. Probably won't find much, but whatever we can get is good. Hopefully it will dry off in time to use it. Maybe I can get a deer too, and our food problems will be handled."

Ryne started to say something but held his tongue. As irritated as he was, the others were right.

The three men got dressed and dispersed. There was nothing left to say as they each resigned themselves to their present duties. Duties were performed in quiet tension as the space between them thickened and cooled. A heavy sadness ran through his blood at the thought, but the truth was not malleable. To pretend like there was anything left besides the empty husks and moaning spirits was a child's wish. Phantoms. That's what they were.

Ryne started the truck and cranked the heat. The frigid wind outside was stiff, but clear. As long as they got back before the storm hit, the drive would be easy enough. Noah came around the side and opened the passenger door. Shawn quickly grabbed his arm before he jumped in and said something to him, low but audible enough for Ryne to hear.

Talk some sense into him.

Ryne put the truck into gear as soon as the door shut and began pulling off towards the pathway back to Wolf's Bone.

EIGHT
NEAR DEATH

Noah tossed the steak into the shopping cart. The fluorescent lights reflected off the wooden planks of the supermarket floor, the resulting glare searing his eyes and growing a sharp ache in his head. He struggled to adjust to it. The thick winter mist had lulled him away from the world of man, and now his eyes rebelled against the unnatural embrace of the fluorescent lighting.

As his head continued to pound, the rest of his body began to slowly fail him. His arms grew heavier with each passing minute, and his legs dragged along the tiles like bricks. Cramping and stiffness held tight around his neck, and he could barely turn his head. Weary breaths escaped his lungs and above all else, he felt utterly drained. His eyelids hung heavy over his throbbing eyes and threatened to close for good at any minute. Shuffling half-heartedly across the wood, his feet slowly pushed his body forward. His stomach groaned as a hunger grew inside him. The breakfast hadn't helped. He'd gotten a lot of sleep in the comfortable loft bed, but not good sleep. Shadows hiding the black eyes of wary animals plagued his dreams. A cloak of drifting snow had fallen upon their vanished forms. He'd awoken a few times to find himself on his side looking out the window at the trees freezing in the Yukon night. He thought about the black eyes that could be watching them from those branches. The fireplace warmed everything inside, but the light only stretched so far outside the confines of the cabin. Beyond that, man's grip ceased to matter and the dark wild simmered and watched and snarled in silence.

"Noah?" Ryne asked. "You okay?"

"Yeah, I'm fine. Tired. Didn't sleep too good last night."

"You look awful."

"I'm okay, I just need to rest. I'll sleep in the backseat on the way back."

The concern was painted in broad, garish strokes on Ryne's face. That same look followed Noah everywhere he went now. Anyone who knew him, knew about his accident, about the day he died, gave him that stare of worry. His parents looked at him like that whenever he would sit quietly at Thanksgiving or Christmas, picking absentmindedly at his food. The girl-friends who never stayed long because it was hard to stay when your partner wakes up screaming in the middle of the night. They all had that look, too. It came from a good-hearted place for most people, but the constant observation weighed on him, and he felt put under a microscope of care. The look reflected a simple question written upon the face of the person looking —*Is he alright?*

No, he wasn't. And he never would be again. His whole young life had been tucked beneath the comfortable blanket of spirituality. He could remember back to as young as three, when he'd play on the church pews during Sunday Mass. From his values to his ethics, those pews, those psalms, had shaped his existence. But now, as a man of almost thirty, those values and ethics lie smothered beneath a different blanket.

The memories were not lost, but rather nailed to the doorstep of his mind. The grain had swallowed him so quickly. One simple mistake, the involuntary flail of an arm, or the struggle of a desperate breath, and the pit pulled him deeper. Alive but stuck under tons of the yellow avalanche, his breathing getting tougher and tougher as he desperately clawed to find little pockets of air. The grain filling his mouth, crusting with his saliva, blocking the last of the precious air. The pressure growing as he was compacted from above and pushed down to a bitter end. The creeping death that began at the edge of his periphery slowly devouring him.

He remembered lying on his back in the grass with an EMT above him. Back, alive, and free. He found out later that rescuers had recovered him from the silo an hour and a half after he'd fallen through the crust. EMTs attempted resuscitation for ten minutes with no luck. And then, miraculously, he came back to life. Resurrected from beyond the veil.

A miracle. That's what everyone called it, from stories in local newspapers to national interviews held from a hospital bed. An absolute miracle. But a miracle was never Noah's perspective. In those quiet nights, when the hospital humming would subside and his room would go dark and empty, he cried. Felt empty, used, and alone. He'd heard the stories all his life. Stories of people visited by the reaper. People given a brief glimpse into the Otherside.

No reaper appeared for Noah. No skeletal figure extending a hand to guide him over. No light at the end of the tunnel. Just a merciless avalanche of grain. No Otherside. Just nothing.

This thought needled at the most vulnerable parts of his soul. As freshly as he remembered his dying breaths, the time between the dark taking over and his miraculous recovery remained as much a mystery to him as anyone else. He didn't remember a thing. That meant one of two possibilities was true.

On one hand, his entire belief system was wrong, and nothing waited for him on the Otherside. Just an empty, lonely abyss. The possibility that everything he had ever believed, everything that formed the structure of his existence, was based on a cruel lie, depressed him. Haunted him. Stripped him of the marrow of life and left him a hollow husk.

Or maybe the Otherside existed; but not for him. Perhaps that place was reserved for people more privileged— more saint-like. It terrified him, snapped a nerve so deep inside he could feel the reverberations in his bones. He'd worked so hard to live his life the way his faith said he should, and to think that only loneliness and misery awaited him in reward now crippled his fragile psyche. To have not been good enough. To have had some misstep along the way damn him. Was there no forgiveness? As frightening as nothing was, this possibility felt much more terrifying.

He put on a mask. A facade of strength and competence to fool everyone around him, but deep cracks had already set in. And they were growing.

Now, standing in the meat aisle, he lost all feeling in his legs, and had to use the shopping cart to hold him up.

"Noah?"

He stabilized himself. "I'm good. I'm good."

"No, you're not. We need to get you to a doctor."

"I told you, I'm okay."

"Fuck that."

Ryne stepped up to his side and shouldered his arm as a small viewership accrued in the supermarket. People from within sight of them all looked heavily in their direction. A blend of native and white faces, hidden beneath heavy hoods of leather and fur.

A hand wrapped around Noah's unsupported wrist. Thin and bony, the fingers long and cold. He turned his head as far as he could. A woman held his other arm. Her dark skin drawn back tightly against sharp bones. Her pale blue eyes beamed with a certain wildness from beneath the fur-cloaked hood. She frowned at him.

"Pe'kake ruc," she said.

"What?" he asked, his voice barely a whisper.

"Pe'kake ruc!"

"Let go!" said Ryne. Noah felt his body being pulled by his friend, but the woman's grip remained strong around his wrist, and she wouldn't let go.

"Pe'kake ruc!" she yelled again. Her shrill cry rang off the supermarket walls in waves of echoes.

"I don't und..." Darkness crept in from the edge of his vision. Then came the panic, peeking its head from the place it ransomed in his mind.

"I said let him go!" he heard faintly. The woman's grip on his wrist broke free, and he felt as though he was levitating across the floor. Doing his best to stay awake, he moved his feet to help as much as possible, but they flopped lifelessly against the wood.

His world went black for a moment and then returned. He was getting loaded into the truck.

"Stay upright," said a voice. Ryne's voice. Distant. Lost.

"Where are we going?" Noah asked. His own voice sounded faint and alien to him.

The truck pulled out of the parking lot and sped off somewhere. Dizziness took over, and his mind swirled in the fog of his wavering consciousness.

And then the dark came back. It started right in his periphery as he felt himself now getting pulled out of the truck.

"Help! I need help!"

A sharp pain seared the side of his head. It worsened with every move as the world in front of him clouded like ink in water. Then his entire inner world, once again, descended into the dark and lonely abyss.

NINE
THE FROZEN WILD

The frozen layer of ice cracked beneath Shawn's boots as he walked between the thick conglomeration of trees. With the rifle slung over his shoulder and firewood filling up his backpack, he trudged deeper into the woods. Cold winters weren't an alien experience for him growing up in the Palouse of eastern Washington, but this cold bit differently. He could feel it slipping through the insulation of his jacket, piercing through the pores of his skin and slowly cutting and burrowing its way down to the bone, resting in the marrow. He could adjust the jacket or his thermals underneath all he wanted, but the cold always seemed to find a way in, like some insect searching for gaps in a house door. He felt something cold and wet against his face and groaned at the arrival of the snowfall.

He struggled to find any firewood not entrenched in snow and saturated beyond uselessness. Thirty minutes in, his surgically repaired knee started throbbing again. He cursed the joint and pushed on, limping through the snow. The leg wavered with each step as stability abandoned him. He hadn't fallen yet, but worry had seeped into his thoughts. A dark awareness that if the knee gave way or, God forbid, tore again under excess stress, it would cripple him.

He was a half-mile from the cabin, maybe more. The forest was thick with old spruce. The spaces between the trees were filled by more trees further into the wild, as though trapping him in a maze of barren walls rein-forced by ice and bark. He'd never felt so claustrophobic in such an open space. The storm lingered in the furthest corners of his view, a blight against the gray wintry sky, visible in brief glimpses through the gaps in the walls of spruce—a python coiled around the forest, constricting with each passing hour, squeezing the breath from the wild. He needed to find more wood.

He hoped the storm might help bring some sense back to their conversa-tions. If he could get Ryne away from the cabin and away from his stupid decision, then he might persuade him. If he could help break whatever bond Ryne still shared with this place, or at least weaken it, then maybe there was a way to walk him back from the edge. But he had dug his heels in again, and now the only thing on Shawn's mind was making sure they didn't freeze to death.

The snowfall picked up, but the air was still very clear and the woods remained quiet. The trees pulsated with silence. Effigies of unblemished nature rendered in green and white. They rose high and stretched out to each other as if desperate for some connection to the place as the heavy snowfall of days past weighed upon them. Their green vitality shrouded by the pale harshness of winter, but still moving within each other's watch. The place was a morgue patrolled by hardened ghosts covered by sheets of quiet snow.

A low, deep growl filled the silent void.

He froze in place. He hadn't seen an animal since leaving the cabin. No birds, no deer. Nothing moved in the white, but the sound was unmistak-able. Listening closely to the quiet of the trees, he heard nothing. But some-thing was there. He knew it. Felt it. The change in the air as something came into the space.

Wolverines were very common in this part of the world and extremely aggressive, but they posed no real danger to humans. Bears hibernate this time of year, but he could have easily and accidentally stumbled upon a hidden den. If he had, the bears most likely were just defending their area and would not pursue him if he left. He tried not to think of the bears that had been outside the cabin last night. How they'd stared with vacant eyes. How they'd violated the basic laws of nature. His mind was filled with volumes of useless knowledge that came from an understanding of animals' natural behaviors. Born from years of witnessing the natural proclivities of the wilderness. Wolves almost always left humans alone or fled at the very sight of them. That was their natural behavior. But so did deer; and Shawn remembered the deer in the road all too well.

Every hair on his body stood at attention, and he thought of the day he'd heard a cougar scream for the first time. Back then, the natural law of the sound calmed him, but there was no natural law to fall back on now. Not in this place. Nothing about this forest felt right, and until he could see what made the noise, he couldn't rationalize anything. It hadn't been the murderous shriek of the cougar that unnerved him, but the soft voice of a singing child.

The forest was quiet and empty again, but he didn't move. Every step he took crushed ice beneath his feet. He didn't want the sound to mask the growl of whatever hid in the trees. Bracing himself for the pain, he slowly turned his body at the hip, rotating his torso to see behind him. His knee screamed as it struggled to hold his weight, but he clenched his teeth together and held in the bark of pain.

Nothing. Another endless maze of trees.

His heart raced. He *knew* he'd heard something. Hadn't he? How many times had he been out in the woods and heard noises just like that one? He trained his ears again, but still heard nothing. Just the eerie quiet hidden within the snowfall.

Then the growl returned, this time louder and without doubt. Closer. Coming from the front. He slowly rotated back to face forward.

Standing in the snow, between two trees about thirty yards away, was a lone black wolf.

He froze. The wolf's eyes cut hard through the light snowfall. Its black coat tinged at the tips with frost. A low, rumbling growl came from the animal's throat. It picked a paw up and out of the high snow. Took a step forward into the space between them.

Shawn slowly pulled the rifle from his back and raised it to his shoulder. The memory of the deer in the road still seared into his mind, he aimed the weapon directly at the wolf.

The animal moved closer, its long legs sinking into snow halfway to its belly. There was no hesitation in the animal's movement. No stutter or pause. It was just taking its time. Shawn's finger gripped the trigger as he stared down the barrel at the beast. The wolf's lips pulled back in a snarl.

The growl echoed off the trees and cut into his blood. His eyes flickered across the landscape while holding aim, looking for the others. The pack. They couldn't be far away, and every nerve in his body told him this was an ambush—this unnatural stalking of prey that had seen the predator. Either this was a distraction from the greater threat, or this was a very lonely, very hungry, and very fearless wolf.

He squeezed the trigger.

Click.

He squeezed again. The trigger moved without tension.

He opened the chamber frantically to unjam the weapon, fighting against the limits of his gloves.

The wolf made a sudden move forward, bounding through the snow towards him.

He turned and stumbled, still trying to pry out the dislodged bullet. The wolf tore through the space, working its way to him, lunging up and down through the heavy snow.

Shawn heard the panting ferocity behind him. The wolf had cut the distance between them in half.

Suddenly, Shawn's knee locked into place, and he collapsed into the snow. He screamed in pain as he rolled over onto his back and faced his attacker. The wolf now stood ten yards away, the snow a white fire against the black night of its coat. Every second that passed, the beast covered another yard of distance. Shawn flailed and fumbled at the rifle, his breathing heavier and heavier as the wolf moved closer and closer. He would need to use the gun as a blunt weapon if—no, when—the wolf got to him.

But— such a fight he knew he would lose. Nobody was coming to save him, and there was nothing he could do. Ice and circumstance had crippled his only chance to run, and now, here in the snow, he would die like a coward.

The wolf now stood five yards away. Then, the sound of metal upon metal as the bullet finally dislodged from the chamber. The wolf moved closer, now three yards away. He chambered the round. The wolf leapt towards him, its body blocking out the dim winter sun as he swung the rifle upwards, halfheartedly aimed at the falling predator, closed his eyes, and fired.

The crack resonated through every bone in his body. Then, nothing.

Snow fell cold against his exposed cheeks, his eyes closed, his teeth clenched, and his face turned away, but still alive. He must have hit it. Somehow, some way, he shot the wolf.

He opened his eyes and looked for the limp and lifeless body of his aggressor, but the white canvas sat empty. No body lay dead in the powder. He looked around for blood on the white but saw none. His knee still locked in place, he pushed himself to his feet through force of will and looked around. Silent and empty. The green of spruce peeking through the heavy white blanket. Peaceful in a way. As if nothing happened.

Maybe he missed, but the shot had been enough to scare the beast off. But how? It had been right over him. Even if he'd missed and startled the wolf, the damn thing would have fallen right on top of him. His eyes trained on the path the wolf had taken, and his heart and throat turned to ice.

There were no tracks.

The wolf had ripped through the loose snow. There should have been displacement everywhere, evidence that a large animal had hunted this area and attacked. He saw where he'd fallen to the ground. Where he'd twisted and roiled. But the path of the wolf was clean. Glistening in the dull light of the low sun. The snow undisturbed. Pristine.

His body frozen stiff, he felt his failing knee slowly return to functionality before he collapsed, not in pain, but disbelief, cold and alone in the silence of the frozen wild.

TEN
MEDICAL ADVICE

R yne sat in the waiting room with his head in his hands and his fingers running through his hair, a migraine searing through his forehead and charring the back of his eyes. Noah had lost consciousness as they stumbled through the front door of the physician's office and was immediately taken into one of the back rooms. If necessary, the doctor could call for helicopter transport to the nearest hospital, wherever it was. Whitehorse, probably.

Noah's condition had come on so quickly, and with so little warning that there hadn't been time to process what was happening. All Ryne knew was that his friend of over twenty years had collapsed in his arms, and he now sat waiting for answers that may never come.

It was more than that, though. He'd been trying for an hour now to place the words from the old woman in the supermarket. *Pe'kake ruc.* Nothing stood out to him at first, but after some digestion and reflection, he was sure he'd heard the word *Pe'kake* before. But he couldn't place it. The second word was more easily familiar. *Ruc* meant "run."

Wolf's Bone had long been home to an aboriginal tribe related to the Gwich'in people who populated the northern parts of the Yukon, usually above the Arctic Circle. Ryne remembered his uncle's history lessons shared over campfires. A small group of natives broke away from the northern tribes and moved south. They renamed themselves the Si'Kualt and settled in the area that would become Wolf's Bone. Now in a place to call their own, they developed an entire society and a unique language. Many of the town's denizens were remnants of that tribe and still used the language today. While Ryne never mastered the tongue, his father and uncle had known it well. During hunting trips, Ryne would often hear Rod whispering these ancient and sacred words. As though he was being respectful towards some unseen audience. When asked what he was doing, Rod would say he was *thanking the land*. From these conversations, Ryne picked up a few distinct words of the language. *Pe'kake* was one of those words. He was sure of it.

The waiting room door opened and shook him from the thought. The doctor, a tall, gangly man Ryne remembered vaguely named Ernest Woods, appeared, and Noah, now standing upright, awake and alert, followed behind him. Ryne jumped up and felt his head erupt with the sudden movement, but he didn't care. He hurried across the room, past the doctor, and embraced his friend.

"Love you too, man," said Noah, patting Ryne on the back. "Can you let me go now? I need to breathe."

Ryne let go. "You're okay, right? He's okay, right?"

Dr. Woods smiled. "Yes, he's fine. Apparently, your friend here is hypo-glycemic."

"What does that mean?"

"Low blood-sugar."

Ryne turned to Noah. "You knew that?"

"Not a clue."

"It's not that uncommon," Dr. Woods said. "Make sure he's getting enough carbs in his system."

"That's it? Just his blood sugar?"

"Well, I wouldn't say that is simply *it*. Low blood sugar can be serious. It's a good thing your friend here realized it before it became a bigger issue. If he starts feeling dizzy again, get some carbs in his system."

"Speaking of food," said a voice from behind them. The receptionist, a middle-aged woman with short gray hair, stood by the door. She held bags loaded with groceries, the same groceries that Ryne had abandoned at the supermarket. "Ted Arnold and his wife just dropped these off. They covered the bill for you."

"Well, that was nice of them," said Noah.

"Now you guys stay safe up there," said Dr. Woods. "They got that storm coming. Make sure you get hunkered down when it hits."

"You're sure he's okay? We don't need to take him to Whitehorse to get him checked out?"

Dr. Woods smiled. "No need. Everything you need to care for him is right here in Wolf's Bone."

"Thanks, Doc," said Ryne as he and Noah turned to leave.

"Anytime. It's good to have you here, Ryne. We were so sorry to hear about your uncle. He was a good man."

The snow had picked up outside, and what had been small groupings of soft flurries less than an hour ago had turned into a full snowfall. Pulling up his face mask, Ryne looked to the east in the direction of the cabin. A wall of darkness approached the area, holding the sky like a vengeful god. The storm was close.

Inside the truck, Noah reclined the seat and laid down. "You mind if I sleep on the way back? I'm exhausted."

"Sure," said Ryne. "You're sure you're okay, right?"

"Yeah. Yeah, I'm fine. Just need some rest."

Ryne cranked up the heater and began the long drive back to the cabin. Shawn had to be worried, but maybe that would ease the conflict between the two of them. Ryne didn't want to fight with his friends anymore.

Twenty minutes later, the storm arrived.

The wind appeared quickly and without warning, and the falling snow turned into a vortex of frost. The truck started to sludge as it made its way into deeper snow deposited by the storm. Ryne could feel the tires straining against the ice, digging in and pushing the truck forward spastically. He'd hoped they could make their way back before the storm hit, but Noah's illness had cost them too much time. Now he fought his way through the initial punch of the blizzard.

The truck lurched and jumped forward in the unpacked snow. The interior of the cab bounced, and Noah jolted awake. He rubbed his eyes for a moment and then grabbed the handguard above the door as the truck powered through more slush and came to rest atop a raised part of the path.

He breathed in deeply. This section of the path was elevated above the quagmire of frost and slush, and its solidity gave some security. He needed a moment. A moment to let his hands unclench from the wheel. For his eyes to refocus. His mind needed a breather. Another breath, and fog filled the cab like smoke. He felt selfish. Spoiled, almost. Of all the times to come and make this idea a reality? God, the storms *always* came during the solstice. Why couldn't he have just waited another week? Just one more week and maybe this would have been easier. But no, he had to do it now. For some unknown reason of profound stupidity, he just had to do it now. God knew how long the blizzard would last. In most of his memories, they lasted only a few hours. But there were other memories. Storms that thrashed and mauled for days on end.

How stupid. How fucking stupid he was to do this *now.*

He grabbed the gearstick to put the truck back into gear when movement crossed his vision. A dark shadow beyond the fogged haze of the windshield. Moving in the swirling whiteout. Towards the truck. Eyes alert and trained on the path ahead, the hair on his neck stood cold and stiff against his jacket collar.

"What are you..." Noah started.

"Look."

They appeared as though born from the blizzard itself. A herd of deer emerged from the surrounding forest and stood in the path. Motionless, as if frozen in the wind. Dozens of eyes gazed upon the truck from all directions. The snow swallowed their thick, tan fur. Long gangly limbs with bulging joints and black hooves dug into the snowpack.

"Behind us," said Noah. Ryne turned his head and saw the unearthly sight, as more deer materialized out of the darkness from their rear. The herd studied them, like children watching a teacher.

A deer on the driver's side moved in with a creeping gait. Ryne watched the animal's slow steps through the snow and realized he wasn't breathing. The animal arrived at the window and looked inside at them. Not in curiosity, but with an uncanny intent. Ryne was astonished by how black the animal's eyes were. There was no glistening in the light, only an empty absence of life.

"Ryne, get us the fuck out of here."

Ryne did not break eye contact. He couldn't. The magnetic abyss of the deer's eyes held him tightly within its empty gaze as an unnatural paralysis flowed through his bones. Within him he felt a mounting nerve, a rising inclination to reach his hand out and open the door. To step into the untamed wild that surrounded them. It simmered within him. The black eyes invited him.

"Ryne!"

He shook out of his trance, reached down, and put the truck into first gear. Eased his foot on the accelerator and slowly released the clutch. The truck slugged forward as the stories of hunters who missed their mark, only to end up gored by the deer they had been hunting, consumed his thoughts. The amount of damage a pissed off deer could do to a person was staggering, and he didn't know if the doors of the old truck could hold one off.

"Dude, get us out..."

"It'll spook them if I floor it."

"They're spooking me."

"I don't want to piss them off."

Slowly, the truck trudged its way across the snowpack. The deer stood their ground. The front bumper tapped one of them with a thud, but the animal did not move on its own, but was eased out of the way by the bumper. To his left, the deer by the window followed them.

Don't piss it off.

The front grille and bumper continued to clear the truck's way, nudging the animals aside. The brave one followed, matching the truck's crawling pace while the others watched and stared, like paintings against the dark backdrop. Ryne kept his foot steady, the tension of the clutch pushing back against his leg. Finally, the last of the herd cleared, and only the brave one remained. Ryne slammed the accelerator to the floor and released the clutch. The tires spun and dug into the snow, lifelessly rotating in the hardened slush before finally catching the grip and exploding down the path. Ryne looked up at the rearview mirror.

The herd disappeared into the swirling snow. The road dark and empty, shrouded by the primeval wilderness. Noah saw it, too.

"What the...?" His voice drifted with the cold fog of his breath.

"I don't know," said Ryne. "Let's get back. We can worry about it later."

"I'm never going in the woods ever again," said Noah, reclining back into his seat. Within a few minutes, he slept again. The truck continued violently rolling through thick snow, but Noah didn't wake.

Ryne was wide awake. A slight tingle shocked the edge of his skin. As they drove away from the encounter, he remembered something. The thought arrived within his mind at the vanishing of the herd, exposing itself to the part of his memory in which darker rivers ran their courses.

He was eleven when he'd first heard the word *pe'kake*. His father had shot a deer, and by the time Ryne caught up to him, he heard Rory praying over the animal. A quiet invocation in a language unfamiliar to his young mind, sharp and jagged at the edges of its words. His father told him that the deer had a spirit inside it. Sometimes a spirit got trapped in an animal's body and required a special prayer to release it from its vessel.

That's where he'd heard the word before, and that's what it meant.

Vessel.

Pe'kake ruc.

Run, Vessel.

ELEVEN
NIGHTMARE

January 2000, Pullman, Washington

I n the glaring light of the midday sun, Ryne looked down a street that seemed to have no end. A street lined for miles upon miles with empty yards and empty homes, unchanging in their sameness. His hair stood rigid in its pores as his eyes flickered across the green lots, searching for the lurking presence. His teeth ground themselves against each other, the sound generating a weakness in his knees. He could feel it. Somewhere in this emptiness was a presence. A looming inevitability.

Surrounded by silence, the smallest sound rang like a bell through the empty street. Ryne whipped his head around and saw it. Living night against the harsh light of day, a black dog moved slowly across the yard to his right. Ryne froze in place, his muscles liquid nitrogen on the verge of shattering the eight-year-old boy into pieces.

The dog crept its way toward him, step by malicious step. Its teeth bared a sinister white against the black of its muzzle. A low, harrowing growl oozed from between those teeth. It was big, bigger than any dog he had ever seen, and it moved with the terrifying grace of horrible intent. Hunting him.

Ryne turned to his left and ran as fast as he could to the nearest house in sight. The dog kept pace with him. Reaching the door, he grabbed the handle and turned with all his strength. The doorknob wouldn't move. It wasn't locked, but it would not move. The muscles in his arms lost their intensity, and his body turned into a strengthless, blubbering mess as he fell to his knees. He torqued his arms and turned with every ounce of will he had, his muscles groaning as he put his little body into the action. But it was useless. Whatever strength he needed to open the door existed beyond him. The black dog slumped its way across the street and into the yard, slowly evaporating the space between them. That growl found its way to him once again, and the eight-year-old boy knew, at that moment, the unfiltered and unyielding truth.

He was going to die.

A sob escaped him, and tears streamed down his cheeks. The dog moved closer. Thoughts raced through his head as he watched the painful end to his young life inch closer and closer with each passing step. He knew it would hurt and sobbed as he thought of the darkness that would follow the pain. The coldness that would take over as what remained of him left his mangled little body and was taken to wherever you go after you die.

He wanted to call out to his dad. To God. To anyone who could hear. But the words stuck in his throat and released only a scared whimper.

The beast moved closer. Now only feet away.

Now he wanted only his father. The safety of his arms, the strength in his protection. He wanted to be held; to be taken away from this broken place and returned to a world of innocence unmolested by horrible beasts. A place that seemed gone now, swallowed by the darkness of the dog as it was upon him.

It opened its mouth and took the eight-year-old boy's throat. The tears flowed from him like faucets. His little voice erupted out of his throat.

"Daddy!"

The beast snapped its jaws shut.

* * *

His eyes shot open to the illuminated figures of dinosaurs on the ceiling of his bedroom, their forms changing color with the soft night light next to his bed.

Just a dream. Sweat saturated his clothes and sheets as the thunder within his chest slowly retreated. Alive. He was alive and safe in his bedroom.

He reached his hand up to his throat but felt nothing. No sensation of touch or feeling or movement. He knew he had moved his arm, but it still lay next to him in the bed, a lifeless form in the darkness. His mind told his body to move, but nothing happened. He could move his eyes, but the rest of him lay still and lifeless. A dark panic set in, covering him like a heavy blanket. His breathing became tired and heavy, and his body refused to comply with any of his mental commands.

Then he felt it. A presence. Familiar. Recent. From the dream.

The presence.

His eyes moved across the dark and empty landscape of his bedroom, searching for the location of the force. And then, on the far side of the room, he found it.

In the shadowed corner of his room, the black dog snarled at him. Eyes black as a damned soul, teeth bared an unholy white. The room filled with a shallow, horrible growl.

No!

He wasn't dreaming this time. There was no waking up. Death had come to his room.

His entire body went into a frenzy within itself. As his insides screamed and fought; the grip of paralysis loosened ever so slightly. Slowly his fingers shook the uneasy sleep out of them, but speech and movement coalesced in the stillness. He had avoided death in the light, but now he would die in the dark.

Daddy! He cried in his head.

The dog's head lowered, and the empty eyes trained themselves on Ryne.

Daddy!

The shadows recoiled and birthed a faint image of what the black form in the corner was—what it *really* was. Not a dog. Its shape was morphed into something more monstrous. What looked like antlers branched in

79

every direction from the thing's head. Inside the blanket of shadow writhed long, thin, devilish arms, cracking and splintering with the sound of broken wood. It growled again, but the growl contorted into a screeching, almost human voice. Like someone getting flayed alive.

The garish form took a step forward, and the snap of dead branches shot through the dark room and echoed off the walls.

"Daddy!" Ryne's voice exploded out of him as his bodily sensation returned. He launched himself out of the bed, through the door and into the hallway, running full speed down the narrow path to his parents' bedroom. The horrible scream flooded the halls of his home. The door in front of him opened, and he slammed into a solid form.

"Ryne, what's wrong?" his father asked.

"There's something in my room!" He gripped his father tighter than he had in years, since he'd started school and hugging your dad became the thing of babies and girls. Now, his fathers' arms were the only place Ryne felt remotely safe, and his tears drenched the man's shirt.

"What do you mean there's something in your room?"

"It's a monster! I had a dream and then I woke up and it was there!"

His father looked up and down the hallway. Ryne refused to look. He knew if he turned around, he would see some hideous, antlered thing standing outside his door. His heart beat out of his chest, and his fingers gripped his father's shirt as tightly as his small muscles would allow.

"Well, let's go see," said his father.

"No!" said Ryne. "No, call someone!"

"Ryne, I promise you. There's nothing there."

"No!"

His father reached down and picked him up. Ryne hung like dead weight in his father's arms, but his dad didn't seem to mind.

"I promise," he said. "There's nothing there."

He held his son as the two moved towards the boy's room. Ryne kept his eyes closed tightly; kept his grip even tighter. He heard the doorknob turn. The soft creak as his father pushed the door open and entered the unlit room.

Seconds passed by and Ryne clutched his father tight, waiting for the sound of cracking wood or that horrible scream. For bony antlers and black teeth to rip into him and tear the two of them apart.

"Look, buddy. I told you, there's nothing here."

Ryne opened his eyes and turned around. His room was empty, the dark corner unoccupied, his bed sheets a soaked mess. Whatever had manifested itself in the darkness of his room was gone.

"I swear..." Ryne said, his voice still coming out between sobs.

"It's okay, I'm sure you saw something. When you woke up, could you move?"

Ryne shook his head. *How did he know that?*

"Were you having a bad dream?"

Ryne nodded.

His father smiled. "That's called sleep paralysis, Ryne. It's nothing to be afraid of. It means your mind was ready to wake up before your body was. Happens to me all the time. It's completely normal."

"I don't like it," Ryne said, still in disbelief. That dark figure burned along the contours of his memory.

"It's not very fun, I know. But you have to remember that whatever you see, it's not real. Your mind is playing tricks on you. Sometimes, our imagination gets the best of us. Sometimes it is hard to come out of a dream. We don't know where we are; and our mind tries to fill in the gaps."

Ryne's eyes moved once again to the corner of the room. Nothing was there but dimly lit drywall. No, no, it wasn't possible. He knew what he'd seen. And he knew where he'd seen it before.

"But Dad, the thing that I saw. It was the same thing I saw when we were at the cabin last month. Remember? When Uncle Rod went outside?"

His father stiffened slightly but kept his smile. "You were sleepwalking, Ryne. Now you're having sleep paralysis. You're just letting some bad dreams get the best of you. I promise nothing is coming to get you."

"Promise?" His quiet voice cracked with shame. He was acting pathetic, childish, but he couldn't help it. Not after what he had just seen.

"Promise, and if something was coming after you, then it picked the wrong guy. Cause it has to go through me first, and that's not happening."

"Okay."

"Try to sleep on your side," his father said. "It usually comes when you sleep on your back."

"Can I sleep with you and mom tonight? Please?"

"Of course."

Ryne changed out of the sweat-soaked clothes into something clean, and the two of them walked down the hallway to the master bedroom. Ryne's mother turned onto her side and looked at the two of them with a deep concern shining in her eyes.

"Is everything alright?"

"Everything's good. Ryne had a bad dream. He's going to sleep with us tonight."

"Of course. Climb on in, sweetie."

Ryne nodded and climbed into bed, tucking himself tightly under the covers.

"You guys go to bed," said his father. "I need to make sure the dog has some water."

Ryne's mother wrapped her arms around him and, for the first time all night, his body calmed in the embrace of safety. Ryne expected to hear the kitchen water faucet turn on, but he heard the phone dialing instead. His father spoke softly; but his voice still carried slightly through the stillness of the house as Ryne's eyelids got heavy.

"Rod," he heard his father say as he drifted off into slumber. "We need to talk."

THE SECOND NIGHT

TWELVE
BLOOD AND WATER

In the cabin bathroom, Shawn sat in blistering hot water, trying desperately to warm himself up. Following his encounter with the wolf, he had trudged his way back to the cabin on essentially one leg. Painfully, he'd pushed himself through the snow as the storm lurked across the dull sky towards the cabin. The temperature dropped to below zero and the snowfall grew heavy and violent in the howling wind. By the time he got back to the cabin's warm embrace, he was freezing. His jacket saturated with ice from the sky and a cold, fearful sweat from within his blood. He turned on the generator in the outside shed that powered the water heater and drew as hot a bath as his skin would allow. He had been fading, but the heat shocked him back to life. His fingers and toes burned hot, and he felt life return to them as warm blood crept from their tips to the rest of his body. He let the warmth enfold him until the chill of the place had cooled the bath; then he ran a new one. Hotter now, well past the point of safe bathing. He needed the heat. Needed something to keep the cold away.

He was alone. Ryne and Noah still hadn't returned, and it had been hours since their expected arrival from Wolf's Bone. With the storm now in full swing, he worried about their trip back. The truck was tough, but old. He'd tried to radio Constable Whitting but was greeted by the hiss of static and nothing else. Useless. And it wasn't like he could simply walk the trail back to town. Doing so during a normal day here would be foolish enough. To attempt it now would be suicide. The only thing left to do was wait and try to stay warm.

The bathroom was the only room in the house that was not visibly accessible to the outside world via a clear window. Rather, the window above the tub was small and glazed. Submerged up to his chin, he looked at the fogged glass with a heaviness in his chest. The rational part of his brain struggled to find a reason for what happened with the wolf, but nothing emerged. Even now, drowned in searing water, he felt something watching him through that glass with a chilling glare. Looking right through the glaze and smiling at him. And all he could do was lie there, a child pulling a blanket over their eyes, hoping that the monster in their closet wouldn't see them. Illogical? Sure. But he couldn't reason the feeling away.

Pain pulsed within his knee as familiar waves crashed along well-trodden shores. He was so tired of these waves, this agony. How long would he live with this? How long could he? The surgeries hadn't helped, and the torment grew daily. Now, beneath hot waters it cried harder than it ever had. At least since the day he'd torn it. The twisting pop had engulfed his leg in fire. But this was a different kind of cry. Cold and hard.

He opened his eyes and gasped. The water swirled milky red as blood poured from gaping holes in the soft flesh around his knee. His whole body went into a spasm. He launched himself out of the water, slipped and fell back into the tub, and tried to stand again. A scream, horrified and primal, escaped him. He looked back down at the gore.

The water was no longer red. His knee, no longer in tatters. No blood. Just steam rising off hot, clear water into the freezing air.

It's in your head.

He heard the cabin's front door open. A chill stalked across the nape of his neck. He lifted his arm out of the water and inched his trembling hand through the space between himself and the rifle leaning against the side wall.

"Shawn?" called a voice from the other side of the door. Ryne's voice. But the chill didn't go away, and his hand held itself firmly on the gun. He knew the voice on the other side of the door just like he knew the sounds of the forest, but they had betrayed him already. He knew the voice of a child, and that had also come without natural inclination. His eyes grew heavy, and the door became a barrier between him and something unnatural, something wrong.

What the hell are you doing? He thought. His fingers, stiff around the wooden stock of the rifle, gradually loosened.

"Shawn?"

"About damn time," he replied, the shakiness of his voice hidden behind a false bravado.

He rose out of the tub, dried off, and dressed himself. He was still cold, but it wasn't a physical cold. The ice that enveloped him was far deeper than his skin. He felt it expanding within him, cracking along his core. He took one last look at his knee and saw nothing. No gore. Nothing but surgery scars and inflammation.

Ryne was unpacking food as Noah lay on the couch. He looked sickly white, as though every drop of blood had been drained out of him.

"You look like shit," said Shawn.

"Good to know," said Noah.

"What took you guys so long?"

"We had an, uh, issue," Ryne said. "Noah passed out in the store."

"Noah did what?"

"It's why I look like shit, thank you very much."

"Are you okay?" asked Shawn.

"More or less."

"I took him to the local doctor," said Ryne. "Turns out, he's hypo-something. He's got low blood sugar. So, we need to make sure he's eating enough sugar."

"Or," he said, "here's a *crazy* thought. We take him out of here and to an actual hospital."

Ryne put his hands up. "Look, all bullshit aside, we aren't going anywhere. We barely made it back. The last few miles were a slog through the snow. The storm keeps dumping more and more snow on the ground and it isn't packing."

Shawn took a deep breath and closed his eyes, fighting back a barrage of anger poised to break through his mental walls at any moment. He walked across the room, sat on the couch, and put his head in his hands, his fingers parting his still-damp hair and massaging the tension out of his scalp. They couldn't leave. The option of escape had come and gone, and they were stuck here in this place of wrongness.

A mass grew inside him. The deer in the road had been its beginning, but now the mass had turned into a cancerous tumor and could not be ignored any longer. The deer. The wolf. The animals. That horrible little voice. This was Ryne's place. His family legacy and inheritance. But something felt very, very wrong here.

"Ryne," he said. "I'm not trying to start a fight with you, but...is there something you need to tell us about this place?"

Ryne turned around and faced him. "What?"

Shawn met his eyes directly. "I was in the woods today and got attacked by a wolf. Not a pack of wolves, just one wolf. I tried to run, but my piece of shit leg gave out, and I fell. He should've killed me, but I shot at him. Then he was gone."

"So, you scared it off?"

"No, I mean he was *gone*. No trace that he was ever there. The son of a bitch tore through a foot of snow and there wasn't even the faintest sign of a footprint. And I did not imagine a giant black wolf in a goddamn snowstorm."

"Shawn, I don't understand ..."

"I don't understand either, dude. Nothing, not one thing, has made the slightest bit of sense since we got into this godforsaken place. Have you *ever* seen animals behave the way they do here? All the years we spent in a tree stand and I have *never* seen animals act this way. You shoot at them, and they don't move. They get out of hibernation just to stare at us through the window. They vanish into thin fucking air! The town's full of creeps, Noah magically gets a disorder he's never had before, and we have the snowstorm of the century moving like a snail over us. Now, I'm open to any and all interpretations: because I do not have the slightest fucking clue what is going on. What I do know is that this hunting trip is over. I am not going back out into those woods."

The room grew quiet, and Shawn realized he had his fists clenched. Noah just stared at him. Ryne held his position by the kitchen sink. The silent air hung like a lead blanket, threatening to collapse upon them with each passing second.

"I'm sorry," Shawn said, sitting back down. "But I would like to know what the hell is going on here. You've been up here a lot. You've been around these animals, this ecosystem. You've never seen them behave like this?

"No," Ryne said.

"Are you sure?"

"Not that I can remember. I mean, there have been some weird things that have happened, but I never thought too much about it."

"Like what?" said Shawn.

"Nothing, just a strange memory."

"Like...what?"

Ryne took a breath and shifted his weight against the sink. He held a hand up; as if trying to manifest words from thin air. He let his breath go and closed his eyes. "The first time I remember coming up here, I had a sleepwalking episode. I walked right out of the front door in the middle of the night during a storm. My uncle was outside. I thought I saw something, but he said he was freeing a deer from a snare."

"What did you think you saw?" asked Noah, now very much attentive.

"I don't really remember. It's hazy. I was sleepwalking for God's sake."

"What did you think you saw?" Shawn echoed.

"I thought I saw my uncle praying to a deer."

Shawn almost had to laugh. He put his fingers to his temples, tried to massage away the insanity.

"Well," he said. "Good to know that nothing strange goes on here."

"Shawn, I was sleepwalking. It was nothing."

"After what I saw today, I don't give a shit."

"Guys," said Noah.

"I'll give you that it's weird, but come on man, what are you saying?"

"Guys."

"I'm saying that there is something seriously fucked up with this place."

"Guys!"

"What?" They snapped.

"Look," said Noah, his voice quiet, trembling. He pointed behind them toward the window.

On the other side of the glass, a large black wolf stood in the driving snow. It was right up against the glass, its black nose millimeters away.

"What the...," said Ryne.

"Told you," said Shawn.

In the failing blue light of dusk, the wolf glared at them, its black fur coated in white frost. Its eyes appeared black and empty, almost hollow, as it scratched the window with its paw.

kitsch. kitsch.

Ice water coursed through Shawn's veins. A sound. It made a sound when it scratched the glass. He wasn't dreaming. He wasn't seeing things. The thing of death was there, in the flesh. Scratching at the window like a dog left out in the cold.

kitsch. kitsch.

His throat filled with terror. What little remnant of understanding that had remained now abandoned him. It was insanity, this place. Rationalizing anything here was foolish. Slowly. he came to another realization. The animal might as well be sniffing the window, but no vapor formed on the glass.

He drifted to his left. Towards the bathroom. Towards the rifle.

"What are you doing?" hissed Ryne.

The wolf's eyes followed him, and the animal moved. With each step he took, the wolf matched his pace. Foot for foot. Their eyes locked, daring the other to look away.

Slow and steady. Logically, he should be safe. If the wolf tried to get inside the cabin, it would have to go through the tempered glass, which was next to impossible. Even if— by some miracle— the wolf broke through, it would surely die from the shards. But he was taking no chances. He had shot this thing point-blank in the chest hours earlier, and yet here it was.

Another step towards the bathroom and another stride from the wolf.

Shawn reached the bathroom door, and the wolf reached the end of the last window on the wall. It sat down and again scratched.

kitsch. kitsch.

Shawn reached inside and grabbed the rifle. He pulled it up to his shoulder.

"Shawn, what are you doing?" asked Ryne.

"I'm going to watch this thing die this time."

His finger tightened around the trigger.

"Shawn, don't be stupid," said Noah. "That thing wants in. You shatter that glass, and it *gets* in."

His fingers curled around the trigger. They wanted to squeeze, wanted to blast a hole through the thing in the glass, wanted to obliterate those black eyes and stand over it to watch it die.

But the logical part of himself knew better. One crack, that's all it would take. Then *it* would be inside.

He lowered the gun.

The wolf continued to stare through the glass for what seemed like hours. Finally, the animal turned and sauntered into the darkness of the forest and was gone. Lost in the lightless void of the Yukon winter.

Shawn dropped the rifle. It fell with a thud against the floor. He collapsed onto the sofa and threw his head back against the cushion.

"What the hell is happening?"

Noah sat quietly in the corner. On his face—a mask—the painted white face of fear and disbelief. Ryne crouched in place, his body slowly dropping to meet the cabin floor, his hands ringing upon themselves with restless nerves. Outside, the trees swayed violently beyond the window, dark shadows thrashing in a black ocean of ice.

Thirteen
The Lake

The storm raged. Heavy and freezing winds battered the trees and ripped branches from their trunks. The blinding snowfall and the pitch black of night had turned into a swirling blackout of ice and shadows. Ryne knew the cabin would hold. It always had. But the cold bore its way into his senses and left him a frozen mess.

He had vetted every thought and explored every corner of his mind, but answers remained hidden in shadow. What was happening extended so far beyond the reach of his comprehension, that all he could do now was sit in disturbed silence.

Noah slept behind him on the couch, bundled up in multiple blankets despite the immense warmth that poured from the burning fireplace. Shawn, too, was asleep, his swollen knee propped up in the recliner. Ryne's mind wandered quickly through tall grasses of doubt and disbelief. In the quiet, he thought about that night when he was a child, the night he sleep-walked right out the front door of the cabin and into the frozen night. The night he witnessed a sight saturated with strangeness. But he knew you could never trust what you see in your sleep. He understood, all too well, the strength of the mind and its many tricks. Perception was a powerful drug, silently efficient in its dealings. But his thoughts labored on the wolf that had scratched at the window. It was a labor of understanding because, deep down, Ryne knew the cold and terrible truth.

He had seen that animal before. In his dreams.

All those nights when sleep had eluded him as a child. Nights spent in bed, eyes trained on the corner of his bedroom, scared to fall asleep. Scared because he didn't know if he'd be able to move when he got up. Terrified at what might be watching in that corner. Every time the old house settled; his ears heard the splintering wood of the thing's arms. Every creak was another step it took out of the shadows. And when sleep came, so did the dog. Always there, always moving closer.

But the dreamcatcher had assuaged him. A week or so after that first nightmare, his father went on a trip. A couple of days to a convention selling new outdoor equipment that he could've sold in his store. When he came home, he had the dreamcatcher and gave it to Ryne. Hung it over the bedpost in his room. Told him that it would stop the nightmares.

And it had. As long as the token of bone and feather hung above his bed, the darkness of that horrible night stayed away. But sometimes he didn't have it. A friend's house. His college dorm. His first apartment. Whenever the dreamcatcher would slip his mind, the dog would always come back. And every time he woke up, he'd see the beast there, sulking in the darkest corner of the room as his body would slowly regain control. It watched him on those nights, the cracking sound of wood softly echoing through the darkness. Those black, hollow, soulless eyes.

But it was a dream, a hallucination. He knew that. As his waking body would catch up to his mind, the thing would dissipate into the night, and all would return to normal. All bad dreamers eventually wake up.

But this time was different. He'd heard the scratching. He'd seen the paw against the glass. So had Shawn. So had Noah. This was not a dream. For whatever reason, his mind's manifestation was alive and present and stalking outside the cabin.

Now the thing was gone, vanished into the black storm that churned outside.

Ryne sat down and ate some bacon. It had been hours since he had last eaten anything. Night had fallen completely, but he could not bear to think of sleep. It felt like he was that scared little boy again. Every fiber in his soul fought to keep him awake, because he didn't know what else would be there when he woke up.

That night so many years ago. The child he had once been, walking out into the black cold. He remembered his uncle kneeling, praying to something. Something wrong. Something that he would see in his dreams and in the dark recesses of his bedroom.

He had been told he was sleepwalking. Rod had said he was simply freeing a deer from a snare.

Just a natural part of these woods.

Ryne wasn't so sure he had been sleeping anymore.

Then, in the silence of the cabin walls, he heard the voice. It came from nowhere and everywhere all at once. It came from out of the sink. It came from the bedroom. It came from the bathroom. It came from the walls.

The voice of a child.

d a d d y

Ryne's head snapped around, looked for the source of the voice, and found it everywhere.

d a d d y, c o m e s e e

A calmness set in over him. A deep, sleepy calmness. He felt the muscles in his body stiffen and then relax to an indescribable state of serenity. Light and free, levitating above himself in an untethered bliss.

d a d d y, c o m e s e e

He didn't recognize the voice, but something about it soothed him deeply.

"Where are you?" Confusion set in. He had said nothing, and yet speech had escaped his mouth.

t h e l a k e, d a d d y, c o m e s e e t h e l a k e

He felt his control desert him and his feet, unencumbered by mental restraint, began to move. He was walking towards the door, but he wasn't. He couldn't be.

Yet, he was.

c o m e o n, d a d d y, c o m e s e e

He opened the cabin door and stepped outside. The wind ripped at his body, like a thousand frozen blades driving themselves into his bones. His eyes stung, but they did not close. The voice called to him.

c o m e o n, d a d d y

He made his way through the ripping wind around the back of the cabin to the long wooden pathway that led to the pier. He couldn't see more than five feet in front of him, but he knew where the path led. The lake was a hundred-yard walk. The voice called to him again, and he felt his legs carrying him forward on that long walk, the cold biting at his skin, slipping through the cracks in his clothes. The trees rose high into the night sky, imposing their will above him. Ancient beyond the scope of his understanding, their roots dug through the snow. Slithering beneath the white. The wind and swirling snow blinded him, but the voice guided him along. He continued down to the where the pathway became the pier, his steps not his own. The natural world contorted around him, melting into the snow like a living thing at his back. The lake sprawled before him, a frozen land below the darkness bleeding from the starless sky.

He reached the end of the pier and the world opened up.

The violence of the storm broke, and the air calmed again. In this momentary peace, the clouds opened up and the moon poured light upon the ice. In this ethereal glow, he could see across the frozen expanse.

Near the lake's center, a small figure stood alone on the ice.

c o m e s e e, d a d d y

From somewhere outside himself, Ryne felt his foot lift off the wooden pier and step onto the ice.

* * *

In his restless sleep, Shawn dreamed of darkness. No image appeared in his mind, no sound in his ears. Savage, shadowed thorns pierced the skin all over his body. He sensed that he was screaming, the aching in his throat sending that abrasive vibrating signal to his head, but no sound escaped his mouth. There was no decipherable direction. The blanketing silence enveloped him and a sharp, piercing pain coursed through his veins, pumped with his blood throughout the rivers of his broken body, climaxing in a single excruciating attack on his knee. Ice suddenly gloved his leg and slowly sunk its teeth into his skin.

He woke in a cold sweat.

Just a dream. God, what a dream. The cylinders of his heart fired away beneath his ribs, slowing as he regained his sense and composure. He closed his eyes, holding them tight. Home. He wanted to go home. He wanted to walk into that one-bedroom piece of shit he called a home and fall down on that lumpy couch right in the middle of it. He'd never wanted to see that small living area as much as he wanted to now. It struck him how claustrophobic the vast openness of the wilderness could feel. Thousands of miles in either direction of nothing but trees made the place seem like some endless, primeval plane.

If only he could get a cell signal. A phone call to his sister. His mother. Even if just to remind himself that he wasn't too far gone, that a world outside of this place still existed. Because it was getting harder now. Every minute in the cabin made his world seem further away.

He opened his eyes and saw the wooden ceiling above. A snowflake, small and white, floated by. A dancer on a breeze that shouldn't be there.

No longer did the warm embrace fueled by the burning fireplace fill the cabin. Replacing it was a biting cold as a gust whipped through the living area. He looked to the windows—they were closed. Then his eyes moved to the front door.

It stood wide open, shaking against its hinges as the storm screamed through the opening.

"Shit!"

He jumped off the couch, landing with a spastic thud. A sharp spiderweb of pain shot through his leg and carried itself through his entire body. He collapsed under his own weight and landed chin-first on the hard wooden floor.

Get up, you idiot, get up!

He pushed himself to his feet, regained his balance and control, and slammed the cabin door closed, banishing the wind to the outside world. A sigh escaped him, and he fell back to the floor. His leg let loose a scream within him that echoed through his body. He shut his eyes, bit his lip, and powered his way through the misery until it finally subsided by the slightest of degrees. When he opened his eyes, he saw Noah fast asleep on the couch as if nothing had happened.

"Ryne?"

There was no answer.

"Ryne?"

Still no answer.

The open door.

Shawn turned his head and looked to the window to his right, staring outside.

No, he thought. *He couldn't have.*

"Noah, wake up!"

Noah didn't move. Shawn pulled himself back to his feet and trudged his way forward to the bedroom. He threw the door open to reveal an empty bed.

"Noah!"

Noah stirred slightly but didn't wake.

"Noah, wake the fuck up!" he shouted, shaking his friend violently.

Finally, Noah shuddered and opened his eyes. Shawn moved into the kitchen and ripped through cabinets.

"What are you doing?" asked Noah.

Shawn found his mark, a flashlight. He clicked the switch, on and off, two cycles to make sure it worked. The light seemed dimmer than it should have been, but it would have to do.

"Ryne went outside," he said. "He just walked out and left the door open."

"What? Why?"

"I don't know, but we've got to get him. The storm is bad."

Noah bounded off the sofa and zipped his jacket up to his chin. Shawn moved to the door and opened it again.

The blizzard had reached what seemed like its zenith. The wind shredded through the trees, ripping branches from their trunks. Only the thickest, oldest, and strongest held their ground. It hit Shawn's face like a frozen hammer, and he felt a sharp fire burning its way up his leg. A low whipping sound moved along the gale. He couldn't see a thing.

Where the hell did he go? He thought. Better yet, *why the hell did he go?*

His leg gave way again, and he struggled to hold his balance. Noah grabbed him just as he lost the last of his strength, stabilizing him in the blitzing whiteout.

"Shawn!" Noah called, his voice pushing through the heavy wind. "Shawn, are you OK?"

"Yeah! Where did he go?"

"Ryne!" Noah yelled, his voice lost in the iced maze, carried off into the wind.

"Ryne, where the fuck are you!"

"Shawn, look!" He pointed down to the ground.

Footprints. Depressions in the snow. Barely visible, but there.

The two of them put their heads down and forced their way through the storm as it flayed and tore at their faces with each step. Eyes tight, they followed the footsteps as they worked their way around the side of the cabin towards the back. Towards the pier. The lake.

Shawn turned to Noah.

"Why would he go to the lake?"

A look of panic spread across Noah's face, as though some memory triggered in his mind.

"Shawn, I don't know how thick that ice is."

"It should be frozen solid."

"I know, but listen, I was there last night, and it looked *really* thin."

"*Really* thin?"

Noah nodded; his eyes still wide from the realization.

They pushed their way further down the wooden path. With thicker bushes and more trees lining the walkway, the wind was slightly less drastic, and he could now pick his head up and face ahead. Even with the wind hampered, the trees still shook and moved like giants in some ritualistic dance.

"Ryne!" Nothing answered besides the screaming wind pushing against the ancient trees. They continued further. The fire burned his leg with each step. His knee felt brittle, and his equilibrium was a house of glass cards balanced atop a jagged stone. Each step felt as though the house would collapse, shattering into a million tiny pieces. But he pushed on with Noah's arm hooked under his shoulder, stabilizing both of them.

They reached the end of the pier. The scene before him faded into an unnerving calmness. No wind swirled in the air here. No snowfall blanketed the frozen lake. It appeared as though the storm suddenly ceased to exist.

He looked up. The powerful borders of the storm wrapped around the lake, but above the lake was the calm of a missing sky. Split open, a hole that turned to a chasm opening to somewhere even further above. Pure black fell like rain from the emptiness as the stars themselves seemed to turn off and on at random, like lightbulbs dying out on the lake's ceiling.

Shawn stood entranced. His eyes stung with the cold, but he couldn't break his gaze away from the abyss above. A pervasive feeling of smallness polluted his thoughts and darkened his senses. This was beyond him. This was beyond all of them.

"Shawn," said Noah, breaking him out of his trance. "Shawn, look."

Shawn's eyes scanned out to the lake where Noah pointed and found his focus.

Ryne was on the ice, walking towards the lake's center.

"Ryne!"

* * *

Somewhere behind him, Ryne heard a faint new voice ride in on the cold and fade away into the night. He wanted to turn his head, to trace the phantom sound. But he couldn't. His gaze couldn't leave the figure of the child, as though he wasn't allowed to.

"Kid? Hey, kid? What are you doing out here? You're going to freeze to death."

The child did not move; but stood silently on the ice with the faintest bob, like a gentle breeze undulating through a branch of leaves.

d a d d y, c o m e s e e

Ryne moved towards the figure despite every single sense in his mind commanding his body to stop. But his body would not stop. A part of him pushed its way to the forefront of his being and compelled him onward, deaf to his internal screaming to turn and run the other way.

i ' m c o l d

Again, he thought he could hear someone calling his name from behind him. He tried to turn his head to look, but the paralysis held, and his body continued to drive forward.

craaaaaacccccckkkkkk

From beneath his feet, he felt the ice move. The sirens in his head began going haywire as the realization of his surroundings grew apparent. He was near the center of the lake, the deepest part. His feet were freezing, and he felt a feeling of creeping movement beneath his soaked socks. Cold and wet.

Like the ice itself was crawling up his leg, cracking apart as it made its way into him. But his body moved against his better sense, and that revolting part of his mind kept him paralyzed and enslaved to the soft, scared little voice.

i'm cold, daddy

craaaaaacccccckkkkkk

Close now, the child stood only ten feet away. Ryne gasped with the part of himself that he still held some command over. The child was a little boy. Five, maybe six years old. Dark hair fell in his face, whisked over glacial blue eyes.

Memories of baby books and photographs filled his mind from a time long before. Those eyes—the same eyes he saw in the mirror every day.

"Ryne!" he heard from behind him. Shawn's voice.

The little boy began to change.

Ryne felt a hand on his shoulder and snapped out of the voice's grip.

"Ryne, what the hell are you doing?" asked Shawn.

"The kid," said Ryne.

"What kid?"

Ryne turned around. The little boy was gone. Empty ice was all that surrounded him.

craaaaaacccccckkkkkk

"Okay," said Shawn. "Nice and easy. Let's get back inside before we go through the ice, or you get frostbite."

The two of them made their way back cautiously across the frozen lake, taking careful measure with each step as the ice slowly cracked and splintered beneath their weight. Upon reaching the edge of the peer, Noah reached his hand down and pulled Ryne up, then Shawn.

The walk back to the cabin was long and cold. Ryne walked in silence, hoping some meaning would resonate loud enough through the embers of his psyche to provide sense, but there were no embers. Only ice. And the only sounds in that ice were the echoes of that voice.

He had just stood there. While the ice cracked beneath his feet, he had stood there like a dumb animal, staring at a vision that wasn't even there. A phantom. But it had to have been there. It had to. The voice had been clear, even more than it had been the night before. He had seen that boy on the ice, heard him, damn near felt him.

It had called him "daddy."

A pit formed deep within his stomach at the thought, and he pushed it out of his head with haste. But it wouldn't leave, not completely. It stayed on the fringes of his mind, like the black dog in his dreams. Still there, in the shadows.

Would it have been so bad? To fall through that ice? To feel the warmth as hypothermia set in? To feel peace and tranquility for the first time in a year? To take his own place beyond the veil?

No, he told himself. *That's stupid. Get it out of your head.*

But the thought did not leave him. It lingered there, in the rivers of his heart. The uncanny welcome of a cold, final embrace.

Fourteen

The Bite

They used the last of the heated water to fill a bath for Ryne. It wasn't very hot, but that wasn't necessarily a bad thing. He only needed to warm up, not go into shock. Now, his body warmed, he paced across the floor in a short-sleeved shirt. Shawn lay in the recliner, his leg stretched out with a bag of ice over his knee. Noah sat shivering on the couch, his arms crossed over his body underneath a sweater and a thermal jacket. The fireplace bled warmth like a fresh wound, yet he was freezing.

Midnight would arrive soon, and the storm showed no signs of moving on. Ryne kept constantly walking to the window, as if scratching some impulsive itch, and looking out in the direction of the lake. The cloud wall hovered stationary each time, dead in the sky above the cabin. The storm was sitting right on top of them.

Noah had seen it, too. The hole that ripped through the sky above the windless, clear lake. A void of darkness hanging from spectral gallows lost in the sky-bound abyss. He hadn't mentioned it. What could he say? How could he possibly describe the sight? There were no words to explain, no clues to analyze. In that moment, he had never felt so small, so insignificant, so pointless. His eyes twitched. His fingers twisted within each other, pulling and squeezing against cold skin. He was losing his mind.

They all were. Something was roosting in these woods. Pushing them further and further into a place of thoughtlessness. It wasn't a dream, a vision, or some post-traumatic hallucination. No, they had all seen the wolf, the deer, the animals, and now the sky.

But Ryne had seen something else. Something new.

"I swear to God I was looking at a kid."

"I didn't see anything," said Shawn.

"You don't believe me."

"I never said that."

"Then just say it."

Shawn sighed. "I believe you saw what you saw. What I'm saying is we couldn't see anything."

"He's right," Noah said. The chattering of his teeth sounded louder than anything else in the space. "All we saw was you."

"You sure it was a kid?"

"Yeah. Or it was. Right before you got there, something was happening. It was *changing* or something, I don't know. I know you don't believe me. Hell, I don't know if *I* believe me."

Exhaustion weighed on Noah's shoulders. There was no question of belief. On the contrary, belief had become a bonding agent. A shared blood that pumped through cold limbs. What wore on them was the growing sense of things getting worse. An escalation that slowly cracked their illusions of normalcy to the point of shattering. So far, each of the incidents had possessed at least some semblance of understanding. Noah's episode displayed a sickness he didn't realize he had. Shawn saw a wolf in the Yukon, which was so deep within the reach of reality that to call it uncommon would seem extreme. Even the deer blocking the road and the animals outside may have simply been wild animals acting like, well, wild animals. And they all found some solace in knowing the others could see and experience the same thing.

But this? This was something else. The link of rationality, however stretched, that had connected all three of them had been broken. Now one of them was being affected in a different, more invasive way.

Noah's head ached. A sudden lightheadedness overcame him, and his vision blurred out any conceivable details of his surroundings. Beneath his skull, he swore something moved. Grew. Pressed against the bone and pushed.

The panic rose from its slumber once again.

"Guys, it's happening again, just like earlier in town."

The woods are lovely, dark, and deep. But I have promises to keep, and miles to go before I sleep.

Not these woods. Dark and deep, yes. But not lovely.

Shawn lifted himself out of the recliner and limped toward his bag sitting on the kitchen floor. He reached in and pulled out a pack of gum.

"Here," he said, unwrapping the stick and handing it to Noah. He took it and placed it in his mouth, exploding the sweet juice across his teeth and tongue. For a minute, he chewed away at the gum as his headache subsided and his vision returned to normal. The panic slumped back into its hole.

"Is it helping?" asked Shawn.

Noah nodded as he felt a calmness return to him.

"I know both of you were sleeping," said Ryne. "But did either of you hear the voice?"

Shawn trained his gaze, his eyes suddenly wide open. "What voice?"

Ryne stopped pacing and fell into the chair across from the recliner. A heaviness dragged on his eyes, and his hands massaged each other. His skin had turned so pale that it made him look sick.

"Remember last night? When the animals surrounded the cabin? Do you remember the sound we heard?"

They nodded in agreement.

"What did you say the sound sounded like?"

Shawn's head dropped, and he studied the floor. Noah stared into space and wished to go deaf so he wouldn't hear the question. Wouldn't think about that night, that sound, ever again.

"Just say it, you know what it sounded like."

Shawn pursed his lips. Noah looked out the window. The storm raged on.

"I need to hear you say it again," said Ryne. "I need to know I'm not crazy."

Shawn sighed and picked his head up. "Like a child singing."

Noah nodded.

A pale sheen glossed over Ryne's eyes, and the bright blue dimmed as light shimmered and died within them. "I heard that voice again tonight.

Clear as day. But it wasn't singing, it was talking. *To me.* It was talking directly to me."

Noah remained still; his eyes focused on his friend. Something about his voice—a dark resignation to the madness that plagued each of them now. Desperately poking, eroding, digging for an explanation. Or, at the very least, direction.

"It told me to come to the lake. It...it..."

He appeared drained. Just empty and lifeless as his mind ran through the next words he would say.

"It called me '*daddy*.'"

The comment struck something in Noah. Of all the things for Ryne to hear. A child calling him *daddy*? Something so specific, so targeted? There was simply no more doubt.

They were all going insane.

"That's why you went outside." said Shawn, his voice low. He knew the darker currents that ran through these words. He'd seen them.

"No, that's the thing. I didn't do anything. I could feel my body moving and I could see everything in front of me, but it wasn't *me*. I wasn't doing anything. I wasn't in control."

Control. That word meant nothing here. Noah hadn't felt the slightest grasp of control since he stepped foot in this cabin. Whatever dominion he held over his state of mind had evaporated into the cold air above the lake when they'd first arrived.

"What is happening to us?"

Shawn stared into the crackling fireplace. "I don't know. But we are being fucked with."

"By who?" asked Noah.

"By the people in that town."

Ryne cocked his head. "What do you mean?"

"Jesus Christ, can you not see it? You hear the voice of a little boy calling you daddy? The one person we talk to *specifically* brought up the miscarriage. Made a fucking point of it. Then the doctor lied to you."

"Wait, what?" asked Noah.

"You aren't hypoglycemic."

"How do you know that?" asked Ryne.

"I gave Noah the gum."

"Yeah, and it helped."

"I know it did."

He showed them the packet. Noah studied it for a second, and then his eyes got wide. He understood the point Shawn was making.

"It's sugar-free gum. Now, how does someone with hypoglycemia have an attack that is solved by a sugarless substance?"

"If the person doesn't have hypoglycemia at all," said Ryne. "A placebo."

"Whatever is wrong with you, it isn't hypoglycemia. They gave you a reason, something to hold on to and believe in. That's why the gum worked. It's in your head."

Noah closed his eyes and let his head fall back limply against the couch cushion. The panic rose again, peeking through the darkness and smiling. It crawled within him, feeling its way out of the black place where he tried to keep it hidden.

The woods are lovely, dark, and deep. But I have promises to keep, and miles to go before I sleep.

A deep breath in and a long exhale followed by another. The panic stopped its intrusion, but it didn't return to its dark hiding place. It was getting harder and harder to restrain it within its place of banishment. He felt it poisoning his veins, an ink filling his blood. The knot in his stomach tightened and retched his insides as bile formed in his throat.

The woods are lovely, dark, and deep. But I have promises to keep, and miles to go before I sleep.

"So, why lie?" asked Ryne.

"I don't know. But I know one more thing. Everything that has happened to us so far has been outside the cabin. Noah getting sick in town, my run-in with the wolf, the whole thing with the lake. Hell, whatever is going on, it had to coerce you outside before anything could happen."

"So, what does that mean?"

"It means we don't leave this fucking cabin. It means we find some way to block that door to where we can't get out and nothing can get in. Not until the storm is over. Until we can leave for good."

Shawn looked as though he'd aged twenty years. His eyes had turned wild and intense, darting back and forth. Noah couldn't hold his gaze for very long. Besides, a separate issue weighed on him.

"We've got another problem," Noah said. "We only have enough firewood to last us until tomorrow morning. And the storm isn't moving."

"What do you mean it's not moving?"

"He's right," said Ryne. "I've been checking out the window repeatedly. It's been over an hour now, and the cloud walls haven't moved. I think the storm is just sitting on top of us."

"So, when we run out of firewood and it's still going on, we're screwed," said Noah. "That fireplace is the only thing keeping this cabin warm. After it passes, how long will it be before we can even get out?"

"I thought you guys got more firewood earlier?"

"No," said Ryne. "Noah got sick before we got to the firewood."

"Christ," said Shawn. He sat back down in the recliner and exhaled a sharp breath as he winced in pain.

"Are you okay?" asked Ryne.

"No, I'm not okay. My damn leg won't work. It hurts like hell, and every time I try to bend it or put pressure on it or even just get it to move it feels like I'm getting stabbed."

"Doesn't it usually act up whenever it gets cold?"

"Yeah, but not like this. Usually, it just aches, and I can't really run, but it's never felt this bad. I think I fucked it up earlier. Worse than usual."

"Pull your pants up and let me see."

"When did you become a doctor?"

"Just do it."

Shawn reached down and pulled the cuff of his pants up. About halfway up his calf, a reddish black liquid was frozen solid against his leg. They all saw it. Shawn stopped pulling. The color gave it away.

"Is that blood?"

"I think so," said Ryne. "Keep going."

Shawn bit his lip and kept pulling up. There was a tacky sound as the frozen blood tore from his skin like a scab, and fresh, warm blood began flowing down to the floor. Shawn groaned in pain, pulling until he exposed his entire knee.

Noah held his breath, and Ryne took a step backwards, aghast at the grizzly sight revealed before him.

Shawn's knee was mangled. Punctures extended around the kneecap and slightly up the thigh. Frozen blood clotted the holes, but the dried gore did not distract from what the wound was.

"A bite? That's a fucking bite! Why do I have a fucking bite on my knee!"

"When did this happen?" asked Ryne as he took another step back.

"I don't know! I hurt my knee with the wolf, but I took a bath right after. This wasn't here! Jesus Christ!"

"Shawn, calm down," said Ryne.

"No, I'm not calming the fuck down! Why do I have a bite mark on my leg? The only animal I've seen all day was that fucking wolf and it didn't bite me!"

"Are you sure it didn't bite you?" asked Noah.

"I would remember being bitten by a fucking wolf!"

Ryne ran into the kitchen and, looking under the sink, pulled out a dusty first aid kit and brought it back to Shawn. He looked at Noah. "I need you to go into the bathroom and run hot water over a rag and bring it out here."

Noah nodded and scurried into the bathroom; his stomach still tied in a sickening knot at the sight of Shawn's mutilated leg. There was no mistake. It was absolutely a bite; the individual punctures were driven deep into the tissue below the skin. And the way his knee twisted—whatever had bitten him had really gotten into the act, ripping and thrashing. Shawn would have remembered that.

He turned on the hot water and waited for a few seconds, but nothing but ice-cold liquid sprayed from the faucet. The generator outside needed to be turned on to heat the water. Noah turned and ran back into the living room, not stopping as he made his way through the room towards the front door.

"Generator needs to be turned on!" he said.

"Wait, don't!" Shawn's voice.

But he had already blown through the door and into the furious storm. The wind hit him like a brick and staggered him, but he regained his balance and trudged towards the generator shack to the right of the cabin. Noah got close enough to see the shack through the blinding gold snow and froze in his tracks.

The snow was a deep, yellowed gold. It fell in solid flakes, falling through the wind as though there was no wind at all. A strong odor filled the air, thick and oily. Beneath his feet he heard the crunch of crust.

Grain. Falling from the black sky. Heavy and dense, it coated the world around him and built up on his jacket and hood.

The panic returned, more eager now. Pulsating within him as he drowned in grain for the second time in his life. Shadows appeared to him in the darkness, creeping their way through the golden flakes.

He was crazy. He had to be. This couldn't be real, couldn't be happening.

The woods are lovely, dark, and deep. But I have promises to keep, and miles to go before I sleep.

He fought for control within his own mind as the panic stepped blatantly out of its dark hiding place and into what little light remained. Nausea filled his insides with bile. His breathing grew heavy. He closed his eyes tightly and wrestled for command of himself.

The woods are lovely, dark, and deep. But I have promises to keep, and miles to go before I sleep.

He opened his eyes again.

The black wolf stood in front of him.

Holding his breath, Noah took a step backwards and swept his sight over his surroundings. The grain blinded him in every direction, but he felt a presence off in the trees, watching him. Surrounding him. Suffocating him in its invisible stare. His gaze returned to the wolf; which had taken a couple of steps towards him. It did not bare its teeth, and it had its ears perked upwards like a friendly dog.

A sudden serenity overtook him. His heart rate dropped, and he was overtaken by an immense calm. The cold whips to his face now felt like balmy touches and, for a second, the surrounding dark lifted. He felt at peace. He felt happy.

This is it, he told himself. This was what he had searched for ever since his accident. The end of the tunnel. The proof he had longed for. The ultimate answer. He had spent so much time in the dark, but now he saw the light. That radiant light of peace and happiness. He felt himself willingly fading into it.

Then he felt a hand on his back, and an arm wrapped hard around his chest and yanked him back out of his blissful trance. The grain had turned back to snow again; white and cold. But the wolf still stood there, no longer the facade of a happy dog, but a malevolent force driving a horrific focus through the storm. Focused on him.

Ryne dragged Noah back through the wintry haze. Noah's eyes never left the wolf. The rest of the world around slowly returned to normal, and he found himself again in the dark bleakness of the frozen Yukon wild. Everything else had disappeared—the light, the peacefulness, the serene happiness that had enveloped him. All that remained was the wolf.

"Ryne, do..."

"I see it too."

The wolf opened its mouth, and a shrill scream rose through the trees, where it was joined by other screams coming from all different directions. The forest turned into a cacophony of ear-shattering shrieks intertwined within the maze of snow pelted trees. The wolf started changing. Its form shifted, rising higher into the trees. Its head expanding into jagged shapes jutting towards the sky. It started to drift off into the dark snow as Ryne pulled Noah into the cabin. He slammed the door behind them, cutting off the inhuman cries.

"What the hell was that noise?" said Shawn, still lying in the recliner.

"The wolf," said Ryne.

"It wasn't a wolf," said Noah, his chest tight, his heart a beating drum beneath his ribs.

"What?" asked Shawn.

"It wasn't a wolf. It was something else. I couldn't see exactly what, but it wasn't a fucking wolf."

"Noah, I need you to fill up a pot with water and put it over the fire," said Ryne.

"Ryne, what was that thing?"

"Noah, focus. It can't get us in here. I need you to get water and warm it up."

Noah stumbled his way into the kitchen and filled a cooking pot with water. He placed the pot atop the grill tray above the fireplace. After a few minutes, Ryne called him back over and stuck his hand in the water.

"Good enough," he said. He dipped a rag into the warmth and wiped down Shawn's leg. Shawn winced in pain as Ryne applied the pressure. The frozen blood gradually melted and dripped down his leg like bloody tears.

The wound cleaned off well, and the more it was cleaned the more obvious the source of the injury revealed itself. Noah mentally traced these wounds across the backdrop of Shawn's mangled leg, letting the shape of the carnage emerge. It was a dog's bite.

But no. That black *thing* wasn't a dog, nor was it a wolf. It was something else, something worse. Noah hadn't gotten a good look as Ryne dragged him away, but he had seen enough to know that a wolf doesn't look like that, and he was damn sure a wolf doesn't sound like that.

He sat in his spot on the sofa and wrapped himself in the blanket. He was freezing. The adrenaline had worn off, and now the chill of the Yukon air had reclaimed its station to plant frost into his bones.

And then there was the light. Noah had no explanation, but the feeling was a familiar one. At the bottom of the grain silo, as the last particles of oxygen died within his lungs, he had been consumed by the same sensation. This time was different, however. Withering away beneath the grain; there had been the feeling of pure darkness, the feeling that nothing was there with him as he succumbed to suffocating death. He had never felt so empty and alone.

But this time, he'd been calmed by an uplifting light and a serene presence. There had been a fullness to the sensation, a happiness and peacefulness radiating from all directions. And he had been ready and willing to accept it.

He now recognized that terrifying feeling. The sensation of death. And he had been happily walking into its embrace.

FIFTEEN
SECRET

R yne finished cleaning and treating Shawn's knee and wrapped it tightly in an old gauze bandage, using duct tape to keep pressure. The wound was bad. Whatever bit him had drilled deep through the muscle to the bone. He couldn't figure out how Shawn hadn't felt the bite or how he'd managed to walk back at all. The only explanation he could conjure was that the wolf had, in fact, attacked Shawn and bitten into his knee. After that, he'd gone into shock and fired the rifle, scaring off the wolf, but couldn't remember the moment. The blood froze quickly, so he didn't notice it when he got in the tub. Then, the warm water in the tub melted the blood, just as Ryne had done, and led to the grizzly scene they had all witnessed.

And none of that made any sense. Not even by the farthest stretches of hypotheticals.

Any possible understanding would be as formless and weightless as a ghost. It was a path that only hooked and curved its way through more questions while the answers hid deep in the dark trees.

Regardless, once the storm cleared, they would need to take Shawn back into town to be treated at an actual hospital. Shawn needed stitches, badly. Not to mention the structural damage to the knee itself. It would certainly require surgery. Ryne didn't voice this concern aloud; Shawn didn't need to hear it. The knee had been the bane of his existence for years. The issues clinging to Shawn's life like a fog bank all started from the dying joint, and now it was more torn up than it had ever been, so Ryne kept silent. Better to let the doctors tell him.

But any recovery hinged on first getting Shawn to the doctor, and doubts filled Ryne's head. There was no way to drive the truck through the loose snow covering the path back to Wolf's Bone. It had been bad enough earlier, and now five hours of heavy snowfall had rendered travel impossible. Plus, the storm still raged on. It just sat hovering over them. Not moving an inch. Stubborn, like that damn deer.

The continued escalation of events caused him to think critically about their chances of getting out of the cabin. How safe were they inside its walls? How long before whatever stalked the shadows outside broke its way through the front door? Before he heard the child's voice calling him? Would he walk right back out again?

Beyond logistical questions and hypotheticals, the circumstances of Shawn's butchered knee remained the most haunting of mysteries. Shawn had walked back to the cabin on that knee. Got in and out of a tub with that knee. Chased Ryne down across the ice on that knee. Something like that should have crippled him immediately. Hell, they should have found him frozen in the snow following the attack, unable to move. But they hadn't.

It seemed as though whatever had bitten Shawn's leg had been gnawing on it for the past few hours, ripping deeper and deeper with each passing hour. As though time itself had cultivated the severity of the wound.

Would it get worse? *Could* it get worse?

They needed to radio Wolf's Bone and try to contact Constable Whitting. An obvious and easy choice to make, but a shadow hung above it. Something was happening to Noah as well. Something the doctors had lied about. Another block pulled out of the feeble tower of half-clues and conjecture.

Why would the doctor lie? What purpose would it serve? Could it have simply been a misdiagnosis?

Ryne reached out and hovered his hand above the broadcast button on the small radio. He didn't know if the signal would get through the gale outside, but he heard the periodical moans of agony from Shawn and understood that, regardless of the questions surrounding the doctor's diagnosis, Wolf's Bone was their only option now. They were a strange bunch, sure, but they were still people. Flesh and blood human beings with whom he shared a distinct ancestry. Whatever peculiarities they possessed would be easily explainable by basic human instinct and logic. No instinct or logic existed in whatever waited for them in the shadowed wood.

"Radio-check one-two, can anyone hear me? Radio-check one-two, is anyone there?"

Static.

"Constable Whitting, come in. This is Ryne Burdette at the Burdette cabin requesting immediate medical assistance, over."

More static.

He checked the broadcast station and confirmed the correct tuning. But no signal broke through.

"This is Ryne Burdette requesting *immediate* medical assistance. There's been an animal attack. Do you copy? Over."

From beyond the static came a low, soft hum. It rode the crackling of the waves and slowly made itself audible through the cracked spaces of sound.

A child's voice. Singing.

j e s u s l o v e s m e t h i s i k n o w...

He turned off the radio. *No*, he told himself. *You're hearing things that aren't there, letting this strangeness get into your head.* But he couldn't bring himself to turn the radio back on. It was useless anyway. There was absolutely no way to get a signal through the storm. Not this one. This storm was behaving strangely.

Behaving. Like it was alive.

Get out of your own head.

The bedroom seemed smaller now. Hell, the entire cabin did. It was as though the space illuminated by the cabin's light was shrinking by the minute. Constricted by wilderness.

He stood and returned to the living area where logs crackled and popped within the fireplace. At least they'd stay warm while their fear devoured them.

"There's no signal," he told the others. "Just static."

"So, what next?" asked Noah.

"I don't know. There's a radio tower that might get a signal through, but it's a five-mile hike."

"We'd never make it," said Shawn. "Not in this."

"Do we wait it out?" asked Noah.

"Might be our only option at this point," said Ryne.

A lie, and he knew it. Shawn needed serious attention on his leg. They could hold out for a while, but the longer they waited for assistance, the worse the injury would get, especially if an infection set in. They had a little time, but not much.

An unease fell across the cabin as the three of them sat in silence. Ryne leaning against the wall next to the fireplace. Shawn in the recliner, relaxing his leg. Noah bundled up on the couch, shivering. Ryne cocked his head, considering Noah.

"You're cold?"

"Freezing."

"It's really warm in here," said Shawn. "How are you cold?"

"I don't know, I just am. I've been cold since we got here."

Ryne got out of the chair and moved over to the couch. "Move over," he said as he sat down on the middle cushion. The air felt slightly chilled, noticeably different from the warmth sweltering the rest of the cabin. He sat there for a minute, the others watching intently. The pores in his skin closed up as cool air slithered up his skin, and he shivered. This part of the room was cold.

"What the hell?"

"It's cold, isn't it?" said Noah.

"Yeah, but why would it be? There's no open window or anything."

Ryne stood. Around him, the warmth returned—except for one spot. His feet and ankles still felt freezing. The cold was seeping out from under the couch.

"Noah, get up."

"What? Why?"

"I need to move the couch."

Noah obliged, and Ryne pushed the couch aside. The floor below was empty, except for the circular rug that encompassed most of the living area. Beneath the section of the weaved cloth that normally stretched under the couch, something bulged. Shawn noticed it immediately.

"Check under the rug."

Ryne pulled the rug up. Cut into the wooden floor was a door with a pull handle. A cellar door.

"Did you know this place had a cellar?" asked Shawn

He searched his memory for anything. Any random remembrance of the cellar being used, or even mentioned. But he'd never even seen the couch in a different location, let alone pushed to the side for access into a hidden cellar.

"No. This is news to me."

He reached down and grabbed the handle. The door was stuck and needed a few seconds of loosening before he finally pulled it free. A blast of cold air filled the room as Ryne fell backwards with the weight of the open door.

"It obviously hasn't been opened in a while," said Shawn.

"Yeah, no shit," said Ryne as he picked himself up off the floor.

Noah bent his head down over the hole. Wind blew through his hair.

"It must have some opening to the outside. All the wind from the storm must have built up until we opened it," said Noah. "That's why I was so cold. I've been right on top of it this entire time."

"Your dad never mentioned this?" asked Shawn.

"No, never. I had no idea this was here." His memories continued to run reports in his head, but Ryne could never remember a single discussion around the presence of the cellar.

They stood over the dark hole in the floor as the cold air pushed its way into the cabin. There was a whistling echo deep within the dark, but no light to speak of. Suddenly there was a need growing within him. A need to know, to illuminate the last mysteries of his family. A desperate compulsion pulling him towards the cellar.

"Anybody feeling curious?" asked Ryne.

"No," said Noah. Shawn shook his head in agreement.

"Yeah, me neither," said Ryne as he began his descent into the dark.

SIXTEEN
THE CELLAR

As Ryne lowered himself into the abyss, a chill ran into his clothes, where it rooted itself into the pores of his skin. A wind blew in from somewhere at his back, softly whistling past unseen obstacles, like a snake slithering around the intertwined branches of a tree. The cellar smelled stale and acrid. The wind helped mask the smell to a degree, but he couldn't deny that lingering all around him was the stench of death long forgotten.

He finally reached the hard ground at the bottom of the ladder. Darkness enshrouded everything around him. Shadows blended into shadows and hid within dark corners of his imagination.

"Are you at the bottom?" asked Noah from above.

A deep irritation swelled within him. There was absolutely no way whatsoever that he didn't know about this place, but he couldn't find a single memory of it. Even if he'd never seen it before, this cellar was obviously used for something. Rory and Rod had to have, at least, made some trips down here. Something was being withheld. Something important and potentially dangerous.

"I can't see anything. Could one of you get me the flashlight?"

"It's dead," said Noah. "All we have are the lighters."

Of course it is. "I guess that will have to do, then."

Rustling sounds came from above him. He heard the floorboards creaking with each step overhead, which made him worry about the structural stability of the cabin.

"Here," said Noah. Ryne cupped his hands at the ladder's base, and Noah dropped a zippo lighter into them. Flicking the lid off, he ignited the flame and a small portion of the darkness eroded away under the virgin light. It wasn't much, but it was enough for him to see the sight emerging before him. The hair on his arms stood, and his heart beat hard and fast against his rib cage, trying to evacuate his chest and run far away from the thing now illuminated by the flickering flame.

"Guys, you need to come down here," he said. "Now."

"Everything okay?" asked Noah.

"No. Get down here."

"What about Shawn?"

"Put him on your shoulder or something— but get him down here."

He stood in frozen silence as the others fumbled above him. He heard Shawn's grunt of pain as Noah helped him up. The floorboards creaked, and the ladder shook under the weight of both men as they descended into the cellar.

"What is it?" asked Noah.

Ryne held the lighter out further in front of him.

"...Jesus..." said Shawn.

The walls of the cellar were not actually walls at all. The only thing seemingly built by man were a set of wooden floorboards placed beneath their feet. The "walls" were hard clay permafrost, like whoever dug the hole into the earth had never finished building the cellar. And those frozen walls were not bare. The grizzliest and most intensely unsettling sight that Shawn had ever seen adorned one of them.

A deer hung dead on the clay, held up by long metal nails pierced through its legs. More distressing than the presence of the body was its condition. This was no trophy kill, no stuffed buck. No, this was something different. This was savagery. An ancient-style torture. A kind of brutality that only existed in the hearts of men too far gone from the edge of sanity. In a state of decay, the rotting of the carcass mixed with the cold air pushing through the underground cellar. But the physical layout of the deer sunk deep under Shawn's skin and left his mouth and mind entirely agape. The dead animal had its forelegs splayed apart in opposite directions with a nail driven into the clay through the base of the hooves. The hind legs crossed at the ankles where the third nail had been forced through two layers of fur and bone. The animal's head hung down limply to its chest.

The deer had been crucified.

Shawn continued to stare; his eyes unblinking at the ghastly sight. From behind him came a lurching sound as Noah fell to his knees and vomited, adding to the acrid stench. Ryne sank to a crouch and struggled to find his breath.

"...God..." said Noah as he finished expelling his guts all over the wooden floor planks.

"Ryne, please start explaining something," said Shawn.

Ryne remained in his crouch. "What could I *possibly* explain?"

"What the hell is this! You have to know something; this is your family's cabin!"

"I swear to God, I have no idea what any of this is."

Noah regained his footing behind them and steadied himself. "How fresh is it?"

"What?" asked Ryne.

"The fucking deer. How long has it been dead?"

Ryne looked at the crucified deer and stepped forward for a closer inspection. The animal's eyes were flat and black, and pools of dried blood coagulated beneath the carcass.

A disgusting odor hit his nose; a rank scent of decay encrusted within a sodden dampness. A swirling feeling of emptiness filled his head, and he pulled back to take a breath and collect himself. This was the smell he had sensed upon his entry into the cellar, now uncompromised by the wind.

"I'd guess a few months," he said, wincing away from the dead thing against the wall. "At the most."

"How did we not smell it?" asked Noah.

"The wind hides it."

"No, Noah's right," said Shawn. "The wind only came with the storm. How did we not smell it when we first got here?"

Ryne lifted the lighter back to the animal. The soulless eyes seemed to follow him as he slowly guided the light to his side, illuminating the other dead things hanging from the clay. The deer was not the lone victim. Others shared the mausoleum as well. Other animals, the entire Yukon fauna record on morbid display. The bodies appeared in various states of decomposition. A wolverine hung next to the deer, followed by the frail corpse of a fox. Deeper into the cellar, the clay walls continued melting into the shadows. As far as the glow from the flame extended, animals adorned the permafrost wall like some sick exhibit. A strong gust blew from somewhere within the cellar and extinguished the flame. Ryne hurried to hit the ignition again, desperate to rediscover some light. Once he ignited the flame, he held his other hand up to block the wind.

"Can we please get out of here?" asked Noah.

Then, without warning, a memory finally emerged in Ryne. Vague and incomplete, but a memory, nonetheless.

"Look on the floor, right at the animal's feet," said Ryne as he turned the light once again to the carcass adorned wall. There was nothing under the deer but dried blood.

Ryne moved deeper into the chasm to where the wolverine hung, its lifeless body slumped and rotted. It had been dead much longer than the deer, years by the looks of it. Much of it decomposed and dried out. The dull gray of its skull shone in the lighter's glow. Its eyes long gone. Looking down, Ryne saw what his fragmented memory told him was there. He held the lighter lower to the ground to get a better look. There was a loose stone on the ground beneath the carcass. Old stone—grimed over from years of languishing in this cavern of sogging decay. Turning the lighter to his left, he could see that a similar stone lay at the feet of each corpse within the lighter's glow, all the way up to the deer. The ground beneath the deer's hooves was strangely bare of any stone.

Reaching out with a trembling hand, he moved the stone from its resting place. Underneath the rock was a folded piece of discolored paper.

"How did you know to look under it?" Shawn asked.

Ryne moved the lighter further away so as not to ignite the old sheet and opened the paper.

"Can we *please* get the fuck out of here?" said Noah again.

"Hold on," said Ryne. He held the lighter closer, and the glow lit up a line of text written in careful calligraphy. The words twisted and wound their way across the page. A spot of what appeared to be dried blood provided a distressing bookend to the text.

Jonathan Burdette.

Ryne's breath caught inside his throat and for a few seconds he struggled to create words. Finally, a whimpering, *"what?"* escaped his lips. He collapsed backwards and began to hyperventilate, his breath a heavy push through struggling lungs. He shifted the light to the next animal; this one a large bear. There was a stone beneath it as well. Ryne scurried over to it. He moved the stone and found another carefully folded piece of linen paper.

Richard Burdette.

"Who is Richard Burdette?" asked Shawn.

Ryne's voice sounded hollow, empty. "My great-grandfather."

Blood boiled beneath Ryne's skin, and a deep ache manifested itself behind his eyes. He felt Shawn's stare even through the darkness. As he turned and saw the intensity all over Shawn's face, he knew what his friend was thinking. He was thinking that Ryne was lying. He had to be. There was no explaining away the godforsaken sight in the bowels of his family's cabin, or the presence of his family members' names entombed beneath crucified animals. Even Ryne could admit that.

"Get the fuck back upstairs," Shawn said through gritted teeth.

Ryne got to his feet and started moving back towards the ladder's base. He felt Shawn's glare track him the entire way. As they reached the steps, Noah froze.

"Move," said Shawn.

"Look," said Noah. He raised a shivering arm and extended a long finger. "Behind the ladder."

Ryne cautiously stepped forward. When he reached the ladder, the lighter illuminated enough of the darkness, and he could see what Noah was looking at. Shawn saw it as well, and gasped.

Behind the ladder was a small alcove, dug another few feet into the permafrost. Tucked away enough that they hadn't seen in coming down, now the lighter provided just enough light to make out another animal nailed to its far wall. This one was fresher than the deer, the blood still shining in the glow of dancing light.

Hanging dead on the wall was a large, black, wolf.

SEVENTEEN
BROKEN PEOPLE

One Year Ago—Washington

The smell of the hospital burned through Ryne's nostrils, singeing the hair inside his nose with the stark aroma of sanitation and sickness. A brightness, artificial and unnatural in its glow, filled the room with an oppressive weight. His head hurt and his mouth ached badly. His jaw had been clenched, his teeth grinding for what seemed like an unfairly eternal amount of time.

Holding his head in his hands, he massaged his temples to drive away the dull pain behind his eyes that bloomed from the hole that threatened to erode his heart. It was 3am, and he wasn't sleepy anymore. Sleep had stopped being a priority the moment Maxie woke him up, still in her pajamas, crying and covered in blood. Now, he sat in a cold and sterile room, waiting for news he prayed he wouldn't hear. Prayed to whatever higher power would listen, all the while knowing it wouldn't change a damn thing.

He wanted to cry, but nothing in his body worked. This entire journey the two of them had taken, through doctor's appointments and fertility drugs, was crashing down, a Tower of Babel specifically erected for him. He had gotten too close to heaven. In the end, regardless of whatever life he'd managed to build for himself, whatever choices he chose to make, and whatever principles he held within himself, he knew he was breaking into pieces. He knew the world did it to everyone, but he thought maybe his mother's death had been the break. But it was just the beginning fracture.

The door opened, and a woman in scrubs appeared, holding a machine in her hand. She walked over to where he sat and, without even looking at him, began pulling papers off a clipboard.

"Hi, Mr. Burdette. I have some more paperwork that I need you to fill out."

"Paperwork for what?" His voice broken and hollow.

"Insurance purposes."

"You have my insurance information from every other visit."

"Yes, but they want to be thorough. You may receive a bill if your insurance doesn't cover anything."

An anger greater than anything he had ever felt swept over him. His vision went red, and spots formed across his eyes as he left his body. He wanted to take that nurse's face and smash it against the tile floor, to obliterate that machine across her skull. He would go to prison of course, but that would be okay. He would take it. Let him suffer in his silence, alone in the dark.

The nurse must have been able to feel his hate-fueled stare falling upon her. "I'll come back later," she said, retracting the machine. She left quickly and Ryne was, once again, alone. So, he sat there, staring a hole through the floor, waiting for the inevitable axe to drop. He wasn't waiting long.

The door opened again, and the doctor entered the room. Her face hanging, her expression sour and sympathetic. He didn't want sympathies. What good were they ever?

"Mr. Burdette, I'm..."

"Just tell me."

She bit her lip and glanced down. Ryne was sure she had delivered this same news to many others before, and it must've hurt her to do so. But he didn't care. He wanted to punch something. Something hard enough to shatter every bone in his useless hand.

"Your wife is being cleaned up. She...I'm so very sorry."

Ryne said nothing. Even the expectation of Hell hadn't prepared him for the heat of it. It burned his insides, and he felt the hole in his chest grow and gorge itself on the shattered remnants of his pride.

"She'll be out soon," the doctor said. "Again, I'm sorry." Then she left the room, and Ryne was alone. Again.

He slammed his fist into the wall to his right. He felt the crack in his knuckles, felt them displace, but did not feel any pain. There was no pain left to feel. There was just rage manifesting itself from somewhere deep inside the recesses of the husk he'd become. It came from a part of him that he did not know, did not recognize, and no longer restrained. A sharp crack extended from the new dent in the drywall, the wood from the stud he'd hit visible underneath. Blood poured out of his fist and pooled onto the white hospital floor.

Moments later, a nurse wheeled Maxie into the room. Her head hung low beneath her shoulders, her eyes staring at the floor. She had wanted this for so long, and now it had been ripped away from her. No amount of begging or pleading would bring it back. She looked empty and broken.

The nurse looked at his hand, then the floor, and finally the wall, and gasped. Ryne stood, helped Maxie to her feet, and put his arm around her.

"Put it on the bill," he said, leading her out of the room and down the dark hallway, fluorescent lights buzzing overhead, like x-rays revealing two broken people.

The drive back home was silent. Even the hum of the asphalt under the car's wheels faded away into a black void of soundless fury. Maxie never picked her head up, not even to look out the window. It was still dark now at 5am, but soon the sun would rise above the horizon line and bring light to every world except the worlds holding each other inside the car. There would be no lights for those worlds. Not anymore. Those worlds were dark paths diverging in opposite directions, fated to separate. To break apart.

The red truck was in the driveway as they arrived home, Rory in the driver's seat. Ryne parked the car and led Maxie inside. His father did not follow.

The house felt as cold as the outside winter. Ryne led his wife to the master bedroom. They passed the room with the name "Christian" hung in bright paper letters above the doorway, and he felt her weight drop slightly as she lost a little of herself. He put her into bed and walked back out to meet his father. As he passed through the door, he heard her finally break as she dissolved into a sobbing sludge of hurt and loss.

Rory was still outside when Ryne returned. His father looked older today. The gray had extended well past his temples, and the skin under his eyes sagged with a sadness of recognition. He grabbed his son and hugged him hard. Ryne felt his body surrender and succumb to the loss. His hand throbbed, and his tears rolled down his cheeks to his hand, mixing with the blood.

"I'm so sorry, son," said Rory.

Ryne could not say or do anything besides melt into himself. Then, the sound of squealing brakes pierced the silence of the early morning as a familiar truck pulled into the driveway. The door opened, and Rod stepped out.

"What are you doing here?" asked Rory, the venom seething from his breath.

"I heard what happened. I just wanted to make sure..."

"How did you hear what happened? I didn't call you. Ryne, did you tell him?"

Ryne shook his head, confused. He had not called or texted his uncle. They hadn't spoken in years. He hadn't even spoken to his father much since his mother died.

Rod looked at Ryne, his eyes filled with sympathy. Or was it acceptance? Or apology?

"You son of a bitch!" said Rory. "You son of a fucking bitch!"

"Easy, Rory..."

"Ryne, go inside. Comfort your wife. I'll handle this."

Ryne silently let go of his father and walked back to the house.

"Ryne, I'm sorry..."

"Shut up. You don't get to talk to him."

He opened and closed the door behind him. Whatever issues were going on between them, they weren't his problem now. He could hear Maxie sobbing in the bedroom. He made one last look out the front door window. The two men rolled in the yard, each of them wildly throwing blind haymakers at the other's face. Ryne had seen this sight one too many times to care anymore, so he closed his eyes and turned away, leaving the two brothers to their own devices as he suffered through the dark, lonely house to his grieving wife.

EIGHTEEN
EVACUATION PLANS

Midnight had come, but sleep stayed a far distance from their minds as the wintry assault continued outside the door, which no longer felt secure. With his head light and aching, Noah had gone straight to the loft upstairs the moment he emerged from the dark place below. He had thrown up twice in the basement in front of the crucifixions and had very little, if anything, left in his stomach. The slightest movements seemed to stir what remained into a bubbling froth. He didn't think the image would ever leave his memory. Who could do something like *that*? Why would *anybody* do something like *that*? The answers eluded his grasp and made his head ache and throb with the pulse of a jackhammer.

The panic was rising again, now wearing a crown of antlers upon a horrific face. Clawing its way out of the pit. He couldn't lock it up anymore, couldn't stuff it back into the depths of his ever-more-fragile psyche. It had carved out its own little nook in this new domain of his mind; and surrounded itself with hanging bodies of dead animals encrusted in falling grain.

He could smell it. The sweet, oily odor slithering along the air. Infesting every part and making the many parts one.

Above him, snow built up atop the cabin roof, and he wondered how much weight the structure would hold before it caved in on him as he slept.

He could hear Shawn speaking down below. His voice was almost a hiss. "You're full of shit."

"Shawn, I swear to God I don't know what is happening or why any of that is down there. Just let me explain."

"Stop lying."

"I'm not lying! Why would I lie about any of this?"

Noah got out of bed and walked to the railing of the loft. The two men downstairs were on opposite sides of the cabin. Shawn's fists clenched against the side of his body as he leaned against the recliner, his bad leg hovering off the ground. The rage on his face was both visible and shocking. Noah had never seen him this mad. There was a hatred, a recognition of betrayal and disgust that permeated into once sacred places. Ryne himself burned with a furious intent at the kitchen counter, and his fight-or-flight response had been chosen. He was going to fight.

"This is your family's cabin. God knows how many times you sat over that fucking door."

"Jesus Christ, Shawn, would you just..."

"Your entire family lineage..."

"Fuck my goddamn family! Would you stop and..."

"You're going to sit here and tell me you don't know..."

"I know about the rocks!"

"Then explain!!"

A hardness formed upon the lines of Ryne's face. "It's what I've been trying to tell you, but you won't shut the fuck up and listen."

Shawn's body relaxed in the slightest way possible, but his eyes did not. "I'm listening now."

"It's an old tradition. Ancient. I don't know how accurate all this is, but it dates back to the tribes who lived here before the Europeans settled on this land. During harsh winters or times of famine, the tribe would designate one person to be..." He paused, his voice now a low tremor as he looked for the right word. "...offered to the land."

"Christ."

"They believed the forest had a soul and that, when it was angry, it would send colder winters, or it would kill crops, or any other normal issue you could think of. So, to make it happy again, they would pick one member of the tribe to be offered up as a sacrificial lamb. They would take these rocks. It had to be these specific types of rocks. I don't remember why. But they would take them to some special place, carve their names into them, and…"

"And what?"

"They would walk into the lake. Drown themselves."

"How do you know all this?"

"Like you said, it's my family's cabin. Rod knew all these weird traditions from around the area. He used to tell me about them whenever we'd stay here."

"So why are your relative's names under those stones?"

"I don't know," Ryne said, his voice a defeated whisper. "I suppose it's possible that my family members gave themselves as offerings."

"Offerings to *what*?"

Ryne held up his hands. "I don't know. Honestly. That's beyond me. I guess the forest."

"Your family believed in all that shit? You're Catholic."

Ryne shook his head. "Wouldn't you? After everything we've seen? Besides, my dad converted and raised us Catholic, but my uncle was into all that stuff. Animism. I'd bet most of the people who live here, native and white, believe in it. I guess my family did too."

Shawn took a deep breath. This was a downpour of bottled emotion, and the sickness was still painted vividly on all their faces. Even Ryne's. The look on his face in the presence of the dead things had told Noah enough. The color still hadn't returned to his cheeks, and discussion of the horrors below only catalyzed a deeper freeze of his blood. If he was hiding anything, he was doing an unbelievable job of selling it.

"The animals?" Shawn asked. "Did your uncle ever mention the animals?"

"No," said Ryne. "No, that was…that was new."

Shawn limped his way around the recliner and fell into the chair, grunting painfully. "What the hell are we going to do?" His hand pushed through his long blonde hair and massaged his scalp. The weight was heavy on him. It was heavy on each of them. Noah could see it slathered across their faces. With each passing hour, a pressure built in his chest. His appetite had abandoned him, and he could feel his energy phasing out. He had recurring headaches, feelings of lightheadedness, and a strange pulsating pressure against the side of his head. Ryne was the only one of them who was in any way healthy, but now a mental obstacle had forced its way into the equation and had targeted him specifically.

"We have to leave."

Noah's voice escaped his mouth quietly and without warning. The thought had been rattling in his head ever since he saw the deer nailed to the cellar wall, but his tongue wouldn't stay silent any longer.

"We have to leave," he said again. Louder now, more certain.

"How?" said Ryne. "You saw the road when we were coming back in from town. No way it's passable."

"He's right," said Shawn.

"No, he's not," said Noah. There was a conviction in his voice that surprised even him. Every word that came out of his mouth was carefully processed and packaged. He knew what he was saying, and he knew he was right. He had never been more certain of anything. "We need to go."

"Noah, the road..."

"I'm not talking about the road."

Ryne and Shawn looked up at him. Their faces, inquisitive and doubtful, darkened in the flickering of the fire. They looked up at him as though he'd finally lost his grip on the last handles still holding him together.

"We can't stay here," Noah continued. "We thought we were safe inside the cabin, but that's changed. The storm isn't moving. Why, I don't know. But it isn't. We are going to run out of firewood soon. You felt the wind in the cellar. There's an opening that goes somewhere outside. Considering what is down there, God only knows what is using it. And the wolf...the wolf was fresh. New. Whatever is going on, it's getting more intense the longer we stay here. And we have no idea how long after the storm passes we would be able to leave. Forget the truck and forget the road..."

He paused. He knew full well the implications of what he was going to say next.

"...we need to go on foot."

Silence filled the warm cabin. None of the men dared to meet each other's eyes.

"I know how it sounds," said Noah. "But it's our best bet."

"It's suicide," said Ryne.

"So was your plan to stay here in the first place," said Shawn.

"None of that matters anymore," said Noah. "It hasn't mattered since the moment we went into that cellar. All that matters is getting out of here. The truck can't make the drive up the trail. So, our best bet is to go on foot where the snow is passable...through the trees, I say we follow the trail back to town, but we stay in the tree line the entire way. The snow will still be thick, but it won't be as bad as the road."

"What about the undergrowth?" asked Ryne.

"The snow is resting pretty heavy on top. It was no big deal to walk through it earlier today," said Shawn. "But there's no way I'll be able to do it now. You two, maybe, but I can barely walk across this cabin, let alone twenty miles through the woods. In a blizzard."

"I know," said Noah. "I'm going to go alone."

"What?" snapped Ryne. "What the hell are you talking about?"

"Shawn can't walk. And his leg is getting worse. You know the most first aid, so you need to stay here. I'm useless here. I bring nothing to the table except a mouth to feed. But if I can get to town, I can get someone with a snowplow or something, and I can come get you."

"This is crazy," said Ryne.

"It's twenty miles. If I leave at first light, I can make it to town by mid-afternoon. I can get help out here by nightfall, and we can get the hell out of here."

"Noah, it's a blizzard. You'll freeze to death."

"I can take the cold. We spent all this money on these jackets and pants. Let's see how much bang we got for our buck."

"We can bundle him up," said Shawn. "Layer him to comfort. If he stays moving, he might stay warm enough." Shawn stared at his lame leg, nothing more than an anchor dragging him down to the bottom of the darkest sea. Noah knew his friend well. If Shawn was able and capable, he would be the one to make the trip. He was the strongest, the most athletic, the most headstrong. Whatever the storm would throw at him physically, Shawn could take it. But the phantom in the chair couldn't. The leg had been robbing him of so much now for years, and now it robbed him once more of an opportunity to feel useful. Noah wanted to pity his friend, but Shawn would be furious at the thought, and, more importantly, the time for pity had long since passed.

"I have a better idea," said Ryne.

He walked into the bedroom and returned carrying a large, folded paper. Sitting on the floor, he opened it and spread it across the carpet. It was a topographical map of the forest. The soft cold air from beneath the sofa fluttered its edges.

"It's twenty miles back to Wolf's Bone. There is zero chance you'll make it alive. But there's another possibility." He pointed at a seemingly random portion of the map. "This is us," he said. His finger traced along a straight line to a marked area. "This is the radio tower. I can't get a signal through on the battery radio because of the storm, but if you could get to the tower..."

Shawn's face snapped back to form. "How far is it?"

"Five miles," Ryne said. "Still a hell of a hike, but.."

"I can make it," said Noah.

"It's our best option besides waiting it out. If you're dead set on going for help, this is the way."

"Sold."

From then on, the decision was simple. Ryne knew more about how to care for Shawn, and that was important. Noah couldn't shake the feeling that the leg was much worse than Shawn was letting on. It was tattooed all over his face. Evident in every grimace and groan. Ryne had to stay in the cabin. End of discussion. Besides, with Shawn crippled, Noah now possessed the single most important characteristic needed for the long walk through the snow.

Grit.

Years of hard labor had prepared him for this. Long, arduous days under the pelting sun or freezing rain. The hours he'd spent fighting for every inch of his life under a sea of grain. Shawn and Ryne were hunters; patience was their greatest virtue. But they could not afford to be patient now. No, now was the time for the worker. The time to get things done. Noah's time.

"You know I'm right, Ryne," he said.

On the hard floor, Ryne slowly lay his head back to rest against the logs. He looked defeated, broken to a point beyond all recovery. He didn't know what was happening. Noah knew him far too well to suspect anything otherwise. If anything, he shamed Shawn internally for even considering the possibility, but there would be a more appropriate time to address that. For now, they had one goal. They needed to get out of these woods.

"Get some sleep," said a small voice from the tall man fractured on the floor. "Get some sleep and get going once the sun comes up."

"That's the plan."

"Take a gun, take food, take whatever you need."

"Okay."

"And if anything happens...if you see anything. Shoot first, ask questions later. Got it?"

Noah's body stiffened at the request and he felt a deep discomfort; but Ryne was right. They didn't know exactly what was skulking in those woods, but Noah had looked into its eyes and knew it was beyond the realm of their comprehension. The feeling still churned within him, this unholy feeling of helplessness and smallness. The feeling that nobody was looking after them, because this was a place man was never meant to go. A place God had abandoned long ago. A place reclaimed by something else, something so very wrong that it sheared the threads of everything real and natural.

He swallowed hard.

"Got it."

* * *

Ryne turned on the couch as the storm battered the window and threaded its wind through the trees. It still just sat there, ripping the cold Yukon air into shredded wisps of freezing fabric. The storms had never bothered Ryne as a kid. They had always seemed so natural, a simple part of the place he observed and respected but never feared. But now, all that existed in him was a deep and suffocating fear.

Strangeness had taken on new meaning in the cellar. The sight still echoed in his mind, bouncing off the dark corners and recesses that he pretended not to notice; yet always reverberated back into the light of his conscious thought. The emerging image of the deer had been shocking, but it was the wolf that stuck with him the most. Because they had all seen the wolf. Noah had seen it outside the window and in front of the shed. Shawn had seen it in the flesh. Ryne had seen it in his dreams. And now they had all seen it dead and decaying, a wild Christ-figure nailed against the earthy wall of an unholy area. The blood was still fresh. They all knew the truth; but dared not speak it into existence. Noah had only alluded to it. The wolf was only a few hours deceased, a day or two at the most. Somebody, or something, had been down there and performed the ritualistic act right beneath their feet as they slept warm and unaware.

He felt his eyelids grow heavy. Exhaustion. Pure, unfiltered, mental exhaustion threatened to push him to an involuntary slumber. But he didn't want to drift off at all. As long as his eyes stayed open, whatever crept beneath their feet in the cold night couldn't sneak up on them. The presence that walked within the trees wouldn't come in the light. As long as he could stay awake, he told himself, these things wouldn't happen. His mind simply could not take much more. Again, he imagined the wolf hanging, and he immediately remembered the nightmare. The visitation he often got in the witching hours of the morning. The dog that wasn't a dog. The dog that he'd just seen crucified in a cellar he'd never known about. The *thing* that would hide within the shadows and mock him from the darkness. So, he would not sleep. Not tonight. Not until Noah made the trip and brought back help. He had forgone his bed in favor of the couch. The thought of being separated from the other two, even by a flimsy door, chilled him.

And then, without warning, his mind gave way, and he fell into a deep slumber which slowly became a light, illuminating his new location. The street. The endless street with the houses that all looked the same.

No.

The dog. The *thing*. Coming to him.

No!

And then he woke, unable to move. A heaviness upon his chest pinned him to the couch and squeezed the air out of his lungs.

There— in the corner, *it* was there. Sitting in the dark. But it wasn't the dog. No, it towered in the gloom, walking upright, a shadow with a hollow face. Antlers jutted from the hollowness and filled the frame of the room. Inhuman noises chattered and spit from its rotten maw.

Then that feeling returned, and a wave of nausea hit him like a brick. He leapt off the couch and ran across the living room, past the sleeping Shawn, and threw up into the toilet. He heaved three times until his stomach was emptied all of its contents. Then he collapsed, a relic of a man. His arms and legs felt like lead, and his shoulders lacked the strength to do anything about it.

Why were his relatives' names written on those papers? Laying beneath what he knew were ritualistic artifacts? Frantically, he searched his mind for any answers but found none. The only images he could conjure up were the dead wolf and the thing in his room from all those years ago. The antlered shadow. These views swallowed the landscape of his sanity, and he began to cry.

Behind him, Shawn stirred and woke, but said nothing for a while. The silence deafened the space before he finally spoke.

"I know you're not okay, so I won't even ask. But you need to get some sleep." Within minutes, he was snoring and twitching in the grips of a dream.

Ryne rose to his feet and began making the slow walk back to his restless slumber. The cabin was dark, lit only by the crackling fire, eating its way through one of the last remaining pieces of firewood. He saw Shawn sleeping in the recliner and heard Noah tossing and turning upstairs. His eyes made their way to one of the large windows and looked out into the snow-driven wild surrounding them.

The animals had all returned. They stood at an unnatural attention, as they had before. Standing silently in the storm, as though part of it some-how. Visible in the flickering mesh of the cabin's fire that bled out through the tall windows. He stared at them for a minute. His stomach twisted and threatened to expel itself again across the cabin floor. Finally, unable to endure anything more, he continued his trek past the couch to his room as they watched him from the snowy world; which seemed so far away and so close at the same time. He lumbered through the bedroom door and into the bed, rolling on his stomach and putting his face into the pillow. If the paralysis came tonight, he'd make sure he couldn't see a single goddamn thing. The dreamcatcher hung delicately off the wooden bed frame, still and motionless in the warmth.

Slowly, sleep returned to his heavy mind, and he drifted off into slumber, oblivious to the pair of black, soulless eyes watching him from just beyond the small window in the corner.

NINETEEN
INTO THE WOODS

They spent the morning in silence as a dim glow from the shrouded sun angled its way through the windows. At 10am, the slightest trace of light in the December sky had appeared. The sunlight was sparse enough this time of year, especially on this day—the solstice. It would be almost eleven before substantial sunlight appeared in the sky, and it would begin its descent by 5:30. If Noah was going to go, he needed to leave the moment he was given the opportunity. They'd flagged 10:30 as the departure time. By then, the light from the winter sun would be just bright enough for sight and guidance.

The storm was still rolling outside. Shawn sat in the recliner; his leg freshly bandaged again in the early hours of the morning; and watched out the window as winter continued its assimilation of their world. While the violence of the storm flayed the land, it wasn't quite a whiteout. It was now growing light enough to see a few yards past the tree line, like the storm was allowing them to see just enough to forget about what prowled beyond. Danger still lay ahead, but at least Noah had a fighting chance, which was more than he could say for himself.

During the night, Shawn had felt a strange sensation in his injured leg. When Ryne woke to change the bandages, the decay in condition was significant. The veins traveling up and down his leg bulged—black, dead, and swollen. But they still worked, somehow. *Something* was being pumped through these dark vestibules. Shawn could feel it swimming through his blood.

This fucking leg. This useless, parasitic shit stain he called a limb. To put any kind of pressure on it was agonizing and futile. It could no longer hold up his weight, and the rest of his body felt so fatigued that his muscles seemed to cease their functions at random moments. Walking was impossible now. Even drinking a glass of water invited a spill, as his arms would spasm without warning. It seemed as though his whole body was shutting down, and it all stemmed from that leg. How much was he going to lose because of the pathetic appendage? Baseball had been his one talent, his one ticket to something resembling a good life. His opportunity to provide for those who had provided for him. That was gone now. He knew it. It had taken a few years for the acceptance to set in, but the illusions had finally faded away in the Yukon snow.

And what about hunting? He was sure now that he would never be able to climb a tree or stand ever again. He would never again be able to track down a mis-hit buck. He would never again be able to brace the leg while cleaning a deer. As he saw the knee rotting away with a pace that shocked and unnerved him, a drip of panic manifested itself within the dark corners of his heart. Something was spreading—he wasn't sure what, but he knew it was nothing good.

Ryne hadn't said much on the matter, but Shawn understood the events in motion. There was no way the leg could be saved. It looked completely dead in its black discoloration and poisoned blood, but that wasn't what worried him. He couldn't have cared any less about losing the leg. Honestly, now it was a burden he couldn't wait to rid himself of. His worry stemmed from whatever he felt flowing through those decaying veins into the rest of his body. Over the past few hours, Noah's quest had taken on an even more paramount importance. If he got lost, could not reach the radio tower, or moved too slowly; Shawn's predicament would become a tragic certainty.

This leg had already cost him his livelihood. Now, it might cost him his life.

Ryne and Noah stood in the kitchen, packing Noah's backpack with essentials for the hike to the radio tower. This wouldn't be a stroll through some temperate Montana brush, orange and beautiful in the fall wind. Shawn had walked through the wild yesterday. The undergrowth was weighed down by the snow, but it was still there. The little hands of the taiga, reaching up from the natural earth and gripping for prey. It could present a major problem if Noah stepped in the wrong place—those little hands grasping at his ankle, holding him while the heat abandoned his body, and he froze on his feet. Winds still ripped through the trees; and walking against it would be arduous and exhausting. The temperature gauge read five degrees Fahrenheit outside, and the combination of cold, wind, and wet could be catastrophic. But all this considered, there was no argument. No further discussion to be had. The truth was well-known throughout the cabin. They had no choice.

Especially now.

Shooting pains splintered the inner contours of Shawn's leg. For relief he bit down on a rag he had grabbed from the kitchen in the night. Ryne and Noah looked at him, but he didn't look back. He hated anyone to see him like this. So helpless. So unathletic. A bum crushed beneath the weight of one dead limb. A limb that had somehow been bit by an animal that never touched him and left no other trace of its presence.

The thought made him shiver. With all the natural elements presenting a grave challenge for Noah, nobody dared mention the decidedly unnatural force hiding in the overlapping maze of spruce. *It* was out there. They all knew it, but to say it would add unnecessary fuel to an already perilous fire.

"Here," said Ryne, loading up Noah's pack with bags of beef jerky and candy.

"No," said Noah. "You need to eat."

"We've got food. Besides, if you get lightheaded, you'll need it."

"I thought that whole thing was bullshit?"

"Just in case."

Noah nodded and zipped up the backpack. He looked almost comical, covered in layers of heavy base clothing beneath the red thermal jacket, his pants stuffed full of insulation. He wore an impossibly thick thermal beanie and heavy gloves. He looked like a red Michelin man. While he wouldn't have much maneuverability, he'd be able to plow through the uncompromising blizzard. But should the *thing* come... Shawn pushed the thought out of his mind. Reaching the tower was priority number one..

"Hey," said Noah. "You guys remember *A Christmas Story*?" He pulled his arms down to his side and then flapped them up, feigning a lack of control under his thick gear, smiling. Ryne grinned and laughed to himself quietly.

Shawn didn't.

"Please get there," he said.

"I will," Noah said. His voice was stern. Determined. "I promise."

He and Ryne shared a long hug and a pat on each other's back. He walked over to Shawn, leaned down, and gave him a fist bump.

"I got you, don't worry," he said. "Be back soon."

Another searing shot of pain spread throughout Shawn's body, and he bit down hard on the rag. "Please do," he said through gritted teeth.

Ryne opened the front door, and Noah stepped out into the raging storm where the wind hit him hard. He buckled slightly but regained his balance and pushed forward into the dim morning light, the ice beneath his feet crunching as he walked across the frozen ground towards the dark forest Past the useless truck. Toward the radio tower. He turned and gave them a thumbs up.

"We're going to be okay," said Ryne. "If any of us can make the hike, it's him."

Shawn nodded in approval but kept his true thoughts in his head. Ryne was correct. Between the three of them, Noah stood the best chance. Both Ryne and Shawn, when healthy, knew the forest and hiking better than him, but he wouldn't make the same mistake both of them would. He wouldn't quit.

But it wouldn't matter. It wasn't about quitting anymore. Or guts, or moxie, or any other stupid phrase celebrated at too many leadership meetings or scouting reports. It was about survival, pure and simple. He couldn't stop the thoughts from creeping into his head—thoughts lingering on the enemy unseen as Noah moved into the woods at the base of the tree line. A coldness encased his heart, and a sinking feeling constricted his body as he watched his friend of over twenty years disappear into the shadows of the storm-ravaged trees.

TWENTY
PROMISES TO KEEP

Noah's feet crunched through the frozen ground as he pushed and willed his way deeper into the thick wood. The branches, long spindly arms reaching out like desperate children, pulled and scratched his jacket as he moved forward through the thicket. He saw where the carved path that led back to Wolf's Bone should be. He was right. The snow had filled in the indentation completely. No way the truck would have made it even half a mile.

The sharp sting of frosted air needled the exposed skin around his eyes. He'd been walking now for three hours, following a hidden and nearly lost game trail that led from the cabin to the general whereabouts of the radio tower. The temperature dropped the further he pushed on, despite the sun getting closer to its compromised zenith in the gray sky. His eyes watered, and his tears froze against his face. The wind blew from the south, and he was walking straight into it. Each step took the energy of five. The muscles in his legs ached and throbbed with the smallest exertion. Around his shoulder, the rifle seemed to weigh a hundred pounds, its weight growing with each stride.

Even with his ears covered by the beanie, the sheer volume of the wind astounded him. The woods around him roared with a deafening hush.

White noise. The snow falling from the unmoving storm slithered its way into the smallest crevices of his jacket at his wrists and around the top of his neck and went to war with the thermal layers he wore beneath.

In the static of the gale, Noah thought he heard a loud crack from somewhere behind him. He turned. Stared into the white. He saw only trees. An endless ocean of snow-covered spruce with waves of loose powder that seemed all at once separate and part of everything else. For the past three hours, he had slogged and ripped his way through this ocean with a guiding light in his head, but now that light dimmed and vanished. He felt like a stranded sailor who had lost his point of navigation.

The panic walked behind him. He could feel the footfalls in the snow. Matching his own. Striding with him. It was out of his head now.

Just follow the path, he told himself and pushed further into the gale.

The game trail appeared faint, barely noticeable unless someone knew where to look. And in this endless sea of reaching trees, the path seemed impossible. But there was a trick to it. The path cut directly through the space between the trees, and he could walk in nearly a direct line and not hit a single one. Sure, there were a few turns and twists built into it out of necessity, but the path followed a mostly simple, straight shot.

He pushed further and further along, head down against the wind, until he stepped into something thick and springy.

It was a tree.

He'd walked right into a damn tree. He must be losing it now, not even aware enough to avoid something that had probably stood in this exact spot for centuries. And then a terrifying recognition filled the still ringing parts of his brain. He had walked *into the tree.* He looked around frantically, knowing exactly what he was looking for. A small indentation in the forest floor where the undergrowth had been cut away and devoid any of trees, where the ground beneath the snow was deeper, its landing more solid.

He could not see the path anymore.

That made no sense. He hadn't changed direction except for when the map told him to. Even the wind was still blowing straight into him, but he had somehow meandered away from the guiding path and deeper into the forest. The trees ripping and thrashing in the wind, surrounding him. Closing in.

Like grain.

The panic crept up again, its presence unmistakable at his back.

Focus.

A wave of terror spread over him. How could he have lost the path? It was his only guiding light. In these thick, deep woods, that path was the only thing that could guide him in the direction he needed, *absolutely needed*, to go. Now he risked getting swallowed up by the vastness of the Yukon wilderness. He felt the air leave his sails as the realization hit that he'd fallen away from safety and into the clutches of the unknown.

The panic's fingers gripped around his shoulders.

He turned frantically, but there was nothing behind him. *It's in your head,* he told himself. The panic wasn't a real entity, couldn't hurt him unless he let it.

But he'd felt those fingers, hadn't he? He'd heard the footsteps behind him for what felt like miles now, assumed they were in his head. But he'd *felt* those fingers. He knew he had.

Focus, he told himself again. He couldn't allow panic to set in. He'd lost the path, but if he let the panic take over, he would fade deeper and deeper into the wild. His mind fought off the encroaching dread, and he clenched his jaw in concentration.

His footsteps. That's all he needed, just a few steps backwards to find out where he lost the trail. It might cost him a little bit of time, but it beat getting lost in the storm.

But when he turned and saw his footprints, his heart sank. They were filling with snow more quickly than he could even move to them. His breathing picked up, and he felt the panic rise again as the wind ripped at his stationary form.

The wind.

The wind hadn't changed direction. It still blew hard from the south, and the storm was still sitting on top of the forest. The wind would stay consistent. He just needed to push against it and continue on in that direction. He couldn't have strayed far. The radio tower remained a reachable objective.

He focused on what lay before him. The wind cut into them, but he held firm, kept them open. The woods in front of him beckoned. A heat combusted within his chest, and he took one step forward, digging his foot hard into the snow and breaking through to the undergrowth beneath. Then another. And another.

Keep moving.

The sound of the wind grew in volume, rising like music conducted by the suffocating forest.

The woods are lovely, dark, and deep.

Another step into the murk.

But I have promises to keep.

His eyes watered and froze. He wiped them off and pushed forward.

And miles to go before I sleep.

The mantra continued in his head as he willed himself through the freezing assault.

Then he felt it. A slight incline beneath his feet, that quickly steepened. He was coming up on a hill, a fairly large one. A hill that the map told him would be there.

A resurgence fueled within his legs as new blood was warmed by a shimmering beacon on a formerly hopeless horizon and pumped through his veins like battery acid. He picked his head up and looked forward through the white haze and labyrinth of spruce.

He could see it. At the top of the hill. He had wandered about fifty feet to the left of where he was supposed to be, but he could see the goddamn thing.

The tower.

He moved up the incline as fast as his legs would push him, grunting as his weary knees struggled to hold him up. He used the trees for balance and support. The frost fell from his eyes and a furious yell erupted from deep within him, a war cry against the wind, against the forest, against the wolf. Against this whole damn place.

The tower stretched just above the highest tips of the trees, old and rusted. An old wooden shack sat dormant at the base of the metal structure. It hadn't been maintained in years, but the light at the top of the tower flashed red.

Working.

The tower was getting power from somewhere. Underground lines maybe? He didn't care. He'd never been so happy to see a flashing red light.

He stumbled into the shack and found the radio controls unused in

God knew how long. Remembering Ryne's directions on how to operate it, he began transmitting.

"Hello? Hello? Is anybody there? Please... Goddammit, what's the phrase? Mayday! Mayday! This is Noah Stratton calling from Tower 1S-32. We need immediate assistance! Over."

Nothing but static. He switched channels.

"Hello? Can anyone read me? Please, this is Noah Stratton calling from Tower 1S-32. We need immediate assistance! Over."

More static. He switched channels again.

"Please! Somebody, come in. This is Noah Stratton calling from Tower 1S-32. We need immediate assistance! Over."

There had to be someone on the other line, right? The constable knew they were out here, knew there was a storm coming. Someone had to be manning the radios. But as he moved through the stations, nothing but static spit from the radio speakers.

"Will somebody answer the fucking radio! Please! This is Noah Stratton calling from Tower 1S-32. We need immediate assistance!"

A crack, a hiss, and a voice.

"Tower 1S-32 please repeat, over."

Noah couldn't press the transmit button quick enough. "Yes! Yes! This is Noah Stratton. I am with Ryne Burdette and Shawn Ackerman in the Burdette family cabin. There's been an animal attack and one of us is seriously wounded. We need immediate assistance. Over."

From beyond the radio, more static. He lost them.

No, no, no!

"Please, somebody answer me! I am trying to reach Constable Whitting. I repeat, there's been an animal attack. We need immediate medical assistance. Over."

"Mr. Stratton, this is Constable Whitting. You say you had an animal attack? Over."

"Yes! Shawn was bitten by a wolf on his leg. It's bad and needs treatment. The storm is too thick to drive through, but we need assistance, and we need it now! Over."

No voice returned from the other side of the radio, but the static vanished. He had the right frequency, and another soul waited on the other end of the line, but nothing was being said. *It's fine,* he told himself. Whitting was probably relaying the information to those who could get out to help. They were going to be okay! They could leave this godforsaken place and never look back, leave all this in their rearview mirror and then smash the mirror, grind the shards to dust, lock them in a box and drop them to the bottom of the ocean.

Sound returned through the radio speaker, but not the voice of Constable Whitting. It wasn't a voice at all.

It was a bell. One knell of a large, old bell. The knell died away, and then another one began. A familiar sound, but where had he heard it before? That one long knell that was allowed to die away, low and steady, before the second one?

The church. The bell from the church in Wolf's Bone. The same sound Noah had heard leaving the grocery store the day they arrived. Yes, he was sure of it. But the sound seemed deeper, lower. Like the radio was inside the bell itself.

As though the transmission was coming from within the church.

And then, as if born from a horrifying dream from the murkiest swamps of his mind, the voices returned. A chorus of words unknown to Noah's ear, a language unfamiliar and unnerving, poured from the speaker of the radio as the deep, low bell knelled in the quiet background.

He dropped the radio and his breathing accelerated. He fell backwards and hurried away from the radio towards the open door.

The cabin. The dead things beneath it. The church. The wolf. The doctor and his lies.

The chant continued from proud, ungodly voices that echoed within each other. Loud, so impossibly loud from the radio's little speaker. A sharp pain shocked his temples and spread through his head. Intense and burning, the pain moved through him like a razor as he struggled to his feet, tried to shake away the pain, tried to move away from the space saturated with the venomous chanting. As he slammed the door shut, a sound broke through the trees from somewhere in the distance. The sound of splintering wood, cracking through the cacophony of wind. A high-pitched wailing engulfed the space and ripped through his ears.

He needed to get back to the cabin.

The panic laughed at him as his first step sent him tumbling down the hill. He wavered to his feet at the bottom of the hill and took a step back towards the direction of the cabin. To Ryne. To Shawn. To safety.

The smell of grain filled his nose.

The panic smiled at him. The snow turned gold.

The wind changed direction.

TWENTY-ONE
DEEP IN THOUGHT

S hawn's snoring filled the cabin with a warmth of normalcy. From the furthest memories of childhood camping and sleepovers, Shawn's snoring had long been the target of ridicule, but the sound now imbued Ryne with a strange comfort. It was the sound of someone sleeping happily, content. It was the sound of something that had eluded the three of them during the past few days. The sound of momentary peace. So, Ryne tolerated the obnoxious snoring. Welcomed it even.

But that peace was still tinged the black ink of worry. He hadn't said anything earlier, and he assumed it didn't need saying, but Shawn's leg was *bad*. The way it twisted and mangled was a visceral reminder of the first injury. Ryne hadn't been in the park when it happened, but he'd seen the video.

Shawn played centerfield that day. Riding one of the hottest streaks of his life, there was some chatter from the Pirates about calling the 24-year-old outfielder to the majors. After six years of chipping away in the minor leagues, everything was coming together. Ryne knew how hard Shawn had worked at the game, how much it meant to him. When he played, the exuberance radiated off him, visible to anyone who cared enough to watch. He was a terror on the base paths, leading AAA in stolen bases, and his combination of consistent solid contact and speed had become a viable and unique weapon. If someone was going to get him out, they were going to have to *earn* it. And if they didn't, they were going to pay.

The pitcher hung a curveball up in the zone, and the batter crushed it.

Shawn's first step was so quick and explosive that it had seemed he was already in a full sprint by the time the ball left the bat. But he misread its path. He had read a deep fly to the left-center field gap, but the ball got caught in the wind high above the outfield grass and drifted to dead center.

For other outfielders, this would've been a problem, but not for Shawn. He turned his shoulder and flipped his hips to change the direction of his sprint. It would be a difficult play, but he'd made a name for himself making difficult plays.

Then his spikes gotten caught in the turf.

A person's leg isn't supposed to bend that way. Ryne would never forget the sight of his best friend lying there, screaming in agony. Taking the first step down an increasingly dark path of denial.

But this was worse. The leg was dying. Ryne had day-one basic first-aid knowledge from coaching and teaching, and, though far from a health expert, he could see the inevitable. There was a blackness was spreading throughout the limb; flesh and muscle decaying by the pound hour after hour. By the time Shawn could be airlifted to the hospital in Whitehorse, whatever infection was present would be too far gone to save the leg. All Ryne could do now was keep him in good spirits and wait for Noah to arrive back with news of help. He didn't care how late in the afternoon help came, but he didn't want to spend another night in the cabin.

Despite his initial desire to make this his new home, he now prayed for the chance to get out of this place and leave it far, far behind him. Whatever comforts he hoped to achieve had turned to snowflakes in a blizzard, and the cabin itself was some horrific idol, a dark effigy. Something representative of a world he knew nothing about. Damn his name. He wanted nothing to do with the atrocities in the cellar. He was content to let it rot, unseen and forgotten in the dark.

Still, his thoughts couldn't stop racing around the track of his family, and a horrific curiosity took hold within him. Their names were still a puzzle in his mind. A puzzle with all the wrong pieces.

"Deep in thought?" asked Shawn.

The sound of his voice pulled Ryne out of his own head. He *had* been deep in thought. So deep he hadn't heard Shawn stop snoring and wake up.

"Yeah," he said. "Lots to think about."

"Like what the hell is happening to us?"

Ryne nodded his head. "That's the big one."

Shawn's bright blue eyes had lost their luster during the past few days. He looked like he'd aged years into an uncertain future. "You got any answers yet?"

"I don't even know where to start asking the questions."

"Well," said Shawn, straining to sit up higher in the recliner. "Let's start with the obvious one. What is the deal with your family and this place?"

"Shawn, I told you..."

"I believe you. But it doesn't change the fact that there's some kind of connection. Do you have the *slightest* idea what it could be?"

"I don't know. This place was never anything more than a vacation home for me. I don't know what my family up here was really like. I didn't know most of them, they..."

"Died, right? Died when you were young, or before you were born?"

"Yeah. Met my grandfather once when I was like three. Don't remember a thing. My dad and Uncle Rod were the last ones left."

"And you." His voice seemed almost accusatory, but not of Ryne.

"And me?"

"Yeah, and you. I don't think that this place was left to you out of sheer goodwill. I think somebody wanted you here."

"Why?"

"Isn't it obvious? You're the last one. Whatever ties your family has to this place, they die with you."

Ryne leaned back in the seat, weighed down by a phantom blanket. Shawn was right. After the miscarriage and the accident, he *was* the last Burdette left. All too perfect. He shuddered at the possibilities presented by the thought.

"You talked about the rocks earlier, remember? And you said Rod told you about those."

"Yeah, when I was ten or so."

"Not your dad."

Ryne paused and cocked his head. "No," he said. "No, Dad never mentioned them."

Shawn leaned as far forward as his condition would allow. "Your dad never liked to talk about this place, this town, or the family in general. But your uncle couldn't shut up about it. 'Matter of fact, every time I remember him saying something about the cabin or Wolf's Bone, your dad got *pissed*."

The fire of recognition ignited in Ryne's memory. His father had hated talking about the family, especially as he and Rod grew apart during Ryne's adolescence. The only stories he ever heard from his father about the "old country" were told here, in the cabin. While he sat and aged through his formative years, the extent of his ancestry was passed down within the logs of this place.

"Unless we were here," he said. "If we were at the cabin, he was an open book. But not at home. At home, all of this was taboo. In fact, he's the one who left Wolf's Bone. Rod just followed."

"And when we first got here, did you not find it weird that Whitting only mentioned Rod, and not your dad? They died in the same accident."

Ryne jerked his head slightly. He *hadn't* realized it. "No, I was too wrapped up in what he said about the baby. I didn't even notice."

"It sounds to me like, whatever the connection between this place and your family is, your dad was trying to get the two of you as far away from it as possible."

Slumping back into the chair, Ryne stared at the window, bewildered. The storm still raged outside. His eyes found the fireplace again, where they glared at the dancing flame. "Then why did we ever come back?" They watched for a moment as the wood turned to cinders, floating weightlessly into the chimney.

"We have to talk about another thing too." Shawn took a deep breath. "The thing that's been watching us. What the hell is it? Because it's not a wolf."

Ryne swallowed. "I don't know." Even during the winter trips where familial histories were shared, nothing like this had ever been brought up. Something stalked them now. A shadow in the dark of the wood. They had all seen it as a wolf, but he also saw it as something else, and so had Noah.

He'd heard it as a child. Something that could not be explained with logic or sense, something that remained unknown to the last surviving Burdette, even as it hid within the gloom of his subconscious.

"You said this area was settled by some specific tribe?" asked Shawn. A hardness shaped his voice. He always had that hardness whenever he was working out a problem.

"Yeah, an offshoot from the tribe up north."

"And that they used to offer people up to the spirit of the forest?"

"That's the legend."

"Well, I think we're pretty much past this being a legend."

The cabin got eerily quiet. The only sound came from the crackling fire. He really didn't want to talk about this any further, and he didn't think Shawn did either, but it didn't seem like silence was an acceptable option. It needed to be out in the air, spoken aloud, and realized in truth.

"Is there anything in their folklore like this?"

Ryne pointed down at the floor. "The things down there. They were crucified. That's not Indigenous."

"Fucking witchcraft, that's what that is." It was a word that neither of them wanted to say out loud, but it had been festering and marinating in their minds since the unnerving discovery. A bleeding sore begging to be scratched. "Right? I mean, who else does something like that?"

"Could be some kind of witchcraft, I guess. Some pagan ritual, maybe? Either way, it's European. So, how did European witchcraft make its way into Native American land?" He searched his mind for any historical information he could think of regarding the Europeans who'd settled the area— his ancestors and bloodlines. They were fur traders, harmless God-fearing folks from France. They weren't black magic practitioners. And yet, he couldn't deny what they had seen in the cellar. It would be seared into his memory, his mind blackened with it for the rest of his days. However many that remained.

"And why the change?" asked Shawn. "The tribes obviously had a very sacred process, with the rocks and walking into the lake, for offering gifts to whatever this thing is. If these people, the settlers, kept worshiping the *thing*, why would they change tradition? Wouldn't that, I don't know, piss it off?"

A nervousness pulsed in Ryne's chest. His spinal cord felt like frozen twine, precariously holding his body together. Hearing it out loud, how casually they discussed something that shouldn't exist; he wanted to laugh at the absurdity of it all. And yet, he had seen the animals outside, heard the childlike voice, seen the wolf, and he knew what was laying underneath their feet.

Their eyes meandered to the burning log and the five others that remained. They'd run out of wood by nightfall.

A slight rush of adrenaline began surging through him. Something connected the pieces, and he needed to know what. These scattered pieces on his family's legacy all interlocked with each other somehow. But the corners were missing, locked away. Hidden in the one place left to look. Every bowl had been licked clean. All but one. The thought of returning to that spot made him nauseous, and his bones hurt with fear. But it was a necessary risk.

He stood and moved the couch back against the nearby wall underneath the loft.

"What are you doing?" asked Shawn.

"There's one place we haven't really looked..."

"Oh, I think we looked at it enough..."

"Why were the names there?" asked Ryne, his voice sharper than he'd intended. "What reason? You said it yourself, there's something connecting my family to what's going on, and I want to know what the fuck it is."

Shawn sighed. "Alright, well help me up."

"No, you need to rest."

"You're not just going down there alone."

"That's exactly what I'm going to do. You stay here and rest. Just talk to me while I'm down there, so I don't kill myself."

"Fuck, man. I don't like this."

"Neither do I, but I'm tired of guessing."

Ryne pushed the couch out of the way and lifted the rug, exposing the door. He reached down and gripped the cold metal handle, twisted it into position, and pulled upward, popping the door free from its slot in the floor. Freezing air slapped his face and escaped into the cabin, flickering what remained of the fire. Staring down into the abyss, he thought of his father and all the things he hadn't told his only son. His hands went limp as a swell of pain and self-pity formed a rising wave in his chest. But this wasn't the time for that. Shaking off the feeling, he refocused himself on the darkness below.

Placing one cautionary foot in front of another, he took a step down and began his descent into the black.

Twenty-Two
The Panic

N oah forced his way against the wind as he tore through the snow. His lungs empty and on the edge of collapse, he fell into the white and laid there for a few seconds, trying to find that one good breath that would restore balance and order to his body. A breath that wouldn't come. Lungs starved by the cold, his airways cried out in pain and presented the horrific truth—he needed to slow down. He was fading into exhaustion and had been sucking thin, freezing air for hours. If he didn't slow down, his lungs would give out, and he would drown in his own blood.

But there was the thing in the trees. The thing that had made the sound at the radio tower. He hadn't heard anything since then, nearly an hour gone, but he could *feel* the heaviness in the woods. The branches that grasped for him through the wind. The presence that lingered just out of view, watching, and waiting.

The panic still walked behind him as well. The snow crunched with each step. He didn't turn to look. If he did, he knew the white would turn gold and the grain would return to swallow him.

He had to slow down. Had to make it back to the cabin. Were both possible? He supposed it didn't matter. Nobody was coming for them. His blood still chilled at the sound of the bell and the cultish chanting bleeding through the speakers of the radio. They would just have to make the firewood last, pray that the storm moved on.

And what of the storm? How had the wind just changed direction like it had? Was that possible? The walk back would've been better with the wind at his back, but now he pushed through it once again. His legs burned as much as his lungs did and struggled to hold up his frame.

He cursed himself for ever enjoying the cold. For taking deep, cool breaths in the hills of the Palouse. The tingle he used to enjoy on his skin was now a razor, slicing into all his pores at once. Every bodily system felt like it was one wire short from instant collapse. All the money he had spent on these clothes, all his experience in the cold winters of eastern Washington. None of that meant a damn thing now, as his heart slammed against a frozen breastplate and his tears froze to his cheeks. He felt his cold and stiff beard against his face, and he could only breathe through his mouth. He wanted nothing more than to walk into the cabin and fall asleep inside the fireplace.

A crack snapped above the whipping wind and echoed through the winter frost.

It wasn't in his mind. And it wasn't the first time he'd heard the sound.

The snow turned to grain again. Deep gold, the oily thickness of the air filling his frozen lungs. His feet were on top of the crust. He took a step and heard the crunch as the ground gave way, swallowing him. The panic laughed, close now to his back.

Focus, he told himself. The white returned, and the grain dissolved away. With every step, the crunch of the ice beneath him threatened to take him back there. To the silo. To that black place beyond the veil where he had lingered upon suffocation. Upon death. He could still taste it in the air.

"The woods are lovely, dark, and deep. But I have promises to keep, and miles to go before I sleep," he said, teeth chattering.

He had to still be close to the path. The wind hadn't changed again, not like it had at the tower. Still in his face, he pushed against it. He looked down, trying to find his footprints from earlier, but the snowfall was heavy. Nothing stayed exposed for long.

But what if the wind *hadn't* changed? What if he had become disoriented by the fall down the hill and was still moving against it, another hour in the wrong direction?

No, no, he couldn't be. He never went around the hill. The wind had changed.

But did that make any more sense?

And then, off in the distance. A shape. Small, covered in fur. An animal? He strained his eyes against the assault of the snow. No, not an animal. A person. There was somebody in the woods with him!

"Hello!" he cried out to the small figure. "Hello! I need help!" His voice choked as it left his throat, gasping in the wind.

The figure looked like the size of a child, wearing the fur of an animal like a jacket. Yes! A child. He could see the faintest features coming together through the gusting snow.

"Hello!" he cried again.

And then, just as quickly as the figure had appeared, it vanished into the trees. A phantom lost in the angry wind. No, no, he had seen it. A child. He *had* to have seen it. But nothing stood with him now. Nothing but the cold, the ancient trees, and the panic creeping along with him. He was losing his mind. Had likely lost it already. Left it frozen, dying in the snow where that bell rang through the radio to the chorus of horrible chanting.

"The woods are lovely, dark, and deep. But I have promises to keep, and miles to go before I sleep." The words were a lost echo, a broken sound from a broken man.

Another crack, closer and louder. *Don't look* he told himself. *It's not real. The panic is not real. It's all in your head. Get it out.* But was it? Was it all in his head? Was the deer nailed to the wall in his head? Was the wolf outside the shed in his head?

"The woods are lovely, dark, and deep. But I have promises to keep, and miles to go before I sleep."

He could almost feel those fingers again, wrapping slowly around his shoulder.

Another crack sounded well above the wind. Undeniable. It was the sound of a branch breaking but magnified beyond the barrier of noise created by the furious gusts. Noah froze in his steps. He didn't turn around this time. The sound died away and the storm's auditory assault continued.

He took another step.

Another loud crack rang deeply through the trees. This one louder than the last two. And closer.

Noah felt his nerves unravel. The sheer volume of the cracks seemed so unnatural, so bizarre, so *intentional*—as if he were supposed to hear them. He felt a weight in the air, pressing against him. A presence lingered in the wind to his back.

Don't look back. Just walk.

Noah took another step, and then another. The presence moved with him. Every footfall through the snow was mimicked by a movement behind.

"The woods are lovely, dark, and deep. But I have promises to keep, and miles to go before I sleep," he said again, pushing his thoughts forward and away from the specter that followed.

Another loud crack. His body tensed with the shock of the volume. Whatever walked behind him *wanted* him to hear it. To hear how easily it snapped those branches, like the hollow bird bones that hung on Ryne's dreamcatcher. To hear how close it was.

A sudden wave of dizziness overtook him, and he fell to his knees. The air left his head, and his vision blurred. His muscles began losing control. *Not now,* he thought and clenched his fists tightly. He raised himself back up, steadied his feet, and continued to march.

"The woods are lovely, dark, and deep. But I have promises to keep, and miles to go before I sleep." The presence lingered nearby. Shawn could feel a strange coldness at his back, even colder than the wind.

Dizziness hit him again, and again he collapsed. This time was worse. A sharp pain reverberated through the sides of his skull. His hands clasped at his ears, and he bit down hard on his tongue. He fought off the pain as blood seeped warm from his mouth and exploded in a splash of red across the white below him. He stood back up and could feel the presence mimic his movement. He wouldn't turn around. Couldn't bring himself to do it, to face it. To look in the eyes of what had haunted him for years. Tears formed and froze against his cheeks as the inevitable enveloped him. It wasn't supposed to be this way. He'd seen a better way. The dog had been right there. He could've gone warm and peaceful. Not like this.

"The woods are lovely, dark, and deep. But I have promises to keep, and miles to go before I sleep."

Then, a pain more excruciating than anything he'd ever felt took over his entire body, and he fell forward. His skull felt pushed to its limits with the force of *something* trying to get out. He rolled in the snow and screamed as a ripping sensation overtook his body, like parts of him were getting torn from the rest of him. But the pain in his head felt even worse.

He heard a loud sickening crack, and his head exploded in a searing agony. The pressure pushed its way out. Warm liquid ran down his hands as they felt the intrusive source. Something hard and rough, with the texture of wood or bone, had broken through the side of his skull.

He rolled on his back and screamed. The pain flayed the edges of his nerves, and he wished nobody had ever taken him out of that damn silo. He opened his eyes slightly. Above him he saw a vast set of jagged shapes blacking out the winter sky. Then he lost his vision as his tears filled with blood.

Another loud, sharp, and agonizing crack, and something broke through the opposite side of his skull. Then a disembodied voice, a haunting echo, moved wistfully through the snow-covered wood.

The woods are lovely dark and deep, but I have promises to keep and miles to go before I sleep...

Noah's screams drowned in blood and faded, lonely, into the snowy wind.

TWENTY-THREE
THINGS LONG ABANDONED

Six months ago, Washington

The church was silent. A serene glow floated from the candles above the altar, like the dim halos of angels feigning salvation across the world. Behind the altar, Jesus hung crucified in plastic and wood on the cross, the crown of thorns gently resting upon His holy head. Lining the walls of the church were stained-glass windows that gave no light at this time of night and displayed illustrations of how Christ himself came to his predicament.

It was a beautiful church; Ryne could admit that. There had been a scheduling conflict at the funeral home, so the wake was held in the church, followed by the service in the morning. The ceiling was vaulted and classic, and upon the higher walls were paintings of angels and saints watching down over the absent congregation. At the altar laid a casket, closed out of respect for the bereaved. But there was no congregation to send their thoughts and prayers, and the bereaved sat alone in a pew wearing an old suit and the wear and tear of too much tragedy on his face. There were no angels here tonight. Just one very lonely man.

Ryne shifted uncomfortably on the stiff wooden seat as he tried his best not to make eye contact with the varnished box that held the remains of his father, or whatever they could find of him. The phone call was still a fresh wound. There had been an accident in the Yukon. His father and uncle had veered off the road about thirty miles outside of Wolf's Bone. The car went over the side of an embankment, had fallen into a deep valley, and crashed into the earth. Then it caught fire. No survivors. Bodies were recovered, but they were disfigured and burned beyond recognition. His father was identified by dental records, his uncle by the registration of the blue work truck.

The most upsetting thing about the call had been the numbness. Ryne heard and processed what was said to him, but he couldn't feel it. And why should he? It was just another shot, another punch, another cruel twist orchestrated by some demented puppeteer. But slowly, the realization set in. His father was gone, and that meant something. Memories shared throughout years of bonding were now just pictures in a rotting scrapbook returning in time to the dust from whence it came. Memories had become few and far between following his mother's death, when Rory became less of a father. When Ryne became less of a son.

So, the memories turned to dust hanging in a dead wind, and he now sat alone in an empty church. It was almost 8:30. The wake had begun at 7:00. The scheduling conflict was last minute, and the new site was further away from the funeral home for most people who lived in town. He guessed they couldn't be bothered to drive the extra miles. A few work associates and the occasional unaware congregant wandered in, but now there was nobody. Nobody left to grieve. Nobody left to care, to lose, or to remember. Maxie had texted him her condolences, but that was the extent of it. That ship had sunk through self-inflicted flooding. He didn't blame her. The way he acted after the baby. The rage that had possessed him. The broken drywall and shattered windows. The *thing* he became, overtaken with an unquenchable anger. He'd burned his marriage in the same pile that he burned Christian's name banner.

The last of the scarce visitors had left half an hour ago. The church was empty aside from Ryne sitting in the same spot he had dug for himself upon his arrival.

The quiet emptiness had dropped a blanket stitched of sorrow and acceptance over him. He simply stared off into the distance, looking past whatever was in front of him, and into the void of space where nothing and everything existed, indifferent to the existence of the other.

He felt everything all at once: devastation, fury, loneliness, dejection, and a million other emotions that stirred within him like some unholy brew in a cauldron of suffering. How pathetic was he? He couldn't even look at the coffin. He cursed himself and felt the swell of anger and shame rise. He wanted to break every single idol in that church.

The door opened behind him. He turned to see what mistake someone had made or who felt guilty enough to make an appearance.

Shawn and Noah stood at the entrance. A lightness in his blood almost threatened a smile beneath the weight of everything else. But the fact that they were there, that they'd shown up...he was just happy to see them.

He rose from his perch of misery and made his way to the back of the church. They had made quite the effort to clean up for the somber occasion. Shawn had cut his hair, which was now neatly styled for the first time in years. Noah had shaved, and Ryne realized it had been a decade since he had even seen his friend's actual jawline. Their suits were pressed and flawless.

He embraced them each. "Thank you, guys, for coming. I know the change was kind of short notice." Shawn had been in an extended tryout for the Reds in Ohio, and Noah was working a farmhand job in Kansas. The two of them had put everything on hold and moved earth and water to make it.

"Wouldn't miss it," said Noah.

"How are you doing?" asked Shawn. The man in the casket had been as much of a father to him as he had been to Ryne.

"As good as I can be."

Noah looked over Ryne's shoulder to the casket.

"They kept it closed?"

"Yeah. Apparently, it was better for everyone." He looked around at the empty house of God.

"Have you heard from Maxie?" asked Shawn.

Ryne shook his head.

"When is the wake for Rod?" asked Noah.

"Tomorrow afternoon. It will probably be emptier than this."

"I still can't believe they were together," said Shawn. "I thought after the last time they were dead to each other."

"Yeah, I thought so too. Listen, you guys don't need to stay. I appreciate you coming, but there's really no point. I'll wait until the end of..."

"Fuck that," said Shawn.

"You're in a church, dude," said Noah.

"Screw that," he corrected. "No, you're not going to sit here alone and drown in all of this. Get your crap and let's go grab some dinner."

"No, it's fine..."

"No," said Noah. "It's not fine. Like he said, get your crap, we're going to eat."

"You don't have much of a choice," said Shawn.

It felt wrong to crack a smile under given circumstances, but he couldn't help it. Everything he had ever loved, held, prayed for; had all been violently ripped from his grasp. His mother, his baby, his marriage, his job. Now his father. But not his brothers. His brothers were still here.

He grabbed his suit jacket from the pew near the front of the church and his gaze found the casket. Images ran through his mind like a home movie. He saw, vividly, memories as they gasped their last breaths before getting pulled beneath the waves of time. His grasp on his own emotions slipped and tears rolled down his face. He moved to the casket for the first time. Placing his hand on the finished wood, he took a breath.

"I know it wasn't always perfect. I know I wasn't the best son, especially after mom died. And I know I was worse the past few months. I wish I could change that. Apologize for it. Do something. But I guess that time has passed now. I'm sorry for not calling as much. I'm sorry for being everything you never wanted me to be. I really am. It's just been hard, and I don't know how to do it. It was hard enough when I had you here, and I was too stupid to call. Too stupid to ask. Now, I have to do it without you, and I don't know if I can." He wiped his eyes with his free hand. "I want to say thank you for everything. Everything before I got lost. Everything after too. I know you tried."

Ryne pulled his shaking hand away from the casket and reached into his jacket pocket. He pulled out the small wooden box. The dreamcatcher, old and frail now, rested in the felt interior. The molded bones browned with time. Cracked at the strong points, barely holding itself together on the strength of the broken places.

He held the little thing for a moment and imagined a life where they were somewhere else. Somewhere warm. Somewhere far away with his mother. Her cheeks ruby fire, full of life. His father content, Wolf's Bone evicted from his memory. Not the man haunted by phantoms, but the man Ryne remembered opening his bedroom door without fear on a cold, dark night so many years ago. And Ryne imagined a little figure in his arms, with small fingers that never got to feel, wrapped in his embrace.

He placed the artifact atop the casket. *No bad dreams tonight.*

"I love you, dad. Sleep well."

Tomorrow he'd walk away from his father for the last time, and he'd reclaim the dreamcatcher then. Replace it with a toss of dirt and extinguish the flame of his fantasy. But for tonight, it was the least he could do. Under the watchful eye of a lonely crucifix, he rejoined his friends and left the church. Empty and dark, the only sounds in the hallowed place were the creaking whispers of things long abandoned.

THE LAST NIGHT

TWENTY-FOUR
DEAD THINGS

The darkness of the cellar was eclipsed only by its silence. A faint whistling sound filled the cellar as wind pushed inwards from some unseen opening lost in the shadows, but the quiet stillness outside permeated through the walls. Ryne held the lighter in front of him, holding his breath, preparing for the illumination of the hidden horrors. His finger ran across the spark wheel. The quiet metallic sound broke the silence, and a bright orange glow manifested in front of him.

It was the deer again. The bile rose into his throat under its empty eyes. Its body slumped against the nails driven through its legs. Against this weight, the forelegs looked as though they might crack in two, surrendering to the mass of the dead thing.

A question had been circulating in his head since he'd first seen the deer. How did the animal die? It had been dripping blood, so it wasn't dressed and wasn't found dead in the woods. But it almost certainly must've been killed prior to the hanging, because there was no way somebody was going to overpower a deer by hand to perform this act. Atop the deer's head protruded an enormous set of antlers. Ryne counted ten points. To attempt something like that with a deer of this size would have been suicide. Shot? Maybe. But what kind of hunter shoots a deer and then leaves it intact?

Someone who's not a hunter. That much was obvious. This wasn't an animal killed for sport or for food. It was killed for whatever purpose it now served nailed to the permafrost.

From a distance, he couldn't make out any sort of exterior wound, but it was very dark. The lighter effectively illuminated the immediate, but not the distant. He leaned closer to get a better look. The putrefying smell eroded the hairs within his nose and raised the bile in his stomach. He turned away and tucked his face into his jacket, taking long, deep breaths from anywhere less rotten. He gagged loudly and then vomited all over the ground.

"Everything alright?" called Shawn from above.

He coughed the remaining gall out of him. "Yeah, it's just disgusting."

Turning back to the rotting deer, he held his breath as he scanned the animal's body. There was nothing. No gunshot wounds, no blade entry, no bruising. The only visible signs of duress were the nails driven through the animal's bones.

His body warmed with sympathy for the animal. The cause of death still eluded him, but the sight was enough. He could imagine the sound of the bones shattering as rusted metal got driven through, splintering them apart at the marrow. And if the animal had, somehow, been alive when this had occurred... God, what a horrific way to go.

Something above the corpse caught his eye. Hanging horizontally over the hideous scene was a torch, still wrapped in dry cloth. He raised the lighter towards it.

The small orange glow quickly grew to a large, revealing flame that exterminated the space's darkness. What had only been a foot of visibility now stretched to ten feet of clarity. The fire lit the cellar enough that the other victims melted into view, hanging silently like martyrs without a cause. Somehow, the more light that shined on them, the more unnerving their forms appeared. As long as they were confined to the shadows, his mind could pretend that the black space was empty and not occupied by these incomprehensible sights.

In the newfound light, he could also see that above each of the animals hung another torch. He circled the cellar, lighting the rolls of cloth and illuminating as much as possible. Moving around from left to right, riding the large column of earth in the middle that held up the cabin, he saw that the cellar extended beyond the cabin's floor plan. On that column he noticed smears of something on the clay. Red and shining in the torchlight. They looked like letters, or maybe symbols. He moved closer as the lighter's glow illuminated the space.

Blood. Fresh blood. Smeared by the hands of unseen visitors. And the letters weren't letters at all. They were runes.

He swallowed. European without a doubt, some sort of spell or ritual. He backed away from the wall, felt his skin chill at the bloody tapestry before him, and turned away.

"Ryne? Talk to me, man," called Shawn from the room above. His voice grew more distant as Ryne pushed deeper.

"Honestly, I'd rather not."

Every step he took another victim hung from the wall, fastened to the frozen clay with metal nails. The animals showed their age. The white bone of a decomposing deer, the wilted pelt of a bear. It was a vision back in time that begged the question of how long these things had been here.

He reached the last corpse. A white wolf, old bone showing from rotted legs and snout. Formlessly sagging against what little weight it had left. Beyond the wolf, he could see the source of the wind. A long, dark tunnel opened before him. Its gaping maw moaned with the passage of the outside world from somewhere near its end.

Ryne stepped back from the tunnel. The surrounding light flickered against the walls, and the fire's reflection swayed in the hollowed eyes of the dead things forever entombed in this place. He backed away from what he assumed was the exit of the cellar, although he couldn't bring himself to think of it like that anymore. This was a tomb, a crypt enshrouded in unholy auras. A place where light was violently and efficiently decimated. A place where life met a desolate and unnatural end. The torches were lit in a semi-circle, stretching from the tunnel across the walls to the stairs. The dead things danced in the firelight.

Ryne felt minuscule, insignificant. He was a speck of dust caught in the middle of a plume of embers from an inescapable fire, destined to ignite and burn with the rest of the ashes.

The other wall was still unseen, hiding in the black. There weren't animals hanging on it, so there were no torches to light. There was just the thick, unyielding darkness.

He closed his eyes and clenched his jaw. Gathering himself, he opened his eyes with a new fortitude. He had come down here for answers, and he would find answers. Scanning the lightened area, he looked down at the ground beneath the animals. Under each carcass sat a rock, as he had expected. He cut his gaze to the white wolf again, bent down, and moved the stone out of the way. Hidden underneath he found a tightly wrapped piece of cloth. Unfurling it, he could see the name written darkly in fine calligraphy.

William Burdette

He inhaled deeply. He knew the name. He'd never known the man, but he knew the name. William had been one of the first Europeans to settle Wolf's Bone. He was a fur trader, a hunter. The man who built the cabin, and it seemed its cellar as well. The rest of the Burdette family lived in town, but William had preferred to spend his time out in the woods. And now, his name was ritualistically disposed beneath the long-decayed corpse of a wolf.

Ryne sensed the pattern darkly manifesting in the crypt. Looking down at the clay wall, he knew exactly what he would find under the corpses, but he indulged himself anyway. He moved silently, not a word escaped his lips. Picked up every stone, one after another. Below each were names:

Peter Burdette
Johnson Burdette
Nicholas Burdette
Benjamin Burdette
Tyler Burdette
Richard Burdette
Jonathan Burdette

His entire family line rested in this crypt, with only their names remaining. Their bodies replaced by slaughtered animals hung to the wall, demeaned beyond reproach.

His family settled in a place not meant for man—a place walked by something man was never meant to know. But man had come, and man came to know. At the center of this grizzly understanding was his family, steeped in blood so far.

It was the stones that told the story. The unassuming rocks told a tale of worship and sacrifice. He knew the legend well, and for good reason.

His family had been the offering. They had been from the moment they set foot in this place over 150 years ago.

His legs lost their strength, and he collapsed on the clay floor. He gasped for breath; his brain overwhelmed with panic. What had he done? What had he walked his friends into? Had he anything left in his stomach, he would have thrown up again.

"Ryne!" Shawn called down. "You okay? Talk to me!"

It took him a few moments to find the strength for language. "No," he said. "No, I'm not."

"Are you hurt?"

No, but you are. Thanks to me. "No. This is just all kinds of fucked up."

"What's going on?"

"It's my family! It's my fucking family," he said as his insides were ripped in two. "Goddamn it, we worshiped this fucking thing!"

Silence from above. "What's the point of the animals?" asked Shawn finally.

"I don't know. I guess it's some kind of ritual, but that still makes no sense. There are runes drawn on the walls in blood. They're not indigenous. The settlers...they must have brought something over here with them."

"God," Shawn's voice was low.

God wasn't here.

Recognition and realization hit at the same time. Why did the names stop at his grandfather? Where were the names of Rory and Rod? His eyes moved again to the deer with no stone beneath it. Why was there no stone? Following the pattern; there should be one for his father.

In the torchlight, he could also see the other animals tucked away in the alcove under the stairs, including the ones he'd missed before. Past the unmarked deer, he could see a wolverine, then the black wolf, and finally an owl.

He followed the pattern. The deer was his father's spot, as he was the oldest. The wolverine was his uncle's.

The wolf was his.

He felt sick again and took a step back to recover. Too many things were pouring into his head and swarming his thoughts. What had they done? What had his family awoken?

Then something else caught his eye. An owl that appeared nearly as far along into decay as the deer, but it had a stone beneath it. Reaching down, Ryne picked up the rock and opened the folded paper.

Christian Burdette

His muscles ceased their function. Dropping the rock, Ryne's head spun as he heard the stone smack against the wooden floor. Every emotion he had ever known flooded him all at once. The flood rose from within, and stability deserted him, dropping him into a void as his body fell at the base of the ladder. He heard Shawn's voice calling from what seemed a million miles away. Slowly, fading into oblivion, he lost consciousness, lying on the ground surrounded by his family's decrepit legacy.

* * *

"Ryne! Ryne, answer me!"

Shawn's heart sank into his chest as his friend went silent. A dull thud was the only noise that had escaped the dark place beneath him in the past few minutes. Now he heard nothing but the soft whistle of freezing wind. The last of the logs flickered and burned. Two remained. They wouldn't last until morning.

"Goddammit, answer me!"

Nothing. Just more whistling and silence, amalgamating in the still air of the cabin.

He looked down at his leg, wrapped tight in gauze and bandages. Beneath the cloth was a pathetic sight as dead now as those things in the cellar. Hours had passed since he'd tried to put any weight on it, when he'd collapsed like a felled tree. The tendons under mutilated skin snapped and popped away with the sharp siren of agony, like shears pulling apart the nerves. His heart pumped the black venom through dead veins and arteries, contaminating new blood.

But it didn't matter now. Something was wrong down there—Ryne wasn't responding. Pain would have to wait, no matter how intense. There were more important things at play than his comfort. He put the edge of the blanket in his mouth and bit down hard, grinding his teeth into the Sherpa before rising to his feet. He planted his good leg onto the floor, and then swung the dead one from its resting place.

He screamed through the blanket as the slightest movement sent thorns scraping across his nerves. His thoughts swam adrift in the darkest waters of his mind, where every doubt or concern he'd ever experienced sat festering in blood, little devils pricking and prodding conceptions of failure into his head.

There was no way he could make any sort of difference here. If Ryne was in trouble, then in trouble he would stay. Shawn felt useless now, a lame horse limping towards an imaginary finish. He laid on the ground and tears filled his eyes.

"Ryne, for God's sake answer me!"

He was alone. Useless, broken, and alone. He wondered how far Noah had made it. Would he make it to the tower? It was their only hope, but the deck was stacked hopelessly against them. If he didn't make it back, if he got lost, or injured, or *it* found him all alone and defenseless, then they were doomed. And even if he had reached the tower and gotten a distress call out, Shawn doubted very much that he and Ryne would last until help came for them. The part of himself he'd always said was the "honest" part felt like it already knew that both Noah and Ryne were gone. The thud was it, the end of his friend. And now, he would die too. He could feel the cold eyes of the deer from the road, hear the snarl of the wolf, see the corpse beneath him as though he were staring into its face. They were never alone, not in this place. The cellar opened up somewhere, and he shuddered at what he knew could have made its way in there. Whatever had taken Ryne would slowly climb its way out the place below and into the cabin. Creep its monstrous shape from the pit. And that would be it. That would be his end. Lying on the ground like the failure that he was.

This fucking leg. The bane of what little existence he had left. This parasite stuck to his body that took and took and took. Everything.

But another part of Shawn existed too, a part rising within his chest. A part of him who understood what it meant to lose and valued every moment given to him. A part who survived as a hungry and scared child under the shadow of a man who'd become a monster. A part who remembered the phone call that told him Noah had died, suffocated in a grain silo. A part who remembered the text from Ryne saying the baby was gone. A part who remembered the empty church where his surrogate father lay inside a closed casket.

Fuck. This.

If failure was his destiny, then so be it. He could fail himself. It was fair. Everyone's life ended in failure, anyway. Failure to breathe a final breath. Failure to hold off the reaper one last time. One day, inevitably, he would fail himself. But he would not fail Ryne.

He reached out and grabbed the leg of the heavy coffee table and pulled himself close to it. Using his three good limbs, he positioned himself upward and, through an immense flood of agony, rose again to his feet.

"Ryne, I swear to God you better not be down there ignoring me, or I am going to be exceptionally pissed."

He dragged the dead limb behind him as he inched his body towards the hole in the floor. It wasn't black anymore but lit up with a dim radiance bouncing with the fires of torches below.

Directly under the opening, he saw Ryne lying on his side. He wasn't moving.

A scream shattered the air. Inhuman. It choked the quiet and reverberated like a siren. Shawn covered his ears quickly as the pain shifted from his leg to the inside of his head. He wavered, and his good leg lost its strength to support him and his frantic movements. His perception dimmed as his balance failed him, and he fell forward into the cellar. For a moment, he saw the illuminated dead hanging on the walls, their faces lit up with the glow of flickering torches, looking almost alive, before he hit the floor and felt the wind kick out of his lungs. A sharp thwack as his head snapped back into the hard ground. The scream died with the impact and his world was silent. In the shock of the fall, he could barely move his body and felt nothing. Slowly, the feeling returned, and he was assaulted with more misery in his leg.

Rolling over in anguish, he saw Ryne lying next to him. Above them, the wolf hung on the wall. Looking down at him. With its head unnaturally angled, its eyes—dead and lifeless—drove an empty glare through the crackling firelight and straight into his center. The same beast. The one who had sunken its fangs into his leg without him even feeling it. Dead and gone, yet very much alive.

His vision blurred, and his periphery blackened.

"Ryne," he said weakly. "Ryne, wake up..." The pain halted his speech and held him down against the hard ground.

In his failing sight, he saw the firelight skip and dance across the walls and the dead things moved within it. He was certain they were moving. Certain they would push their way off the wall and come to him as the fire died. They seemed so alive in the crackling giggle of the torches.

"Ry..." He started, and his body gave up. His consciousness abandoned him in the cold depths of the subjugating hell.

Twenty-Five

Legacy

H e was a child again. Sitting alone and lost in the middle of the empty road, a destined orphan waiting on the inevitable. Long, dark hair fell across his forehead and became drenched in the tears that filled his eyes. He cried freely. There was nobody left to impress, no toughness left to salvage. He was a child who knew the future. He would lose everything. He would meet the love of his life and lose her. He would be granted the gift of fatherhood and lose it. He would continue a long family heritage of loneliness and sacrifice into a bottomless pit of unquenching misery. So, he cried. Like lonely little boys do when the stone in which their future is set becomes an anchor dragging them to the abyss.

The houses all looked the same on either side of the empty road, and they would always look the same. New people would move in and move out, and their lives would never alter course because nobody ever altered the course of their life. They just made the turn already dug into the tracks.

He heard the beast well before he saw it. A growling pant, deep and guttural from behind the fence. He looked to his left and saw the hideous source of the sound. The dog was long gone. What stood now, feet away from his face, was something beyond comprehension. As large as a bear with a long and dark face, almost canine, its broad shoulders stretched into long arms ending in decrepit hands. A monstrous set of antlers jutting from

173

the sides of its head and stretching towards a desolate sky. Its snout peeled back to reveal blackened muscle and bone and unnatural teeth. Long, yellow, and dripping with saliva. Its skin was taught and rough, like the gnarled branches of ancient trees, twisting and rolling for centuries. But of all the visual horrors possessed by the thing, its eyes were the most haunting. Black, dead, and soulless. If eyes were the windows to the soul, these windows showed a space of vast nothingness spotted by tiny stars of vile death and hatred.

He cried. This was his reaper, and he knew it. Maybe not now, but someday. The thing his family had worshiped would be their destruction, his too. Maybe one day he wouldn't fear it, maybe one day he would fight it until the last breath left his lungs.

But he was a child. A little boy. And little boys weren't ready to fight. No, all he could do was cry. He wasn't ready to die. He didn't want to go into the darkness. He was scared, the way that all children fear what waits beyond the only thing they've ever known.

But he could go now, couldn't he? Forget all the misery he hadn't suffered yet? Just let go now. Accept it.

The antlered thing opened its mouth and screamed at him. Shrill and hateful, the world went black at the sound. He squeezed his eyes shut, tears still streaming, and cried for his parents as the beast closed in on him.

* * *

Ryne's eyes shot open in the shimmering light of the crypt. An emptiness hollowed his head and his stomach as he rolled on his back and took a long, deep breath. The rotten air filled his chest, and he coughed violently. The wolf hung above him, with its dead glare angled down. Sitting up, he pushed his body back out of its stare.

"Good," came a voice from behind him. "You're alive."

Shawn had backed himself up against the nearest wall and sat there in stillness. Blood dripped from his ears, and his eyes stared ahead with the glazed focus of a soldier who'd seen one too many battles.

"What the hell are you doing down here?" Ryne asked.

"I came down to get you. I fell. Hit my head pretty hard. Think I have a concussion. Was going to try to climb back out when I woke up and saw you were breathing, but..." He pointed down to his knee. The joint bent unnaturally to the side, his leg a broken stick. The only thing connecting his thigh and calf now were a few tendons and ligaments.

"Oh my God," said Ryne as he felt the vomit rise in his throat. He covered his mouth. Choked it down. Still, he turned away. "Does it hurt?" he asked through the gag. What a stupid question.

"Very badly."

Ryne pulled himself up and sat against the ladder. Very little light shown from the cabin above. The fire seemed to have gone out, and the windows were darkened by night.

"What time is it?" he asked.

"About six-thirty."

He had been out for six hours. His skin went cold as he thought about what could've transpired in those six hours of unwilling sleep. Then, a more sinister reminder alerted itself within his head.

"Noah never showed up?"

Shawn didn't even alter his glance. He just shook his head solemnly. "What were you talking about earlier? About your family?"

Ryne took a breath, deep and heavy. He had wanted to forget every revelation he had suffered through in this pit, but he couldn't. The image of his ancestors' names stuck in his head like a dart.

"All the animals have a stone beneath them. Every one of them has the name of a male member of my family. Generation by generation from the man who built the cabin to my grandfather. Whatever this thing is, I think my family worshiped it. I don't know why they crucified the animals, but I think it's some sort of offering. The runes are written in blood, I'm guessing was from the animals."

"Didn't you say when you were a kid you saw your uncle praying to something outside?"

"Yes." It was the first time in his life he had acknowledged that fact soberly. It hadn't been a dream; it hadn't been a mistake. He hadn't been sleepwalking. He had seen what he thought he had seen. "It stops at my grandfather. My dad and uncle's names aren't under the animals they should be, and neither is mine. But..." his voice trailed off in horror at the next sentence he knew he had to say.

"But what?"

Ryne jerked his thumb behind him. "You see the owl next to the wolf? There was a stone underneath it. The name says Christian."

Shawn's eyes widened. He now looked awake. "Christian?"

"Yeah." Ryne's heart dropped at the sound of his own voice.

"Jesus Christ, man, what have we gotten into? I can see your family making offerings and sacrifices and shit, but how exactly is an unborn baby going to do that."

"I think..." said Ryne, his voice low and sad. "I think Rod had something to do with it."

"What do you mean?"

"When we lost the baby, I didn't tell anyone but my dad. I didn't even text you and Noah until that night. Just my dad. We got home, and he was there. Then Rod showed up. He knew about what happened."

"Did your dad tell him?"

Ryne shook his head. "No. In fact, they got into a fight in my front yard about it. But Dad seemed to know something, and so did Rod. It sounds crazy out loud, but I don't know what's not crazy anymore. I think Rod did something. I think...I think he was the reason we lost the baby. And I think that reason has something to do with this place."

"What reason could he have?"

"The names stop at my grandfather." He pointed to the deer. "That should be my father." He moved his finger to the wolverine beside it. "That should be Rod, and...," his eyes met the wolf's. "That should be me. But there are no stones. No names. It's almost like it just stopped, but then there's the owl, and Christian's name."

"They died."

"What?"

"Whatever they were supposed to do, they couldn't...because they died. That's why you're here..."

"Fuck that." Ryne felt the anger rising again. He never agreed to any of this. What kind of lie had he been living? How many untruths had his father been feeding him? Until he lost Christian, he had been in church every Sunday. He remembered the seriousness with which his immediate family had always taken their faith. And now? Now to find out his ancestry worshiped this...*thing?*

"I had another thought while I was sitting here, wallowing in my own misery," said Shawn. "About our friendly stalker. How many stories have we heard about the woods? How many legends? We had those stories burned into our minds so we would respect the forest. And now, dammit, we find out they weren't make-believe."

"Just legends. Stories."

"To us. They are legends to us. We know nothing about this place. Even *you* have no idea. What do you have? Stories passed down for generations? Generations that were strangers to this place? All stories come from some basic truth, right? Whatever this thing is, what if this is the original truth? What if all the legends are true? What if different people saw this thing differently and assigned their own names to it? Labels? Gave it their own identity and let the legend grow?"

Ryne thought about Shawn's theory. It made sense in principle. Human history is full of countless cultural legends eerily similar to the legends of other cultures. Could it be possible that the same thing inspired multiple legends across multiple cultures in this part of the world?

Shawn stared forward; a stoic gargoyle confined to the ground.

"Where the hell is Noah?" Ryne asked.

"You know where he is." His voice was flat and direct, and his eyes never moved from the spot on the wall.

"Don't say that."

"We sent him out there to die."

"Shawn..."

"No." He was crying now. "He was our best friend, and he was talking stupid, and we bought into it and sent him out to die."

"He went out there for us..."

"No, he went out there for *me*. The two of you didn't need a rescue, you could have waited it out. There's no waiting it out for me. I know where this train is going. I can *feel* it. Every second I can feel whatever is inside of me moving. There's only one place this is going."

He'd never seen Shawn so defeated. This was the same man who was ready to rip his head off just two days ago because he wanted to stay in the cabin, and now he was giving up?

"Fuck you," Ryne told him through his teeth.

Shawn stifled a laugh and looked at him as though he'd lost his mind. A new resolve born from anger. "Really? Fuck me?"

"Yeah, fuck you. You don't get to quit. You don't get to stand there and patronize me about wanting to stay behind and then turn and quit now. That's bullshit. Noah's coming back, and we're getting you out of here. Yeah, you're going to lose your leg, but you hated the piece of shit, anyway."

"I would say the situation has changed slightly, wouldn't you?" said Shawn.

"I don't care. If I can't quit, you can't quit. Or do you want to stay down here and die a spineless hypocrite?"

"Alright. What's your plan, huh? Cause our last great idea probably got one of us killed."

"See that tunnel? It opens up outside somewhere. That's where the wind has been coming from. Either Noah's almost back with help on the way or...or he's not." Ryne shuddered at the image of his friend gone, his body lying alone out in the snow, forgotten amongst the primeval trees. But he couldn't entertain the thought now. Noah was coming back, but there was no telling how long it would take. Their earlier estimates of a six hour trip had been an aggressive one, which didn't consider something going wrong, and Shawn was in a bad spot and getting progressively worse. They desperately needed a backup plan. "If he isn't, we still need to get out. I'm going to walk down the tunnel and see where it goes. Somebody's been using this place, so it has to go somewhere. I need you to get over here and wrap your arms around my neck. I'll pull you up the steps. You can't walk at all now, but nothing has happened in the cabin yet, so it's the safest place for you while I try to find a way out."

Shawn stared at him. It was hard to read him anymore. His eyes were different. Changed in a way.

"Alright," he said. "But you better figure out what you're going to do. Because what's going to happen when you see this thing, huh? You going to talk to it? Rationalize with it? Get angry when it won't listen? When it doesn't care? What are you going to do when you're faced with something you can't hit?"

TWENTY-SIX
THE TUNNEL

By the time he got Shawn in the recliner, Ryne's arms and legs ached, and a dull pain nestled its way deep into the small of his back. Stretching out, he heard and felt his vertebrae snapping back into place.

It was past seven now, and there was still no sign of Noah. No headlights coming from the path. No helicopter sound of impending rescue. There were just the woods, the snow, and the night as the storm continued its fury upon the natural world. The air itself lonely and lost within the vastness of the desolation.

Ryne placed his friend in the recliner and turned to the hole in the floor.

"I want to ask you something," said Shawn.

He thought about ignoring him, about walking down that ladder and pretending he didn't hear him. He didn't have the time nor the desire to be lectured. And yet, he paused. Took a breath, let it go, and turned to his friend. The crippled mess of a man, broken in mind and body, laid back in the recliner with his head tilted to the side and his eyes heavy. He'd thought about ignoring him, but he'd turned around because in the rational part of his brain he knew a very real truth.

This might be the last conversation he ever had with his best friend. His brother.

"What?"

"I've never asked it before, because I was scared of the answer. But seeing how our story is being written out, I want to know. When you and Maxie split up, did you hit her?"

The words stung harder than the freezing wind outside could've ever dreamed. Bored a hole deep into him and shredded the sinews that held him together. He opened his mouth to speak, or thought he did, at least. But no words came out.

"I remember how angry you were. How angry you still are. I was scared you and her wouldn't make it after losing the baby, but to see it happen so fast. And then for her to not even show up at the funeral? I just need to know now, because I might not get a chance to know later. Did you hit her?"

He felt the water form behind his eyes and then bleed out onto his cheeks. After everything, this is where it had led. What it had come to. What his brother thought of him.

"No," he said. "No, I never hit her."

But there was a truth to the tone of the question. He had been changed; become something he didn't recognize. The feeling in his bones had been red with rage that threatened to erupt at any moment. In fact, he'd taken that anger out on everything *but* Maxie.

"I never hit her. But I hit everything else. Broke a few windows and some drywall. I...I couldn't help it. It had to come out, and I couldn't live with myself if I went there. So, it had to go to other places."

"That why she left?"

"No." He took a breath, deep into himself. Held it there and let it build up the courage for him. "We had this banner that ran across the nursery door. It spelled Christian's name. She...she refused to take it down after we lost him. I don't know. I guess it brought her some kind of comfort. But I couldn't stand it. It was like some constant reminder that *nothing* would be the same again. That I'd failed to protect the most helpless thing, the *only* thing that mattered. I kept asking her to take it down, but she kept saying no. She said she could still feel him. Inside her. Every once in a while, she would hold her stomach and smile a little bit, like she'd felt something. Phantom kicks. I guess the banner and the kicks made her feel like he was still there, somehow. But I couldn't take it anymore. So, one night when she was working late, I ripped the thing down. Brought it into the backyard and lit it on fire."

Shawn stared at him, his eyes still heavy but open and alert.

"She came home early. Brought dinner. Literally left work and stopped to pick us up something nice to eat so that we wouldn't have to settle for leftovers. She tried to do something nice. For me. And she came home to... well, the kicks stopped after that."

The log on the fireplace crumbled and burned toward its end. There was only one left.

Ryne walked into the bedroom and grabbed the other rifle, made sure it was loaded, and gave it to Shawn.

"The hell is this gonna do?"

"If it comes, hurt it."

Shawn nodded. Ryne made his way back down into the crypt where death and decay were proudly displayed. He looked at the wolf, its fur as black as the night sky. He held absolute hatred for it, the kind of hate that viciously consumes whatever sliver of good someone has left in their soul. It was a destiny he was now determined to eschew. He reached above the animal and took the torch. Lit the old wrapping with the lighter.

Wide and dark, the empty mouth of the tunnel invited him with the eagerness of a viper. It exhaled darkness with the faint wisp of trapped wind. Ryne's spine froze in place, and he took deep, slow breaths. The only movement of his body was the nervous twitch of his index finger. He closed his eyes tightly and settled himself before opening them again with new resolve. Stepping into the void, he held the torch out in front of his face, stretching a glow to either side of the tunnel. He looked above him and considered exactly how much ground sat between him and the surface world. The top of the tunnel was held in place by wooden beams extending into the earth, and he wondered how sturdy those old beams still were.

Aside from the wind, it was quiet. So quiet, the silence itself seemed alive, moving in place beyond the glow of the torch. The tunnel must have been five yards wide, the clay walls carefully dug out of the permafrost with precise planning. The history of this place had become an ever-evolving mystery to him, filling his mind with irrational and impossible thoughts. Thoughts that had been scattered in the roaring wind. Now, as he found and collected them, his answers seemed just beyond reach.

If the thing in the woods was the original legend which had inspired so much folklore throughout the written history of mankind, was this tunnel dug by the first people to witness it? Had his ancestor built the cabin where he had on purpose? For what reason?

Fear cracked its way through his bones. The presence of whatever stalked these woods, the recipient of worship from his own kin, made him nauseous. But the feeling extended well into his own guilt and blame as well.

From the moment they'd arrived, everything had been off. The strange behavior of the people in town, the deer in the road, the animals on the first night. Every instinct should've been screaming at him to leave. But he hadn't. He'd dug his feet into the ground like an idiot and ignored every reasonable thing that had come out of Shawn's mouth. He'd justified every stupid decision he made with nonsensical logic, and now, because of his own incompetence, Shawn was facing the genuine possibility of never making it home. Noah was still nowhere to be found. He could put a brave face on all he wanted, but the stakes were clear. It was his own fault that his two best friends were now staring down the frosted barrel of a loaded gun. Sickness filled his stomach at the thought of his own culpability in their predicament. His own stupid decision-making aside, it was his family that had enabled all this. Shame and humiliation coursed in his veins at the thought of men he used to look up to, kneeling like cowards before...whatever this thing was. He wanted to hit something, to explode his frustrations on something that wouldn't die, so he wouldn't have to stop until his hands broke apart.

Every step he took was another step into the darkest recesses of his own mind. His breath came in short, hurried gasps as the walls of the dug-out earth constricted around him. He was freezing through his jacket. The wind held within it a palpable tension, like something was guiding it through the weak points in his clothing.

Suddenly, the wind picked up. The torch flickered and died. Darkness once again became the sole proprietor of the tunnel. Panic spread through him, and he struggled to strike the ignition again, fumbling with his lighter until finally finding the catch. With the torch useless now, he re-ignited the flame and moved sideways, using his body to shield it from the gusts.

He had to be getting close to the end of the tunnel. The wind grew in strength, and the pathway in front of him gradually widened. He guessed he'd walked over a mile, and now the end, whatever that held, seemed in sight.

In the distance, at the edge of his vision, he saw a light. Not a bright light, but a dull aura that swayed with barely enough of a glow to warm up the dark. He wanted to break out into a run. To drop the lighter to the frozen ground and sprint away from the darkness to whatever promise the light might hold. But his better sense took over, and he moved slowly and cautiously towards the unknown. The tunnel continued its gradual expanse as the light loomed closer with each step he took. Then more lights appeared, dimmer. Glowing orbs. They emerged, born from the shadows one by one.

Then, almost without realizing it, he was out of the tunnel. He stood in a large opening, a hundred yards wide in either direction. The storm still raged overhead, and the wind ripped through the passage, throwing snow into the cavernous night. The glowing orbs of light were everywhere, and their origin was revealed. Makeshift lanterns, small glass structures wrapped in crooked braces, hung from wooden poles that were erected every few yards within the opening. At the edge of the tunnel along the tree line stood more of these poles, arranged in such a way that a border of lanterns separated the clearing from the frozen grip of the forest.

And the trees. Beyond the lantern wall, they stood with their branches jerking as the frozen gusts gutted them. He squinted against the wind and beheld the sight. Like a forest full of Christmas trees, lanterns hung from the old branches. Hundreds of them, tied tightly somewhere around the wood. It was almost angelic, a taste of magic in desolation.

In the wind, the lanterns tossed and swayed, and their light dulled, but within the glow Ryne saw what filled the clearing. There were small wooden structures everywhere, each one slightly smaller than the cabin with a steeply sloped roof and exteriors of wood held together by a thick, black substance—some sort of mortar. There was no spot in the clearing unoccupied by either a house or a lantern.

He was standing in the middle of a village.

Twenty-Seven

The Return

Shawn's leg pulsed beneath the bandages, and waves of torment scorched through his nerve endings. It was getting worse. Earlier the pain had been restricted to quick movements and changing positions, but now it was constant. He wanted to unwrap the bandage, to see just how bad it really was, but he knew he wouldn't be able to do it. He couldn't even look at it now. The angle revolted him. His leg had been bent and broken before, but never like this. Inside the knee, he could feel the space between his calf and thigh now unoccupied by the biological glue that should have been there. It made him want to vomit, but he was scared the action would push him well beyond the threshold required to hold on to what was left of his life.

The cabin was dark, empty, and freezing. The fire had gone out, and the warmth that usually filled the walls of the woodland retreat had dissipated. The war with the cold was over. One last bullet remained before the creeping frost mounted its final and fatal assault. The storm outside had somehow gotten worse. The wind no longer brushed against the side of the cabin windows with a soft whistle. Rather, it pounded against the glass like some feral animal trying to break in.

The last log sat on the table in front of him next to the matchbox and some old newspaper. If he wanted to, he could light it. It would hurt; but the fireplace was only six feet away. An easy hop or two; reignite the fire and return the warmth to the cabin and hop back to the recliner that was now his hospice bed. If he was going to die, he may as well die warm.

He wasn't going to kid himself. There were only two ways he was getting out of this. Either somebody was going to pull up at any moment in a snowplow or a helicopter with a pilot crazy enough to fly in this storm, or Ryne was going to find something at the end of the tunnel. Each scenario was unlikely, bordering on impossible. It wasn't a lack of faith in his friends. Not even close. He had all the faith in the world in both of them. Despite everything they'd been through, they were as dependable as the winter snow. Even Ryne's stupid decision to stay here was born out of a momentary lapse of composure. Shawn knew it. He had seen the real Ryne in the crypt a half-hour ago. The fire that had been missing from his eyes during the past year had returned. Whatever doubt had remained about his friend got extinguished with his answer to Shawn's question. Because the truth was that he wouldn't have been able to take it if his best friend had turned into his father. If he had crossed *that* line. But he hadn't. He'd done something horrible, something beyond words, and he had paid the consequences. But he hadn't done *that*. And Noah, despite the things that still chewed and gnawed at him daily, was still a rock of a man. The lack of hesitation to embark into the storm for a five-mile hike was impressive— but expected.

No, the issue wasn't his friends. The issue was that they were going out into the domain of something they had no business knowing about. Something that didn't care about how tough or how dependable they were.

How could Ryne's father have never told him? Rory Burdette was the most honest man Shawn had ever known, and it shook him to his core to think of the chasm of lies the man had created around his son. And now, the chasm engulfed them too.

His bones ached with the cold as it devoured the cabin. He looked again at the lone remaining log. *Fuck it*, he thought. Three possibilities. Noah arrives to save the day, Ryne returns to save the day, or neither of them comes back at all and Shawn dies a slow, frigid, and miserable death. In none of those possibilities was there a reason to save the final log until the inevitable.

He bit down on his blanket and used his arms to lift his body out of the chair. Balancing on one leg, he grabbed the log and hopped twice before throwing the log into the open fireplace along with some paper for kindling. Struck a match. The fire caught quickly, and warmth spilled out across him like an ocean wave of peace. He hopped back to the chair and fell back in. The pain was excruciating, but he didn't care. He smiled in the heat. If the fire could last long enough to see him take his last breath...well, there were certainly worse ways to go.

thewoodsarelovelydarkanddeepbutIhavepromisest okeepandmilestogobeforeIsleep

Shawn jolted up in his seat. His leg erupted in pain. Had he imagined it? No, there was no way. He heard that voice. He knew that voice.

It was Noah. He was back! An ecstatic explosion of glee filled his empty husk. They were saved! Thank God, they were saved! Everything waiting for him back home flashed in his mind: a dog he needed to feed, a girl he needed to talk to, a bed he desperately needed to sleep in. Apologies needed to be made and plans for an uncertain future needed to get ironed out.

"Noah!" he called. "Noah?"

Nothing. No lights appeared outside the windows and no door opened. But he was sure he had heard...

thewoodsarelovelydarkanddeepbutIhavepromisest okeepandmilestogobeforeIsleep

There was no mistaking it now. It was Noah's voice. He was even saying the rhyme from that stupid poem he liked so much.

"Noah, where the fuck are you?"

thewoodsarelovelydarkanddeepbutIhavepromisest okeepandmilestogobeforeIsleep

Impatience ate at him, and he looked frantically in all directions. But there was nothing to be seen.

"This shit isn't funny, man. Tell me you brought help."

thewoodsarelovelydarkanddeepbutIhavepromisest okeepandmilestogobeforeIsleep

Shawn focused hard on the sound, but it wasn't coming from any one location. It seemed like it was bouncing off the walls from every direction possible. It sounded familiar in that strange way, the way it felt everywhere and nowhere all at once.

The child's voice. The singing they had heard on the first night. That's what it sounded like. *Exactly* what it sounded like.

It wasn't Noah.

The thought cut him to the marrow. What was talking to him? How was it mimicking Noah's voice? How did it know that phrase?

thewoodsarelovelydarkanddeepbutIhavepromisest okeepandmilestogobeforeIsleep

He listened more carefully and realized that the voice *was* everywhere at once. Like an echo. And echoes have sources. He closed his eyes and focused. Drowned out the reverberations of sound playing off the walls. The epicenter of it all traced to his left. He turned his head and looked out the window.

A deer stood outside. Standing right up to the window. An adult, but not a particularly old one. It had a small, six-point rack and a deep tan color throughout its coat tipped with snow. But its eyes drove a stake through Shawn's chest. They were black and empty. Not really eyes at all, just black spaces devoid of life and feeling. A chill crept through his blood. What looked like a dark gray piece of fabric hung off the deer's antlers. His eyes got wide with a horrifying recognition, and his heartbeat doubled in pace. The fabric was the color and texture of Noah's beanie.

thewoodsarelovelydarkanddeepbutIhavepromisest okeepandmilestogobeforeIsleep

The deer stepped backwards and disappeared into the black winter night, and for a moment, the world was quiet.

Then, out of the darkness, the deer charged the cabin window.

TWENTY-EIGHT
THE VILLAGE

The village seemed empty. Moving through the spaces between the small wooden houses, Ryne struggled to find shape in the shimmer and darkness. Desperately, he looked for someone. For anyone. The lanterns were the only sign of life. Hanging, glowing, burning with a flame of recent light. Someone had lit these candles. Someone had to be here.

"Hello!" he called out. "Hello! Please, if there's anybody here. We need help!"

The wind blew harder now. Empty silence rode along the violent breath of the forest as Ryne moved deeper into the eerie space.

It was an old Si'Kualt village. He knew there were a few of these that were spread throughout the woods surrounding Wolf's Bone, but he had never seen one. Many of the natives of the land had moved into the town itself; shacked up in the shanty homes while holding on to their language. He'd always assumed that the villages eventually died out. Standing in the emptiness, he felt himself proven correct.

But for one to be so close to the cabin? All the years he had spent hunting in these woods, and to have never come across it?

And the lanterns? They swayed like sparkling ornaments along the tree line, high in the thick, snow-covered spruce. Others hung beside the old wooden huts. Yellow light radiated from them, restraining the night for just a moment of clarity that would soon flicker away. Under the aura of lanterns, the night was strangely comfortable.

Something moved to his right. A slight disturbance in the shadows.

"Hello?"

He looked closer. The movement had come from the side of the house just beyond the light of the nearest lantern. A chill crept into him. Either his eyes were playing tricks on him, or they weren't, and he couldn't decide which one was worse.

"Hello?" he called again, his voice almost a whimper.

Movement again, but obvious now. He was startled backwards, but regained his footing. The shadow emerged into the light, exposing its form, and ran.

It was a child.

"Wait!" Ryne said. But the little figure didn't stop. It ran along the side of the houses deeper into the village. He ran after it. The snow beneath his feet slowed him considerably as he fought through the storm, but he kept the child in sight.

"Wait! I just want to talk!"

The child momentarily disappeared into the night but reappeared in the light of the lanterns. It was like running through a park during Christmas time. Through trees filled with lights of holy merriment. Ryne passed through the space between houses, stumbling in the snow. The child was getting further away. At the edge of his vision, he saw the form take a hard left and go inside one of the homes.

Ryne slowed and eased through the slush towards the house. The door had a border of glistering light that seemed to rise and die like the house itself was breathing.

Every instinct told him to stop, to turn back. Nothing good could be waiting within that dancing glow. But the child went in there. And now, this stood as his only hope to save himself and his friends. Reaching out, he felt the cold iron handle even through his gloves. The door slowly creaked open.

A shelf stood next to the door. On that shelf sat a candle. A small, innocuous flame burned through its wick and the aura felt its way around the small interior room of the house, throwing momentary cycles of light and shadows across the room before him.

In the middle of the room between those two worlds stood a man.

He was a short man, a head's height shorter than Ryne. He was bundled in a heavy coat made from the fur of what Ryne guessed to be a bear. A balding head that possessed thin eyes and a thinner mouth rose on a short, narrow neck from the fur collar. His eyes shone in the candlelight, and his skin was a dark, rusted tan color. The man was a Si'Kualt, a native. Behind him, the child hid, concealed by the rhythmic bouts of dark and light. The changing light also revealed something else.

The man held a long, curved blade in his hand, fastened into place by a tight grip and a tense wrist.

Ryne put his hands up. His head nearly reached the ceiling of the small house.

"Why are you here?" said the man. *Good*, Ryne thought, *he speaks English*. A stroke of luck in an otherwise hapless string of events.

"I need help."

The man glared at him through the narrow slits of his eyes. Ryne guessed he was in his fifties by the early signs of age that crawled across his face. Heavy bags beneath his eyes begot the wrinkles that ran down his cheeks and neck.

"My friends and I, we're in trouble. One of us is really hurt, and the other is missing."

The man looked him up and down before coiling his head to the side to look around him.

"We're staying in a cabin. He's still there. The hurt one."

The man shook his head and refastened his grip on the knife. His eyes closed briefly and then reopened to reignite their dark shine in the dancing candlelight.

"There is no help here," said the man. "Go, now." Ryne's eyes continued to find the knife fixed in his grip.

"Please, I need help. Even if it's just medicine or firewood. Please, if you don't help, we are going to die."

The man looked down, and his grip around the knife softened. He looked at the child and said something in his language. The child nodded and walked under a hanging cloth into a room in the back of the house. Ryne's guard sprang into action. Did the man not want the child to see what he was about to do? His hands clenched into fists and his eyes found the blade once again. The man shook his head. Then he put the knife down.

Ryne relaxed. "My friend. He was bitten by something, an animal we think, but the wound is getting worse, and his leg is dying. It's turning black and I think there is an infection spreading. Do you have *anything* that can help me?"

"No," the man said. "There is no help here. I am sorry."

"There must be something?"

"There is not."

"But you don't even..."

"It was not an animal that bit your friend. There are few animals left in these woods." A sternness in the man's voice echoed sharply off the walls of the house. "Sit," he said.

Ryne didn't move for a moment. The knife now rested on a small table in the corner, but this didn't comfort him.

"Do not fear me," the man said as he lowered himself to the floor. "There are many other things to fear."

Ryne thought back to the first night. The animals outside the cabin, dozens deep. He thought of the herd of reindeer in the road on the drive back. "What do you mean there aren't many animals left? They're everywhere in these woods."

The man's eyes hardened. "No. They are not."

Ryne sat down, the cold floor beneath him shocked through his pants.

"You look like him," said the man.

"Like who?"

"Your father."

Ryne flinched.

"You knew my family, didn't you?"

"We have known your family for a long time."

Ryne's ears perked, and he leaned forward, focused. "How did you know my father?"

"Before I came to this village, I lived with the others. In town. Many of us here did as well." Suddenly, his language proficiency made sense. "As a younger man, I worked jobs with your father. He was a good man. But... even good men have demons."

The candle continued to burn, and the room felt like it was breathing, inhaling the pressure and holding it in. Ryne looked at the man in mystery. He'd grown up in town but had left to come here. To live his life the way his ancestors had. How many others had done the same? The house was stripped of all conveniences, aside from the warmth provided by a single, solitary candle. Ryne realized he may have misread the man's age, mistaking the scars of a hard life for the signs of aging.

"Your people came here a long time ago," said the man. "They came and claimed this land as their own. My people tried to tell them the truth, but they didn't listen."

"This land is sacred?" asked Ryne.

"No. Not sacred." The man's eyes were even harder now.

"Is it cursed? There's something after us. I don't know what it is, but I've seen it as a wolf, and...as a child. Is that what it is? A curse? Is that why it goes after my family?"

The man shook his head. "No."

"So, what? What is it?"

"There are no curses, and there is nothing sacred. What is here has always been here. It was here long before we arrived, and it will be here long after we go. There was no special reason for your family's involvement, just as there was no reason for my peoples'."

"What is it? What has *always been here*?"

The man shook his head. "It does not have a name. A name means there is respect, but we have no respect for it. Others have witnessed it, and they have given it names, but we do not."

"So, what is it? I don't care about the name, but what exactly is it?"

"A spirit," said the man. "These trees are very much alive. My people knew that when they first arrived, but were never allowed to leave. The spirit would not allow it. It would let them stay in peace, but there had to be offerings."

"The stones. That's why your people did the ritual with the stones."

The man nodded.

"But why the animals? The ones in the tunnel? That's not your people's doing, so why are they there?"

"The path was dug by my people as a guide to the place of offering. The chosen would leave the village and move along the path. The place where the animals hang now is the place where my people would complete their offering. It was a selfless act to ensure the survival of our people. It is the very heart of the forest itself. The offering would be made and accepted in that place, and then the chosen would walk into the lake. There, the offering would be completed."

"So, why the animals? What purpose does it serve?"

"A soul cannot just vanish. By offering ourselves to the spirit, we allowed it to feed on our souls for as long as it needed to. But for the spirit to feed, the offered must become part of the forest. Their bodies would be used as vessels."

"*Pe'kake.*"

The man nodded. "For my people, this act was easy. There would be a hunt, and an animal would be chosen and placed in the offering place, removed when the offering was complete and then used as it always had been. Your people were different. They had their own rituals."

"My people were fur traders." He knew the lie the moment it left his lips.

The man shook his head. "They swam in darker waters, and they used their own rituals to make their offerings."

"They crucified them."

"Yes."

The candle burned. The darkness snarled.

"Then the change would begin. The offered would then become one with the animal of their offering. The animal would be reborn from the vessel. They would become part of the forest, and the spirit would feed. Their soul would be one with the animal of their offering until the feeding was complete."

Ryne's stomach turned. The animals hanging on the walls in the crypt, the deer in the road, the wolf at the window. It was the reason his father and uncle had always been so forceful about not eating the meat from these wilds.

There aren't many animals left in these woods.

In his mind's eye, he saw Noah eating the backstrap of the deer.

"Oh, God..."

"Your people learned the truth not long after they arrived. They would not be allowed to leave this place, and sacrifices had to be made. It was your ancestors who took upon themselves the responsibility of protection. They built that home above the offering place to stay close. But, in time, they began to worship the spirit. For them, it was an act of devotion, not selfless-ness. Power and control. The spirit became something of great reverence. It seems you do not share these feelings, but I am afraid that your fate has already been written, and those of your future bloodlines. You are here, and the spirit will not let you leave."

"What happens when the cycle stops?" Ryne asked. "What happens when the bloodlines run dry?"

The man turned and looked behind him to the hanging cloth and the back room where he had sent the child. His eyes hid in shadow, but the candlelight's glow caught small and fleeting glimpses of his face. He looked very sad.

"Then my people will begin our responsibilities again."

"Is that your son?" Ryne asked.

The man nodded.

"I am sorry," he said. "But your path was made by those who came long before you."

The candle burned out, and the room was shrouded in darkness. From the black, the child cried and ran into the main room as the man struck another candle. The boy ran into his father's arms and buried his face in the man's chest. Ryne watched him and remembered doing the same thing so many years ago.

"He does not like the dark," said the man.

"Can't blame him." The village streets were lined with lanterns. The trees held stars of light from their ancient limbs, as though the night wasn't welcomed here.

The little boy turned his head to Ryne and showed his face for the first time. He was around seven or eight. His eyes were wide, wild, and scared. He had lived under the shadow of this spirit his entire life, and, in that, Ryne felt a type of kinship with him. The same weight had blanketed his life as well, but at the very least he got to pretend it didn't exist for most of his years. This little boy was living in the shadow that Ryne had been spared. For a moment, he felt eternally grateful that his father had hidden certain truths from him. He must've thought he was giving his only son a chance that nobody else in his family could've dreamed of having, buried by paternal sin. But those rivers always flowed to blood, and that blood pooled in these woods where he had always been destined to return.

Because we always came back, didn't we?

The man whispered something to the little boy in his language, and the child released his grip. As he pulled away from his father, Ryne saw something in his arms.

"What is that?" he asked, pointing at the small artifact.

The boy extended his hands and showed the item.

It was a dreamcatcher. Small, intricate, decorated with the hollow bones and feathers of the snowy owl that populated these woods. The same kind that was hanging above Ryne's bed back at the cabin.

"Where did he get that?" he asked.

"I made it for him," said the man. "It is a custom for a father to make one for his son. It protects him from bad dreams and the voices of the spirit."

"My father made me one just like it..."

The man nodded. "Your father cared for you very much."

It was after the first time, the sleep paralysis. His father knew what he'd seen that night. He had gone on a business trip that weekend, and he came back with the dreamcatcher.

No. He came here. He came here and had the item made. After that, the nightmares stopped. In other people's homes, or his dorm room...or the living room of the cabin. Yes, in those places, the thing came to him at night. But never in his own room.

He quickly got to his feet and ran out of the dwelling. What had been a ghost before had come to life with people now standing outside their homes, looking at him from the glow of their lanterns. The village looked half-full as dark eyes filled the clear air.

The clear air. The storm had stopped.

"It has begun," said the man. "The offering."

"I never made an offering."

"One has been made for you."

Ryne looked at the man in horror. The wolf had been fresh, its blood still dripping down snow-wet fur covered in a rancid scent. His offering had been placed there recently.

The villagers. They had placed the wolf...*his* wolf. When his cycle ended, theirs would begin again. They were scared and desperate, and in their fear and desperation, they had damned him.

"I am sorry, but there is no help here for you. You will run with your wolf soon."

Ryne broke into a sprint and made a beeline directly for the tunnel. There was a loud crashing sound to his right at the edge of the tree line. The trees shook and swayed as something monstrous moved within them. Human cries joined the chaos as the villagers ran inside their homes. An inhuman scream engulfed the air. Lanterns fell from the trees and erupted into brief flames on the ground before getting extinguished in the snow.

He pumped his legs with a surge of adrenaline as the thing in the trees continued to bellow and crash its way along the border of the village. As he reached the entrance, the abyss consumed him again. With no light, he extended his arms out to either side to feel for the barriers in the dark as the hideous, unholy scream scraped its nails through the Yukon air.

TWENTY-NINE
BROTHERS AND SONS

Six Months Ago—Yukon, 32 miles outside Wolf's Bone

T he wheels of the blue truck raced along the black asphalt, winding through the taiga. The side of the pavement rose into great trees forgotten by time. They closed in the small, two-lane road that cut through the heart of the Yukon summer.

Rory Burdette sat in the driver's seat. His hands cramped with the tightness of his grip, and his knuckles hurt. He removed one hand from the wheel and flexed it, hearing the soft pop as the bones in his hand returned to their original places, then repeated the process with the other hand. The truck moved along the winding road through the taiga. It was a land mostly untouched by the hand of man, but Rory knew why. Man was never meant to touch this land.

"You haven't said a word since we crossed the border," said Rod from the passenger seat. The long, lanky man with sunken dark eyes shifted and lit a cigarette. Rory hated smoking, and Rod knew it.

"I don't have anything to say." said Rory.

"No, I guess you don't." He took a long drag off the cigarette and exhaled the noxious smoke. It stung Rory's eyes, but he let them water and focused on the road.

The trees loomed larger and larger as the truck pushed on. Rory kept his eyes open and alert at the space in front of him, waiting for the landmark he was looking for. It wouldn't be long now. The trees were always the first sign. He'd made this trip so many times, but he had never planned out this particular maneuver. So, he spent his time preparing and mapping, waiting for this day. His hunting trips were really road trips. Trips to this spot, to find the perfect moment and to recognize when the moment would present itself.

Any second now.

His brother shifted again, dragging out the cigarette with a care he had never bothered to show anything else in his life. Memories of a wooden pew in front of a decorated altar filled Rory's head, mental photographs colored in the broken light of stained-glass windows. How many times had he sat in that pew and looked up at the man on the cross while another man talked about forgiveness? Rory tried, he honestly tried, to remember those lessons and teachings. He tried to be more like the man on the cross, but there was nothing divine, nothing inherently good, about him. He was a broken man, no more or less. All the prayers and adoration intended to install some holy program into his system had failed. He looked at his brother now, those thin arms and deep, dark eyes. Thought about everything the monster had done. His own blood.

He had tried. There would be no forgiveness.

For either of them.

"I made our offerings," said Rod through the smoke. "I came up last week. Deer for you, a wolverine for me. Like we'd always planned."

Rod had been planning, too. After all the years of running. Of denial and recovery and relapse. Rory felt it just as Rod did. Their time had come.

"I figured you already had."

"You're not mad?"

The second sign was the small climb in elevation. The slightest slope rose along a hill above the trees. The view through the windshield showed more sky than road now. A deep sky painted with the most careful strokes of blue. It somehow seemed larger here. For everything he hated about this place, he had always admired just how big the sky got. All that space for so many possibilities, had he not been chained to the dirt of his family.

"What did you offer for my grandson?"

Rod stopped smoking and looked at him. His eyes were the eyes of an animal, and Rory struggled to see him as anything else. He wondered if he'd ever seen him as anything else. Nothing stirred behind those eyes. If there had ever been a shred of humanity, of decency, behind those dark orbs within the abyss of his skull, it was long gone now.

"I know you did it. At least man up and admit it. What offering did you make?"

The cigarette returned to Rod's lips, and smoke inflated his dying lungs. "Owl. Figured that was fitting. Since you gave Ryne that dreamcatcher. Ashes to ashes, dust to dust, right? Isn't that what you believe?"

"How'd you pull it off? That was a hell of a trick. An offering of the unborn."

"I have my ways. We didn't all abandon our home. I still remember the rituals."

"You had no right."

"No, big brother, you had no right. We have a legacy that you refuse to see. So does Ryne."

"No," he said. "It's not his legacy. His legacy was going to be born to a loving family away from all this horror, but you took that away from him. And then you had the audacity to show up and apologize for it."

"I did what had to be done. You were never going to tell him. You would spit in the face of our father and our grandfathers. I'm sorry it came to that. I really am, but if you want to blame anyone for it, look in the mirror. Had you just told him, he could have raised his family in the light and been proud of his heritage."

The third sign was the small clearing beneath them as they climbed higher. A valley of beautiful green that would be covered in desolate white in a few months.

"Now he can understand and be proud of his people. And he can try again."

There was no reasoning with Rod anymore. Rory hadn't stopped believing, for he knew the subject of his family's worship was far too real. But he had stopped idolizing it a long time ago. He'd been unable to break out of the bonds which had ensnared the men in his family to each other, but he had tried his best. Moved away from Wolf's Bone, married an exceptional woman, and hid the truth from his son. But his family's nature ran deep within him. A monster swam through his blood and was always there to pull him under if he ever got too close to shore.

"You left him the cabin, didn't you?"

Rod nodded. "I did. It is his, by birthright."

Rory remembered the day Ryne was born. His son had been so small and fragile that he never would've suspected him to grow into the tall, strong man he became. A little thing with dark hair and bright blue eyes. The first time he held him, his skin so soft and tender against his bare arms, a feeling of holy euphoria and vulnerability swept through the fibers of his soul. When he pulled him up to his shoulder and rocked, he felt a love unlike anything that could be described in any sort of cosmic sense. His wife had been his entire world, but the little boy had been his existence. A universal truth that spoke to the deepest longings of his broken places. He knew from that moment on, he would do anything for his tiny miracle.

Anything.

He wondered how his father had seen him, seen his brother, upon their birth. Wondered if he'd experienced the same level of emotion, the same level of weightless bliss, Rory would experience himself twenty-four years later.

Or was he another offering? Another body on the wall? Another footstep lost in the white of the Yukon's teeth.

Rory's tiny miracle had grown up to be a kind, thoughtful man who had married a good woman and created his own miracle. When he'd heard the news that Ryne and Maxie were expecting, he'd broken into euphoric tears. He remembered the emotions, how they swept him out to a sea of purpose; and delighted in the fact that his own son would now get to savor the experience as well.

But it was stolen from him. Everything this family touched withered and died in a blackness as dark as the hearts of the people who fed into it. He looked at his brother and felt nothing but contempt and hatred. Beyond the smoking figure in the passenger seat, the expanse of the wild stretched out to an inevitable horizon. He hated that too, even more profusely. He knew what moved within those trees. He knew who lived in that town. He wanted to burn the broken place down. Every splinter of bark, every nail of home.

And he'd always come back. God help him, he'd come back every year. Even took his miracle with him. It was like a frozen noose around his neck that guided him, a pathetic dog, back to his cage. As much as he hated his brother, his deepest disgust was reserved for himself. He'd tried, but he hadn't tried hard enough. He should've fought the noose. Should've left Pullman. Left Rod. Moved to Florida or something and damned his memories to their graves in the black trees. But he didn't. And it ripped him apart.

The last sign was within sight. Half a mile in front of them. The final curve would lead them into the long stretch towards Wolf's Bone. The embankment that structured the curvature. The steep drop into the valley below.

"You know something, Rod? Our entire lives we lived in admiration for that thing in the woods. We made it all the offerings we could make. We prayed to it. We sacrificed everything to please it. Our ancestors built that cabin to be close to it. And what did we ever get in return?"

"Watch your mouth, brother."

"What did we ever get? Not a damn thing. It took and took and took. We didn't have a childhood; we had a preparation. It turned us into monsters. We don't even need the offering, do we? We're already changed. Have been for a long time."

The road in front of them eased into a slight curve.

"I'm not letting it take anything else."

Rod turned his head to his brother, his eyes wide. The cigarette fell out of his mouth and into his lap.

Rory smiled. Closed his eyes.

"What are you doing?" said Rod.

"What I should've done a long time ago."

The tire bumped as it moved over the paved line to the bumpy shoulder. "Our Father..."

Rod was now incensed. His animal eyes glazed with anger and hatred. He looked feral.

"You fucking heathen!"

"Give us this day our daily bread..."

Rory felt his brother's fist connect with the side of his face, bouncing his head off the side of the window. A fuzziness slipped into his mind, but it didn't matter now. The truck swerved slightly, but he steadied it.

"And forgive us our trespasses...."

Another punch and the fuzziness became pain. Rory hit back, throwing his brother against the passenger door.

"As we forgive those who trespass against us."

As the truck made its way into the curve, Rory kept the steering wheel straight.

"Stop! Damn you!"

"And lead us not into temptation; but deliver us from evil."

In front of him the road disappeared, and the sky became the view beside the small metal guardrail at the edge of the embankment.

Rory didn't know what happened to a person after life's cruel end. He didn't know if his prayers would be answered or ignored. He didn't know if forgiveness would find his soul. He didn't deserve it. But he knew one thing.

He would not be in the body of damn deer.

The truck plowed through the guardrail and into the air. There was a moment where gravity didn't seem to exist, where the truck hovered above the trees like a dying bird on its last glide.

He spoke a silent prayer in his head. A prayer of apology for his son, a prayer of forgiveness for himself, a prayer of protection for his grandson. He closed his eyes and accepted the next and last step.

The truck titled nose down and plummeted over a hundred feet down into the valley.

THIRTY
METAMORPHOSIS

R yne's lungs burned as his legs pumped harder, driving his body down the dark path back to the crypt. As the tunnel narrowed, his body bounced off the permafrost like a pinball. Sharp, jarring pains hammered into his shoulder with each contact, but adrenaline fueled him along. His blood was like gasoline pulsing through exhausted cells. But as fast as he ran, the murk never seemed to end. It just birthed more and more darkness, materializing into nothing.

The logic of events in his head was crystal clear now. The misery that ran in his blood was unique, fostered by deceit and adoration. His father was going to stop it, remove Ryne from the equation and end this horrific cycle, and allow it to resume with the natives. As the cycle ended with him, it would resume with them. A feeling of horror washed over him at the thought of willingly subjecting a group of people to the spirit. But there was the image of the man holding his son, the same man who had played a part in making Ryne an unwilling offering in the desperate hope of holding back the return of the spirit for just one more generation. Two fathers who did what they felt they had to do for the only things in their lives worth living for.

It seemed it wasn't necessary to be present at your own offering. He didn't know exactly how he did it, but he knew Rod was responsible for Christian. The thought of his uncle made Ryne's vision go blood-red with hatred. He wanted to get out of these god-forsaken trees and find his uncle's corpse and desecrate it in the worst possible way. Damn his soul and damn eternity. Hatred now ruled his roost concerning that man. The thought of his son, pulled from his tiny, helpless body from inside the one place he was supposed to be safe...it was too much to bear. Nothing would've made him happier now than to have been there—to see the truck hit the valley floor, to watch the sub-human's face crunch against the dashboard as the car compressed upon itself. He wanted to see the light leave that monster, wanted to see those dark eyes go black like the rest of this fucking forest.

But he couldn't have that. Now, he needed to get back to the cabin, to Shawn, as quickly as possible. He hadn't run this far since high school, and his body burned under the crushing weight of fatigue. He willed himself forward.

The pathway was getting even narrower, and the ceiling began opening up. In the distance he saw a dim light. *The torches.* Somehow still burning. A newfound energy swept through him and lifted him onward. Soon, he reached the end of the tunnel and stood in the crypt once again.

He stopped and collapsed into the dirt. His battery had run empty and needed a recharge. He placed his head on the hard ground and took long, gulping breaths of cold, acrid air. He began to cry. It didn't offer a warning but arrived upon a zephyr of feelings that had been pushed aside for a year.

The thought of little hands that would never hold a crayon. Little feet that would never play in mud. A smile that would never grace the world with a light so pure that the world didn't deserve it. It decimated him. He wanted to melt, to die at that moment so that he could test the chances that there was an afterlife and see that little boy. But the anger took over, because the anger knew that he wasn't waiting for his daddy in the afterlife. He was rotting away in the hollow bones of an owl.

A dull, heavy wheezing sound slowly filled the surrounding air. Sitting up, he looked around and saw the torches burning above animals mercilessly hung upon ancient walls. The light crackled and slid across the visage.

The wheezing continued, heavier now. Something in the crypt was breathing.

He was a hunter in a bush again, training his ear to find the source of a sound lost in the density of a virgin forest. The room was large and empty, but the wheezing echoed with intensity. From everywhere. It was impossible. He was hearing things. He had to be. This was a place of ancient death. How could...

His ears picked it up. The loudest of the sounds was coming from behind him. Slowly, he turned his head to see the white wolf, the offering of William in his original awe. The animal was long decayed, bones visible between flesh that had rotted away beneath the degrading hand of time.

It was breathing.

Ryne was startled upwards, lost his balance, and fell again. The dead thing's head twitched as a sick cracking sound of locked bones loosening from their resting places resounded through the crypt. He moved away quickly on his backside as the dead thing's head slowly rose from its chest and glared at him with eyes that were no longer there.

He screamed, a primal scream from the deepest part of his gut. The crypt filled with more cracking as other heads animated themselves, their wheezing growing louder and more baleful.

"Ryne, is that you?" came Shawn's voice from above. "Get up here, now!"

Ryne stumbled to his feet and turned away from the lost eyes of the soulless beast. He ran through the cacophony of wheezing and cracking as the dead regained their fervor. In his panic, he almost ran through the ladder on his way back up to the cabin.

The black wolf, destined to be his vessel, stared at him from the alcove, its head fully erect and animate. He locked eyes with the unnerving sight in front of him and froze in a strange combination of fear and fury. The thing's mouth opened, and a familiar scream filled the crypt.

Ryne broke away from his trance and hurried up the ladder, leaving the dead things wheezing, cracking, and screaming. Exploding through the door to the crypt, he slammed the door closed behind him and fell to the ground. He scrambled to his feet and looked around. Shawn was on the floor of the kitchen, his leg lying limp in front of him. His face was chalk white and tight across his cheek and jaw bones with the tension of a stroke. He was panting, almost wheezing like the things below.

"What is it?"

Shawn pointed a finger at the window on the far side of the cabin to Ryne's back. Turning around, he saw blood smeared across the glass. It was sprayed across the entire window, deep red in color.

"What hap..."

A deer materialized out of the night and rammed into the window, shaking the cabin as pieces of its antlers broke away with the impact. It shocked Ryne backwards, and Shawn's face grew tighter.

The deer slipped back into the dark. A few moments passed and nothing happened. Ryne felt relief of the slightest possible degree.

Then the deer appeared again, crashing against the window, shattering more fragments of bone from the antlers. Blood exploded from the creature's head and joined the macabre painting along the exterior glass. The animal stepped back again; but stopped. It looked inside at Ryne, like it was shocked to see a new face appear. It only had one disfigured antler coming out the left side of its head. The other side of the deer's head was bleeding profusely from a hole where the other antler had been. The pieces laid out unseen in the bloody snow.

Shawn sucked the air into his gasping lungs as the deer turned and again became lost in the oppressive blackness beyond the cabin's lights.

"It's Noah. It's fucking Noah. I don't know how to explain it to you, but that thing is Noah!"

A lump arose within Ryne's throat, and everything he'd learned in the past hour recounted itself once again within his psyche. The clear image of Noah devouring the backstrap from the deer presented itself vividly across a grim and bloody canvas of tempered glass as the deer emerged from the night again with a sickening crack.

* * *

The deer crashed again into the window, and the remains of its second antler broke away from its head in a spray of blood. An inhuman cry escaped the animal as it stumbled away in pain, shaking its gored head. It vanished from the view through the glass, and silence reigned again, aside from the distant cries screaming through the night air. Ryne shook away his panic and scurried along the floor towards Shawn.

He was breathing erratically now with eyes as wide as headlights. Shaking, he shifted his gaze to Ryne.

"I don't know how," he said. "But that was Noah. I swear to God I know how it sounds..."

"I believe you. I believe you. I know," said Ryne. "You're not crazy, calm down."

Shawn's breathing slowed as if calmed by the fact that someone else understood the bizarre and incomprehensible things coming from his mouth.

Their gazes returned to the window. A serene glow had overtaken the night outside the cabin. The tree line was now visible, as was the sheer amount of blood that had been spilled in the snow.

"The storm stopped," said Shawn. A tangible hopefulness sounded in his voice, and it crushed Ryne to extinguish it.

"No," he said. "We're in the center of it now."

The air outside was calm now, and the darkness was now more of a filter than a wall. The hole in the sky above the lake was now atop the cabin, and an almost ethereal aura seemed to extend downwards from it. Animals appeared from behind the tree line as they had on the first night. Dozens of them arrived in a staggered unison, filling the space between the cabin and the trees. All species were represented once again, the deer in particular. Among the deer stood one with blood running down its face from where its antlers once protruded.

Noah now stood with the deer, with the others like him who'd been confined to be feasted upon within the bounds of this forest. The offering his father had tried to avoid was now complete, but a new soul had been found instead. A deep pain ripped through Ryne's chest and his eyes swelled with tears. Hatred flowed through him, ate him from the inside. Gnawed on the tender nerves. Noah looked back at him, and Ryne knew he was still there. He'd tried to break back into the cabin. To rejoin his friends in a moment of furious, pitiful desperation. But whatever shred of him existed within the bleeding deer was just that, a shred. His friend was gone. Again.

Shawn groaned and punched the floor.

"What is it?" asked Ryne.

"My fucking leg!"

Ryne pulled up the leg of Shawn's pants and looked down at the knee, struggling to grasp what he now looked at. It was black, completely black. How could it have died this quickly? Ryne looked closer, and to his horror, noticed an unseen detail.

There were small, black hairs emerging from the dead tissue.

"What is it?" asked Shawn. "Goddamn it, why do you have that look on your face!" He looked down at his leg for the first time and revolted in horror.

Ryne felt sick again, and he wanted to get as far away from his friend as possible...but he didn't move. *It's going to be alright*, he told himself. *All we have to do is fight, and everything will be ok. What happened to Noah happened because he was alone, but we're not alone now.*

He believed it—until Shawn looked up at him with eyes that had changed.

* * *

The change started in his leg. The feeling that coursed through his veins had now worked its way deeper into the rest of his body. His leg felt like it was on fire, a searing pain seeping into every pore. But the hair disturbed him the most. Small black hairs, coarse to the touch like dead grass, now grew out of him.

Shawn looked up from the horrific sight and met Ryne's gaze. His friend's eyes were wide and terrified. The color drained from his face. Then the color left everything else as Shawn's vision slowly turned to shades of gray with little definition.

An intense pain took hold in his arms and legs that forced him to double over in agony. His bones stretched and cracked apart at his ankles. He screamed, but the sound that came out of his mouth wasn't his scream, but something else entirely.

crrrraaaaaaacccccckkkkkk

His ankle exploded in an eruption of anguish as he felt the bones break and realign themselves. He thought of Noah, what he had become, mindlessly ramming his head into that window, and vomited.

Ryne had backed away from him but hadn't abandoned him, not yet. And he wouldn't; they might argue, might get angry, but they would never abandon each other. This is what it would take, a change so drastic and unnatural that it perverted their very nature.

crrrraaaaaAAAAAAACCCKKKkkkkk

His spine extended, and for a moment, he was paralyzed. He tried to speak, but now no sound came from him but a repulsive whine.

A wave of smells emerging from every molecule in the air assaulted him. He heard Ryne's heart racing like a jackhammer from within his chest. Then Shawn's skin broke apart as alien forms and textures arose to claim a stake in their new residence.

He felt it in his mind, too. An urge, an instinct unknown to him prior. A presence leaked its way into the inner rivers of his thoughts and demanded obedience. A nameless influence stabbed and pricked at his better judgement and told him to kill.

For the last time, he looked at Ryne and remembered the promise he had made while crawling across the floor. His time was now. The reaper had come. But it would only take him. He had failed to hold this off as he always knew he would, but he would not fail Ryne. He'd already failed one friend.

He attempted to put some sort of expression on his face, but knew it was useless. He felt this new instinct ripping control away from him. But, behind Ryne, he could see the fireplace and, within it, the last log burning away in the flame.

It wouldn't be long now before he wasn't himself anymore, and that could not happen. They were all doomed, but he would not become a monster. He refused to become the very thing that had sired him and then abandoned him.

Shawn mustered every ounce of control he had left and stood before falling back down onto all fours. His wrists wailed in torment as the bones continued to shift beneath his skin. He wanted to scream in pain, but nothing would come out. Regaining his composure, he trained his eyes again on the fireplace.

In three bounds, he crossed the room and launched himself through the opening of the fireplace and into the flames. He felt the new hair on his body immediately singe and catch. A scathing, burning sensation overtook all the other pain, and a hideous scream erupted from within him. But it wasn't his scream. A putrid smell filled his nostrils as both he and his newfound form burned to death, the flames licking and melting the fibers of his new skin. He felt every lick, every singed hair. The violent final throws of whatever he was becoming. Through the pain, the searing sensation that set his nerves alight. For all the pain he felt, he knew the new form felt it too. And that in itself was more than alright for him as he slipped away softly into the burning dark.

THIRTY-ONE
THE BROKEN PLACES

R yne watched in horror as the remains of the half-changed abomination smoldered and blackened within the stone fireplace, embers cackling and erupting around what used to be his best friend. No words could qualify what he had just seen, a man changing into some other form of the natural world before his very eyes, but it had happened regardless. The forest had never felt so big to him, and yet the cabin had never seemed so small and so pointless in the grand scheme of things well beyond his pitiful comprehension. As a child, this place had been something special —a place of family reverence and happiness. As he'd grown older, the cracks in that foundation had turned jagged and apparent. Now, it was a useless pile of logs, rotted from within, cursed and begrimed by the souls of the very people who built it.

A sudden impact bashed at the front door as something heavy threw itself against the wooden barrier. Ryne leapt to his feet in shock and backed against the wall beneath the loft, putting as much space as possible between him and the unseen force. Another shock against the bracing, and the door buckled as the metal hinges stressed and bent in resistance to the impact.

A burning smell filled his nostrils, and he gagged. The creature in the fireplace was now completely aflame, cremating within its stone tomb. It hadn't stopped its changing process and had metamorphosed into a smoldering pile of what looked like the incinerated remains of a wolverine, its black fur simmering in the heat of the blaze. The burning corpse had once been the closest thing he had ever had to a brother and was now resigned to the furthest distance from humanity.

A mixing swell of fury and hopelessness swirled within him. To the left of the fireplace, was the window smeared with blood. The blood of his other brother rendered inhuman by this sick place. It cackled at him with the snarl of victory as the forest's reserve troops stood behind the horrid portrait, awaiting their orders from somewhere down below.

A deer and a wolverine. All that remained was the wolf.

Along the bushy tail of the creature in the fireplace, a single flame licked the wall just past the stone mantle. The first few licks resulted in nothing, but then one of them caught the dried wood and a small flame feathered upon the grain.

An ear-splitting scream erupted from all around. Ryne fell to the floor and put his hands over his ears, but the sound still forced its way through him. Within his inner ear, he felt a sharp, intense pain, like a needle being slowly inserted into the deepest parts of his head.

And then there was nothing. The scream died away, fading off into silence that had suddenly become the norm. He looked around frantically, his eyes moving from spot to spot across the cabin. There was no sound. The front door still shuddered and buckled under the weight of whatever force was behind it, but the crashing sound had disappeared.

The horrifying realization of deafness washed slowly over him as the front door broke loose off its hinges and fell into the cabin's interior. A shape filled the doorway.

The black wolf bared its teeth and leapt into the cabin, bounding towards him. Frozen in shock, he couldn't move as the wolf struck him in the chest and knocked him against the wall. Its large teeth furiously ripped at his throat. He held his arms up in defense and felt the searing pain as teeth sunk into his forearm. He screamed in silence.

The wolf shook him violently. Blood sprayed across the wooden floor. Through his panicked stare, Ryne locked eyes with the animal. Black and empty. Nothing lived in those eyes, and Ryne understood why. An empty space filled the beast, devoid of any soul, because it was reserved for his own. The offerings had already been made, even with the deaths of his father and uncle. The sacrifice of the deer and the wolverine had been accepted regardless of the lack of family connection. Now it was Ryne's turn. The final offering. The main course that would feed the spirit of the forest for one more generation.

The wolf ripped and tore through his arms. An enormous paw slashed at his throat. He went lightheaded and faltered on his feet as blood spilled soundlessly across the floor. He reached and felt his throat. The paw had missed his neck. But its sharp claws had found the side of his jaw, splitting it open and knocking him off kilter with the force of the blow. Lightheaded and dizzy, he fell to the ground.

The floor beneath him moved. The grain of the wood passed by his face as a pressure formed around his ankle. Gathering himself, he rolled on his back and turned his head. The wolf had his right ankle in its mouth, dragging him toward the front door. This was the largest wolf he'd ever seen, and it pulled him easily. It hauled him out through the door.

He felt the cold of snow as the wolf pulled him off the porch into the wild. His head swirled in pain as the underbrush, mostly buried beneath the days of snowfall, pulled at his jacket and hair. The cold air shocked him alert.

He lifted his head out of the snow and looked around. Dozens of animals now surrounded him. Every conceivable species of fauna the Yukon sheltered now crowded around him like some cultish congregation. The image of Shawn's transformation and his insistence of the deer's identity rang a hellish siren, animating the feeling of change. How many generations of people stood watching him now from the eyes of vessels? How many of his relatives now watched their descendent be damned and dragged through the snow in accordance with their own sins? The thought of it made him feel sick. A tradition of pain, suffering, and ritualistic death passed down through the bloodlines, even without the consent of the sufferer.

A trail of bright red poured from his jaw across the white glow of the night snow. Through blurry vision, he could see the blood curving away from the front of the cabin. He was being dragged towards the rear.

Towards the lake. The stomach of these woods where the sacrifices were made and digested—a fate that Ryne was now involuntarily resigned to. A ceremony for him not granted to Shawn and Noah. They'd been changed, screaming in the dark.

The cellar's wall of animals surrounded him. Above, an owl perched on a lonely branch. Ryne turned his head and looked at the animal, small and delicate. The dead thing from the crypt had become the dead thing in the trees, kept alive with the soul of the most unwilling of participants.

Anger surged within him, uncovering a new resolve. He thrashed around in the snow, kicking his free leg as hard as he could into the animal's head. In a wince of pain, the wolf let go.

He quickly gathered to his feet and limped back, following the path of blood. He didn't look over his shoulder, but he knew the wolf would soon be in pursuit. The other animals didn't move. They just watched with empty eyes as he hobbled through the front door and back into the cabin's den. The fire crawled across the walls and ceiling, as the wolf exploded into the space behind him, knocking him off balance.

He couldn't stop moving. To stop meant to die. As the wolf rolled across the floor towards the kitchen, he saw the front door consumed by flame, blocking his way out. The stairs up to the loft were too close to the wolf as it returned to its feet. The only option was the bedroom door a few yards in front of him. Through a fuzzy head, a ravaged ankle, and a gushing jaw, he harnessed what strength he could find and ran through the door before losing his balance again and crashing into the bed.

The wolf stood in the doorway. A snarl stretched across its black face, and it bared its teeth—now stained with Ryne's blood. But the animal didn't come in. It just stood there, growling in the open doorway, hatred painted all over its face.

Ryne was done. What little strength he had left was gone, depleted into the frigid night. His hearing had vanished, and his vision didn't seem too far behind. He laid there, a wounded animal without the resources to fight back—a predator's dream.

But the wolf stood there and did nothing but snarl and hate.

That's when Ryne realized that the animal wasn't looking at him...but at the item that hung on the bedpost above his right shoulder.

The dreamcatcher.

It can't come in.

A new energy surged within him as he staggered to his feet, holding his shredded ankle slightly off the ground. The tiny artifact, thin threads and the feathers and bones of an owl, looked so unassuming, so dainty. And yet the darkness at his door stared at it with a certain, special kind of abhorrence. Ryne had hated the hospital, hated that nurse, hated every loathsome day of this past year. But there was nothing in this world or the next that he could've hated as much as this presence at the door seemed to hate that tiny, harmless gift—a small caring token of adoration passed from a concerned father to his terrified son.

The smell of smoke filled the room as the wooden walls behind the wolf ignited into flame. The fire was now engulfing the logs and furniture, turning the cabin into an inferno.

But that same little lick of fire hadn't just started this burning, it had done something else, too. The moment it had touched the wood and caught —something had screamed. It had screamed so loudly that it had turned his world into a painful deafness.

Pain. It was the cry of pain. The fire had touched nothing but the wood, but something had screamed in ungodly agony. It was a scream he knew far too well.

His mind quickly ran through the legends he knew growing up. The wendigo, the wechuge, the witiko. The Slavic legends of the woods. These stories varied across different tribes across North America and the rest of the world, but one thing seemed to persevere through the separate tellings and retellings—the role of fire. Nature's ultimate tool of destruction.

Just a natural part of these woods.

Suddenly, another memory materialized in his thoughts. The man in the village.

He had said the trees were alive.

Ryne understood. A shroud still hung over this area, this spirit. A shroud far too dark for human eyes to see through. But that tiny flicker of flame had burned away a small part of that veil, and Ryne had seen beyond it. He knew what this thing was.

The fire now raged behind the wolf, and it was getting difficult to breathe. He pulled a sheet off the bed, a bed he would never sleep in again, and put the dreamcatcher around his neck. In the doorway, the fire had now ignited the black fur of the wolf. It stared in continued hatred at Ryne, its mouth open and its face melting into contorted agony of blood and bone.

Scream all you want. I can't fucking hear you.

Wrapping his fist in the bed sheet, he punched through the bedroom window. The glass shattered. Some of it cut through the bed sheet and into his hand, but he didn't care. He had already lost a lot of blood, so what was a little more? He climbed out the window and fell with a thud to the ground, momentarily knocking the wind out of himself. Slowly, he rose. He stumbled as pain coursed through his ankle, but he steadied himself.

Every available space within the forest was now filled with animals, but none dared approach him. He turned and grabbed the wooden window shutter and, with a hard jerk that took most of the fuel he had left in his tank, he pulled it free. He moved his way around the side of the cabin to the front, the cabin now completely engulfed in flames. The embers drifted on the rising drafts up into an impossible sky. Painted across that sky was a hole leading off into somewhere else, somewhere beyond the visage of good men. Light seemed to be born and die simultaneously within this vastness, and Ryne's feeling of smallness returned. He knew he was a speck of ash, destined to dissolve away into a universe that didn't care enough to even register his existence. But he was also a speck of ash with knowledge that transcended his importance.

He stopped in front of the campfire pit. The air felt treacherously cold, but the wind had stopped.

Daddy

Ryne's eyes snapped up to find the source of the little voice that had just somehow filled the silence. A small boy stood on the other side of the pit. He was the spitting image of Ryne himself, dark hair and light eyes, but with a darker complexion, like that of the woman Ryne had married.

Daddycanwegotothelake

It wasn't a sound that he *heard*; that was long gone. It was in his head. A soft, innocent voice Ryne had always assumed his son would've had. Tears formed in his eyes and froze to his cheeks

Pleasedaddyiwanttogotothelake

But a darkness lurked inside that little voice, hidden within the tones and pitch. Something that didn't belong.

"Stop," Ryne said. He couldn't hear himself talk, but the words sounded clearly in his mind. "Stop it, now."

Pleasedaddywecanbetogetheryouandme

"No," said Ryne.

Pleasedaddyimcoldandscared

"Damn you, I said stop!" He had found his resolve. That little boy wasn't his son. And he would not stand by and let this thing mimic the greatest loss of his life anymore.

AS YOU WISH

A new voice. Deeper and intensely dark. It filled the soundless void.

A sight of horrific breadth now stood across the pit from him. He had seen glimpses of it in his last nightmare, but now it towered over him unencumbered. Its head reaching high above the blazing cabin. The immense antlers on its head blocked the night sky. Its face—a hideous amalgamation of the Yukon fauna—was only briefly illuminated by the inferno as it stood on all fours. It spoke to him within his head, the voice of the child long forgotten and replaced with a deepness not of the natural world.

I DO NOT LIE TO YOU. YOUR SON IS HERE. I CAN GIVE HIM TO YOU.

"No."

YES. YOU WILL SEE HIM AGAIN. YOU CAN BE TOGETHER IN MY GARDEN.

"You've already taken him." The world got smaller and colder as he fought back the new arrival of old tears.

I HAVE ONLY ACCEPTED WHAT WAS OFFERED TO ME BY YOUR PEOPLE.

"They aren't my people. They are your people."

I HAVE ONLY OFFERINGS. I HAVE AN OFFERING FOR YOU.

"No."

STAY WITH US IN MY GARDEN. REBUILD THE PLACE OF OFFERINGS. DO THIS AND I WILL GIVE YOU YOUR SON.

Despite all his knowledge, he wanted to say yes. To end it all now and hold the little boy he never got a chance to hold. To end the misery. End the pain. But he understood too well what was being offered. Pain doesn't go away—it just takes on fresh forms. Lingers like a ghost, tethered to a place irreparably familiar as it changes. And when it has starved its new form, it changes again. And it will keep changing until it has eaten through everything and left the sufferer a husk.

A phantom.

Ryne sat in the snow. His eyes burned bright with rage, melting the frozen tears from his cheeks. He spoke sternly to the living wild. "I know why you're offering this. The cabin is a part of you, isn't it? All of it is. The thing you are now? It's a phantom. Because you are the forest. The lake is your stomach, and the cabin... the cabin is your heart. Built from your bones. Without it, without the offerings, you can't live, can you? Before it was the animals, they served you. But then you ran out of the animals, didn't you? Then the tribes came, and they feared your threats. You didn't give them a choice. So, you found a way to combine your servants. And when my people came, you went from being feared, to being loved. Worshipped. They made you a god. You liked that, didn't you?"

YOU SPEAK OF WHAT YOU CANNOT UNDERSTAND.

"But you indulged too much. And now, the woods are barren; with animals that are no longer animals. You've drunk them dry. Your followers are empty shells. And you're starving."

The grotesque face lowered toward him and came into view. The antlers dripped with the blood of a molting deer.

HOLD YOUR TONGUE.

"My bloodline stops here. And your heart is burning. So, you need me to carry it on. But I won't. You'll go back to the town and find another one of your worshippers to take over. Eventually, you'll run them dry, too. Then you'll go through the tribe. And in the end, there will be nothing left. Nothing but an empty, starving forest."

He reached inside his jacket, pulled out the dreamcatcher and held it up to the spirit. Hatred filled the air. He then dropped the window shutter in the snow and brandished the lighter. With the flick of his ungloved thumb, the lighter erupted to life, and soon flames consumed the old wood. The spirit visibly recoiled in pain, and Ryne's head filled with its unearthly howl.

"You would have taken me before. Into the lake. But then your heart started burning and now... now, you can't touch me, can you? So, you want to bargain. Without your offerings, you starve." He looked toward the cabin. "Without your heart, you die. Starvation takes too long. I'm going to stay here until the last ember of that burning pile of shit is stamped out. And I'm going to enjoy it; because I know it's going to hurt. Like you made my friends hurt, like you made my father hurt. Like you made my son hurt..."

He felt himself break. The strong parts of him broke the loudest, and he collapsed into the broken places. He cried, but the tears froze as they left his eyes. When he opened them, the thing across the pit had changed again. The little boy looked back at him, the fire dancing in the darkness. He wanted so badly to hold him, to tell him it would all be ok. But he wouldn't cultivate the pain any longer. He couldn't. He had no more blood to bleed.

The little boy spoke one last time, the soft voice carrying across the wild and into the night air.

T h e c o l d w i l l t a k e y o u

Ryne sniffed hard and wiped the ice from his eyes. He thought about the pain that the spirit was about to feel, and the price he had to pay to ensure its suffering.

"I know."

The inferno of the cabin erupted even higher, and the child cried out in pain, as if making sure that Ryne could hear through his deafness. But he simply stared in hatred as snow froze to the tips of his hair.

* * *

As the hours drifted along, the spirit's screams grew in intensity but fell upon uncaring and unworking ears. Ryne sat in perpetual silence as he watched the cabin slowly corrode into burning, smoldering ashes. By the end of it, the sun was still an hour away from rising above the horizon, and a large pool of blood had saturated the snow next to him. His vision had blurred to the point of near blindness and the tips of his fingers and toes felt numb with frostbite. When the initial burning was complete, he limped among the wreckage, stamping and grinding out the still hot ashes. Only the stone chimney remained. The fire had spread into the crypt as well, and he thought of the dead things below. Thought about how they had probably cracked, wheezed and screamed weak cries as the flame consumed them. But Ryne hadn't heard it and wouldn't have cared if he did.

As he finished his final destruction, he collapsed onto his back in the snow and closed his eyes. The animals had long since disappeared, retreated into the dark sanctum of the trees. He was freezing, and his jacket had finally lost its war with the cold as the warmth from the burning cabin died with the spirit. He didn't know if it was permanent, if it was really gone, but he knew that he'd made it hurt. Badly. And that gave him satisfaction. The first satisfaction he'd felt in a long time. He hoped, as he lay in the snow, that the villagers could rest easy now, despite what they'd done to him. He understood their actions in a way that only a father could. He thought of that little boy, scared of the dark, and prayed that he could now live in the light, untethered to some primordial shadow.

He opened his eyes. Above him, an owl, pure white in color, perched on a branch. It looked down at him, as if it somehow wanted to talk but couldn't find the words. Its eyes were wide and full, a vibrant amber around the black pupil. Not an empty void, but the eyes of an animal untouched by the influence of malevolence, as if whatever soul had been condemned within it had now been released into the place it was rightfully always meant to go. It was this sight that preceded a comforting warmth that washed over Ryne as he lay in the snow.

Two Months Later

THIRTY-TWO
PHANTOM KICKS

T he black jeep rumbled atop the frozen blacktop, the exhaust blowing hot smoke from the panting engine. The world outside was clear, aside from scarce flakes floating on the wind that scraped and clawed its way across the Yukon. The jeep slowed into the long sweeping curve and then accelerated through it as the town appeared in the windshield. The chained tires cut through the ice, and the jeep came to a rest in front of a building with a sign. Conway's Deli.

Maxie opened the door and stepped out into the frigid world. She pulled her jacket up to his chin, but still shivered in the horrid chill. A breath of thin air that didn't seem to fill up anything. A slow exhalation of fog. She should be used to the cold. Hell, she was part Inuit and had lived in eastern Washington all her life. But this cold was different. Darker. It had a weight to it and a special bite that unnerved the piece of her still cognizant of her ancestral respect for nature.

This had to be the place. Wolf's Bone. Ryne had mentioned it so many times, and the image fit the descriptions. The streets branched off and meandered through the town of old buildings as the place seemed to unfold before her like a postcard. She scanned the streets, looking for the landmarks she remembered from past conversations. And yet, the sight before her couldn't have been the same. The buildings were supposed to have with-stood time, but the structures she saw were ramshackle, eroded, and decayed. Grime was frozen on the windows and the signs had faded almost to the point of invisibility. Ryne had always said the houses were little more than shanties, but the homes she saw made shanties look downright respect-ful. At least, the houses still standing did. Many of them had collapsed, burned to the ground, or been reclaimed by vegetation. And all this was made even worse by the silence. The streets were completely empty. The stores closed in the middle of the day. Not a soul was to be seen.

But that couldn't be. The missing persons reports were filled out a few days after Ryne, Shawn, and Noah didn't return home. Wolf's Bone, that's where they'd gone. She was sure of it. Shawn had told his sister, and Noah had informed his job. But the place laid out before her had no business being the destination for anybody living.

She stood there staring at a ghost town that had been dead a long time.

"Hello?" she called out. The only answer was the whistle of winter wind as it moved through the open street.

She returned to the jeep and drove further into the remnants of the village. The place was unequivocally dead. There had been an investigation when the missing person's report was filed, and she assumed that the corpse of a town she saw now must have been exactly what the investigators had found. But how? Dammit! Ryne had talked about this place before. His father still made visits all the way up until his death. Hell, from what she understood, he'd been on his way here when the accident occurred.

As she drove through the ghost town, she thought about Ryne. About what they used to be. *Who* they used to be. It had taken her a while, but she'd stopped blaming him. Blame was a dangerous game played by hypocrites, and she realized far too late that she had changed too. For so long, the burning banner had been the image of him ingrained in her mind. What he'd done was wrong, but he'd borne the weight of loss on his shoul-ders as well. She, of all people, should've understood. She hated herself for suffering in silence, dealing with the pain in private while he fought his own wars on a front without allies. It had been a grueling process, and she'd had to work at it, but the burning banner was no longer her impression of who Ryne was. She chose to remember the man she married. The kind man who wanted nothing more in this world than to be a father. Even if that man was now a ghost.

A ghost lost somewhere in this place.

As she drove through all avenues and side streets, the death of the town became its face. There was nobody here. It looked like there had been no one here for years, if not decades. Every turn she took led nowhere, and every building appeared as dead as the winter itself.

She reached what she assumed was the town's end. On one side of the road, she saw a supermarket with broken windows and snow piling on the inside. On the other side stood a church, and she thought at first that maybe church was in session, and everyone was there. She stopped the jeep and stepped back out into the chill. Walked up the steps towards the wooden double doors at the church's entrance. Pushed them open.

The church was cold and empty, the smell of dead leaves and soaked wood hanging in the still air. The stained-glass still held its color, but it didn't reflect light the way it was supposed to. Everything was dark and dull, the fading radiance from outside lost in the gloom. But through the darkness, her eyes found their way to the altar where she expected to see a crucifix. What she saw instead was something she couldn't explain. Propped in a Christ pose, its long thin arms stretched out to either side, fastened to the back wall of the church. The idol's head slumped to its chest, crowned by an enormous set of antlers that nearly reached the vaulted ceiling. The effigy was carved from wood, black and rotten, and falling apart with age. Rows of old candles long dead stretched from the decrepit sight, making a circle which wrapped around the seating of the church. In the center of the dying building, a large bell lay cracked and quiet.

She held her breath for a moment and beheld the sight before her. A knot formed in her stomach, and she turned away from the horrific effigy. A sickness bubbled within her, and she ran out of the church towards the jeep. Her lungs gulped deep breaths as she tried to calm down.

"Hello!" she called out again with the last gasps of her voice, but nobody was listening. No one was here. She didn't know what had happened to the Wolf's Bone she'd heard about, but this place was a relic. Wherever Ryne was, it wasn't here. And, judging by what she was seeing, and what she'd *just* seen, that was a good thing.

As she reached the jeep, a clacking sound joined the whistling wind—

the sound of hooves on concrete. From the ruins of the supermarket, a deer walked across the road in front of her. It paused and raised its gaze to Maxie. A buck, but the holes on the side of its head signified the recent loss of antlers.

It watched her a bit longer, and she returned the stare. Finally, it turned away and walked towards the edge of the forest next to the church and disappeared into the trees.

Maxie stood in the cold, dead town for another moment before getting back in the jeep. There wasn't a soul here.

But there was one more place to look.

She didn't remember exactly where he'd said it was, but the cabin was the only other place Ryne might be. Digging through her memories, she tried to locate anything that might tip her off to where the place was.

Then, as she almost drove out of Wolf's Bone, she saw the path. A clearing cut into the woods. A space between the trees was just wide enough for a truck. And then, like a flame ignited in darkness, she remembered.

It was a path, miles into the woods.

This had to be it.

She turned the jeep into the clearing. The surface was jagged, as though wind bad sheared off the top layer of snow, and the ride was extremely rough. Her tires cut and dug into the snow. She had to keep it steady. Slow.

Her skin crawled as the trees seemed to converge around her, and she prayed she wasn't driving on a false path and burying herself deeper into the wild. The ancient branches choked the path like a firm grip, and she felt unnerved by the compression of the natural world.

* * *

It took her nearly an hour to reach the point where the pathway opened up to a small clearing thick with snow. She pulled the jeep to a stop, set the parking brake, and got out. Night would arrive soon, and she didn't have much time to waste. The area before her looked like where a cabin might stand, but it was empty. She looked around, searching for separate paths that might lead elsewhere, but saw none. No, this had to be it. But there was no cabin, just a circular clearing surrounded by the reaching fingers of dying trees. There was a strange feeling about this place that she struggled to name. None of the words seemed quite right, but the closest she could get was *heartbroken*. The place felt like a broken heart.

Then she saw it. A wooden post peeked out just above the snow. She walked towards it, her feet sinking about six inches or so before the snow held her weight. The wood was black in color, charred by some old flame. Next to the post was something half-buried in the snow. Stones.

A cabin and its chimney.

A sickness overtook her, and she nearly collapsed into the snow. The darkest thoughts enfolded her mind, and her ears filled with the imagined sounds of crackling flames and screaming. She could almost feel the heat on her skin, despite the freezing wind.

But she remembered the town, the dilapidated shell of bone she'd left behind an hour earlier. She doubted anybody had been there for years, so it was just as possible that this cabin had burned down long ago. There were no other signs of life, and no indication anyone had been here. She was back to square one.

Unless...

She looked around at the heavy blanket of snow and wondered just how much could fall in two months. What could it conceal? Her heart darkened at the thought, her world reduced to shadow.

No, she told herself. Ryne wasn't here. Maybe he had been here once before, but he wasn't here now. The only thing in Wolf's Bone was that horrible effigy of dead wood with its antlered crown. The only thing here were the remains of something so far removed from the present it may as well have been a ghost.

She looked around and felt the full sensation of winter. The deep white encased the trees with ice, freezing the life from the world. As she searched the trees, something caught her eye. She'd nearly missed it, but it was there. A little piece of life tucked into the tree closest to her.

An owl. Small and insignificant against the vast white of the land, but living, nonetheless. It watched her, and she watched it.

She let herself cry for a minute. Felt the pain of separation build inside her before gasping. Because she knew she felt it this time. A little kick against the side of her stomach. A flood of euphoria seized her for a moment, and she forgot all about the misery, all about the change, all about the sleepless nights and barren tear ducts. Remembered a time when she'd nestled herself happily into her husband, and he'd held her close. Tucked away from the monsters of the world.

She turned away from the owl, and then froze. On the opposite end of the clearing, standing at the tree line, stood a large black wolf. Her heart stopped for a moment and the sudden warmth disappeared, replaced by an unconscionable cold. She fought within herself to find a breath as the animal glared at her. It didn't move, didn't advance or retreat, but stayed rooted in its place. Black against the white of winter. Her legs unworking, she waited for a sign of aggression—a growl, a baring of teeth. But nothing came. The animal just stared.

Feeling returned to her legs, and she stumbled through the snow towards her jeep. Her blood cold, she waited to hear the shuffling of snow as the animal attacked. But she heard nothing. No advance. No noise. Just empty silence. Quick glances showed the animal in the same spot. Unmoved.

She reached the jeep, hurried into the driver's seat and slammed the door shut. When it was secure, she looked out the windshield to where the wolf stood.

But it was gone.

She surveyed the entire clearing, but there was no trace of the wolf. No sign it had even existed. She breathed deeply, trying to calm her racing blood. It was gone. She was sure of it. She didn't know how, but she was sure of it. Gone for good, vanished into the snowy trees and lost in the darkness of the forest.

But the owl was still there, sitting in its tree outside the driver's side window. With its head turned to her, its deep amber eyes cut through the winter's white.

There. She felt it again. That little kick that promised so much. A strand of memory so brightly lit against the darkness of a world so cold. A memory entrenched so deep it was as much a part of her as her own blood and bone. She knew she felt it, as sure as she'd felt the cold wind against her face. She cried at the feeling, felt the embrace of promised futures and lives not lived. Somewhere deep inside, she felt that little kick and thought, for the quietest of moments, that maybe all of it had just been some horrible dream. Maybe she'd wake up soon to the embrace of her husband and the life inside her.

No, she told herself. *It's just a phantom kick.* But, in the back of her mind, she filed the memory away, somewhere she could find it again when needed. When the world got dark again, and the monsters returned. For now, there were more places to look. So, she put the jeep into gear and rolled away from the remains of the cabin and let the memories of little kicks guide her away from that broken place.

AUTHOR'S NOTE

A book is not born from the singular imagination of its author, but rather requires the help, guidance, and support of so many. Too many, in fact, for me to accurately name here. For anyone not named who played a role in helping this book become a reality, please know that my gratitude is unending.

First, I want to thank my wife Lyndie for her constant support, even in the throes of my self-doubt. You never wavered in your support or your belief that this book was worth something. In the same vein, I want to thank my parents—my mother for all the lessons and support of my reading habits from the years of my earliest memories, and my father for being my gateway into horror and the music that inspired the creation of this story.

I also want to thank two of my best friends in the world, Marty and Trina Trosclair, for being my first readers. Without your advice and feedback, this book would have never become what it is now. Also, thank you to my colleague Danielle Faucheux for reading a more polished version and providing even more valuable feedback. I would also like to thank the entire team at Wicked House Publishing for their belief in this story and their constant guidance and support.

Finally, I would like to thank anyone who has picked up my little story and given it a read. I sincerely hope that you enjoy this story as much as I enjoyed writing it.

ABOUT THE AUTHOR
BLAINE DAIGLE

Having lived his entire life deep in the gut of Louisiana, Blaine Daigle grew up surrounded by ghost stories of haunted plantations and cursed woodlands. He still lives in Louisiana with his wife and two children and can't wait to pass on the nightmares to his kids once they are old enough. During the day he teaches high school English. At night, he enjoys diving deep into the fears that shape and mold the world around him. The Broken Places is his debut novel.